LIVE LIKE A WAISTER?

Think and spit like a Waister? The thought was more horrible than any he could recall.

"They're people," Ranes had said. "Not like us, but still people."

Jonson remembered the calm resolve of the Drones, the helpless wailing of the orphaned Dog. Would it really be so difficult? He recoiled as if struck, for *that* was the idea he'd been running from.

It wouldn't be difficult. No, it wouldn't be difficult at all.

AGGRESSOR SIX

"Wil McCarthy brings thought and insight to the realm of fast-paced, action science fiction. *Aggressor Six* is a taut, vivid adventure that never rests. A splendid debut for a bright new light on the SF horizon."   —David Brin

Wil McCarthy

AGGRESSOR SIX

A ROC BOOK

ROC
Published by the Penguin Group
Penguin Books USA Inc., 375 Hudson Street,
New York, New York 10014, U.S.A.
Penguin Books Ltd, 27 Wrights Lane,
London W8 5TZ, England
Penguin Books Australia Ltd, Ringwood,
Victoria, Australia
Penguin Books Canada Ltd, 10 Alcorn Avenue,
Toronto, Ontario, Canada M4V 3B2
Penguin Books (N.Z.) Ltd, 182-190 Wairau Road,
Auckland 10, New Zealand

Penguin Books Ltd, Registered Offices:
Harmondsworth, Middlesex, England

First published by Roc,
an imprint of Dutton Signet,
a division of Penguin Books USA Inc.

First Printing, July, 1994
10 9 8 7 6 5 4 3 2 1

Printed in the United States of America

For Bruce Hall and Richmond Meyer

I am very grateful to Gary and Nancy Snyder for their technical, moral, and nutritional support. Others to whom I owe thanks include Richard Powers, Dorothy Taylor, Charles Ryan, Shawna McCarthy, Amy Stout, Cathy Polk, and the membership of the Northern Colorado Writers' Workshop, most particularly Ed Bryant and John Stith.

Chapter 1

The woman was heavy and tall. Her brown hair hung down just past her shoulders, framing a squarish and businesslike face. She wore an officer's uniform, three stripes on the collar. "Ah, Corporal," she said. "Come in."

Ken cleared his throat, brushed a finger against his throbbing temple. "Th . . . Thank you, Captain . . ."

"Talbott," she said. "Marshe Talbott, Exobiology. Call me Queen, if you like. Might be a good idea to get used to it."

"Queen." He tasted the word. It seemed strange, a familiar sound that had dressed itself up in new meanings.

"I understand you haven't been briefed?"

"Uh, no. I mean, I hope not. This is some kind of think tank? That's all they told me."

She nodded slowly. "Some kind of think tank. Yes. Come in, please. Once you meet the group I think things will be a lot clearer." She ushered him in through the doorway and down a short corridor. "I've been reading your dossier. We weren't sure who they were going to send, but you seem like an appropriate . . . Everyone, this is Kenneth Jonson, our Marine corporal."

The corridor opened into what looked like the control room for a holie studio, its walls covered with screens displaying schematic diagrams, planetscapes, bright yellow lists of scrolling numbers. Lighted shapes flashed here and there on dark, gloss-black control panels. A ring of chairs faced inward, two vacant, three occupied by uniformed men who eyed Ken curiously.

"Dog! Good dog!"

He was startled by the sharp voice, and even more startled when its owner raced toward him on four legs, its tail wagging. It was a *dog,* a big black and tan one with a thick collar around its neck. "I am Shenna!" said the animal. "Shenna is a good dog! I am Shenna!"

"Go sit down," said Captain Talbott. For a moment, Ken thought she was speaking to him, but then the dog hung its head and turned back toward the chairs.

"Shenna will sit. Shenna will sit. Shenna is a good dog."

The captain smiled, her face turning pleasant for a moment. "Sorry. That was Shenna. Maintenance Corps."

Ken blinked stupidly as the dog went over and sat between two of the chairs, her tail thumping against the metal floor. Not only had the animal spoken, it had done so without moving its mouth.

"You've never seen a Martian retriever before," said the captain, catching his look. "They're, ah . . . It's all webs and voders, the talking I mean. No magic involved. Anyway, meet the crew." She pointed at one of the seated figures, a slender man with yellow-brown skin and short, black hair that stood in tight curls. "Lieutenant Sipho Yeng, Astronomy. Born on Mars, lately of Ceres Mainstation. He's one of our Workers."

The man looked at Ken and nodded slightly, his face virtually free of expression.

There was a pause. Ken's mind was crammed with the language of the *Hwhh,* the Waisters, but none of their words seemed to mean "hello." He reached back and rubbed the tender, swollen flesh at the base of his skull. The doctors had told him that the Broca web would not interfere with his conscious thought process, just as they had told him that the emplacement of it wouldn't hurt. Right.

"There is," he said, and stopped. *Standard,* he told himself. *Think in Standard. It's only your native language.* "Uh, I feel this urge to attack you. Crazy. I think the Waister language doesn't contain any greetings for strangers. I'm . . . very pleased that you're an astronomer?"

The yellow-brown man laughed at that. "Relax, Corporal. The Broca web is strange at first, but you'll reach an accommodation with it. Its job is to advise, not to compel."

"After my operation I was confused for a solid week," the captain admitted, then pointed at the next man in the circle. "This is Worker Two. Roland Hanlin, sergeant, Ceres Ordnance. And this,"—she pointed at the last man—"is Drone One."

"Ranes, comma, Josev T.," said the man. "Navy lieutenant, U.A.S. *Century City.* Straight pleased to meet you, Corporal. I was part of your backup on the final boarding action. Of course, I was cooped up in a navigation creche at the time, but I guess we all do our part. Anyway, good show. Damn good show."

Show? The terminal phase of the Flyswatter operation had been many things, but the word "show" was not one Ken would have chosen. Nor was "good," for that matter. He wondered, briefly, if he should take offense at the comment, but decided to let it pass. The roll and twang of the young man's voice were unmistakably Southimbrian, and although Lunites were not widely known as a sensitive people, they were very rarely malicious.

"Thank you, sir," Ken managed to say. Then, with even greater effort: "It's ... nice to acquaint ... to *meet* you. Nice to meet you. All of you."

The captain nudged his elbow. "Well, Corporal? Queen, Dog, Worker, Worker, Drone ..."

He frowned. "I'm the other Drone? We're supposed to be Waisters?"

"Aggressor Six," said Josev Ranes. "They teach you much history in the M'rines? Tactical forecasting is traditionally one of the hardest jobs in warfare, even when your enemies are human. Most standing armies maintain a unit whose job is to live and think and spit like the enemy."

Think and spit like the enemy? Ken remembered the Waister Drones feeding their twisted, bruise-colored bodies into the wiregun abattoir of battle, fluid drooling from their sandpaper mouths ...

What could the thoughts of the *Hwhh* be like? How could anyone possibly know? As a child, Ken had often thought he'd grow up to be a dramatist. He practiced, sometimes, using exercises he'd learned in class or seen on holie. *I'm a tree,* he'd say, stretching his arms out in what he imagined to be a treelike manner. Then, he would empty his mind as best he could and stand very still, sometimes for twenty minutes or more.

"I see," he said.

"No argument," observed Captain Talbott with a nod. "That's good. We don't need any individualists here, we need a nice six-part harmony."

"Yes, ma'am."

"At ease, Corporal. Excessive formality is a team-buster."

"Should I call you Marshe?"

She laughed. "Call me Queen. Get into the spirit of it." She smiled for a few moments, but then a dark expression swept across her face like the shadow of a moon. "We've been monitoring the realtime holies from Lalande. The Waisters just crossed the orbit of Tenebra, which is the outermost planet. Two stations offline so far. It doesn't look good." She gestured at an empty chair. "Sit. Watch for details. For the moment it's all we can do."

Ken shuffled a little. "Ma'am. Queen. Respectfully, I'm not feeling too good right now. They hustled me onto a clipper right out of post-op, and I've spent the last forty hours at three and a half gee's."

"Oh," said the captain. "Well. Let me show you your quarters, then. You don't have any luggage?"

"No, they wouldn't let me."

She led him across the room, through the stares of a dog and three men, to another corridor.

"Sleep tight, chum," said Josev Ranes as Ken passed by.

His room proved to be first in the short hallway. The captain, the *Queen*, slid the door open and went inside. Ken got as far as the doorway and stopped.

"Shit," he said, looking into the room. The walls were purple-gray and padded, slick with clear varnish. The corners had been blocked off with triangular braces, making the room look vaguely octahedral. There were human things here: a dresser, a capsule-shaped sleeping-berth set into the wall opposite the hygiene area with its bathing and sanitary facilities. But these things, these human things, looked decidedly out of place, like palm trees on a cold, airless moon. "Shit, shit. You can't be serious."

"Come in, Corporal," said Marshe Talbott.

"Captain, I can't sleep in there. Please, I *mean* it."

"Get in here, Drone Two. That's an order."

Ken started to protest again, bit it back. This was like a bad dream, or a bad joke. A space-black coffin would have been more inviting than these quarters. *I can't be ordered to sleep here,* he thought. But he knew that wasn't true. A Waister armada was en route to Sol system, six months away at best, and if it were deemed necessary or helpful in some way, Ken could be ordered to consume his own entrails. These were not nurturing times.

He took a breath, and stepped into the room.

"Nothing to be afraid of in here," the captain said, not unkindly.

"Yes ma'am," Ken replied tightly.

Talbott ran a hand up and down her cheek. "You really are upset by this, aren't you? I'm sorry. They gave me a lot of trouble about the decorations, waste of war material and all that. I fought for it. If it helps, even a little bit . . . But you're just back from the boarding action. I didn't think about that. The tip of the Flyswatter. Was . . . Was it bad?"

Ken looked at the soft, glistening walls around him. "Yes," he said quietly, almost choking on the word. "Oh, yes. Very bad."

The captain looked hard at him for what seemed like a long time. "I'm not here to mother you," she said, finally. Her voice was gentle but impersonal, like the anonymous comfort of a couch in a public lounge. "If you've got a problem with this, I'm sorry. I wish things were different. You've borne the brunt of this war, much more than the rest of us, but that doesn't give you the right to fold. I'm going to leave you alone now. You can cry, scream, kick the walls, whatever you want, but tomorrow morning you join the team. Are you following me?"

"Yes ma'am," Ken replied, machinelike. Comfort and enjoyment were wasteful luxuries when life, all life, hung in the balance. The commanders would spend his life as they saw fit.

Talbott's probing gaze withdrew, sought out his

shoes. "I really am sorry. When I was stationed here—
God, it's almost four years ago now—it hit me that I'd
seen my last rainstorm, my last summer day. It seemed
so tragic, but now I can't even cry about it." She
cleared her throat. "Good night, Corporal. I hope you
feel better."

Woodenly: "Thank you, ma'am."

When she was gone, he went over to the bunk and
threw himself into it, killing the room lights with a
slam of his fist. *Was it bad? Was it bad?* How could
she ask him that?

He trembled as the weeks-old fear curled and
stretched within him, settling in for the night. But fatigue was dragging at him already, a soldier's fatigue,
always there, always poised to perform its duty. Within
seconds it was tugging him down, down toward the unwelcome embrace of sleep.

Of course it had been bad. Oh, yes. Very bad.

Chapter 2

Firefly lights winked in the distance, each flicker marking the end of a human life as the Waister disintegration beams, themselves invisible, swept back and forth across the dappled velvet of space. Every now and again, one of the beams would touch the bright pinpoint of a human battleship, and the speck would brighten and expand like an exploding star, then fade away. More lives erased.

In the distance, the Waister ship looked small, the size of a wine bottle, and that was bad, because Ken knew the ship was seven kilometers long. More distant still, the Milky Way cut across the view like a knife wound, its stars cold and unwinking.

Operation Flyswatter, that was the name the officers had given to the disaster that was unfolding around him. *We expect casualties,* the X.O. had said, *but the Navy will be covering your advance, drawing the Waisters' fire, neutralizing their weapons if possible. We have a lot of cause for optimism at this point.*

But the X.O. had known, as had Ken and everyone else, that this was polite fiction, a murmur of sweet nothings to lubricate the thighs of virgin troops. A more forthright paramour might have said, *It's a swarm attack. One million men will be sown across space like seeds of corn, and we expect most of you to die. We simply hope to present the Waisters with more targets than they can respond to.*

Not that it mattered, at this point.

Ken felt the scooter humming between his legs, much like the autocycle he'd once owned. That was back when he'd lived on Earth and had a life of his own, some measure of control over his destiny. The feeling of the sun on his face, the dusty wind in his hair, was a balm that soothed his troubles away as he raced down the ancient beltways of North America. Now, the sun was shrunken and cold behind him, and the "wind" in his face was the rebreather kicking his own exhalations back at him. The scooter was his life, he knew. He drew his air from it, through the slender rape hose that ran from his chest to the tank-rack below, but more importantly it was his only means of propulsion, his only way to catch up with the retrieval tugs.

By slapping the wide, brightly colored membrane patches on the top of the oxidizer tank, Ken could order the scooter to DIVE, EVADE, TRACK, or SPIRAL, all of which involved zooming in toward the Waister ship. There was no RETREAT command he could issue. That was okay, though, since his commanders had thoughtfully decreed that the retrieval tugs would only search for survivors who were within one kilometer of the Waister ship, after it had been boarded and pacified.

Right now, Ken was DIVING toward the ship. Why waste time EVADING, or doing anything else but attacking the enemy? Even a mouse would bite when it knew it could not escape.

Slowly, slowly, he approached.

They were called Waisters because they came from the waist of Orion, and were not to be confused with Belters, who were the human inhabitants of asteroids in Sol system and the five colonies. *Three,* he reminded himself. There were *three* colonies, soon to be two if the fighting went badly at Lalande. And the fighting *would* go badly; Waister technology was insanely powerful, and the aliens themselves knew nothing of mercy. Even at nine-tenths lightspeed, they had traveled for something like twelve hundred years for the privilege of squashing the human race like a nest of bugs.

But they were not invincible! The ship before him, with its melted drive motors and blistering hull, was proof enough of that. Ken clutched that thought to him like a beloved pet.

The ship was the size of a small child's sleigh, now. Lights winked around it, brighter and more yellow than the stars. *New Year's,* he thought, remembering the way drifts of winter snow would glitter in the night while fireworks detonated above them. But that was Earth, a part of his freshly cauterized past.

He'd come from a city called Albuquerque, one of the unlucky sites in the Waister scouting raid. His family, his roots, his heritage, had been vaporized by a handful of sand which passed through the center of town at point-five-cee, half the speed of light. Kinetic energy became heat, and in a flash, two million people were economically removed from the war effort.

He pictured Shiele Tomas, melting, the sidewalk melting beneath her. Look of surprise on her vanishing face.

Sand had figured heavily in the fighting, as it turned out. Of the thirty-six sites the Waisters destroyed, the cities and stations and asteroid warrens, thirty had been hit by sand. And it was sand, blasted relativistically across the path of the scoutships, that had turned the tide, however briefly, in favor of the humans. Three ships destroyed outright, one crippled, unable to maneuver, sailing past the sun into the frigid depths of interstellar space. The other two had been forced to slow down, and humans had descended upon them like locusts.

One of the ships had died in the fighting, going up like a supernova, taking tens of thousands of human lives with it. The other ... The other was before Ken Jonson right now, bitterly fighting for its life. Doomed, surely, its motors reduced to slag so that it was pinned forever between the orbits of Saturn and Uranus. But Sol had lost a third of its fleet already, hundreds and hundreds of ships, and it seemed they might lose the rest before the Waister defenses gave out.

The ship must be captured intact, the X.O. had told them. *We need prisoners, artifacts, intelligence. The survival of the human race depends on this.* The obvious corollary, that *any number* of lives could be sacrificed in the process, had gone unspoken.

The sparkling New Year's lights swept closer to Ken for a moment, as the Waister beams probed his region of space. Terror swept him, like cold water sluicing through the marrow of his bones, but the beams moved away again, the winking of death becoming more distant. The burden of doom had been shifted to others, for a while. The terror faded a little.

He felt exposed, incredibly exposed. If he could choose to be standing nude right now in the middle of an Antarctican blizzard, he would gladly do so. He was like a spider on a wide, white wall, climbing desperately but knowing that a shoe or a rolled-up mat would strike him long before he reached safety, crushing him to anonymous pulp. No, it was worse than that; he didn't even have a wall to cling to, only the pale and heartless stars that hung lifetimes beyond his reach.

Oh, God, he said to himself. *Oh, God. Oh, God.* He repeated it over and over in his mind, like a mantra, until the words lost their meaning and became simply patterns. *Oh God oh God oh God . . .*

The sky lit up as a navy gunboat flashed and died somewhere nearby. No time for fear, no time for the men and women aboard to gasp or scream or grip their consoles with whitened knuckles. They simply existed in one moment, and then in the next moment, did not. Much better, it seemed, much more *humane* than the lonely strobelight deaths of the marines.

The scooter bucked beneath him once, like an angry horse trying to throw its rider, and then fell silent, the soothing autocycle hum of its motor cutting off suddenly and completely. *Part of the plan,* Ken assured himself. Nothing wrong, NOTHING WRONG, the scooter was supposed to do that when he was halfway to the target.

Halfway. God. Could it really be true? It seemed like days since the "people cannon" had expelled him from its dark and claustrophobic womb, but still the Waister ship looked tiny, distant. He looked around it, his eyes hunting for human figures, but that was ludicrous, of course. His nearest comrades, kilometers away, were dull pinpoints of light. On the hull of the ship they would be like bacteria.

Ken felt a vibration in the scooter, faint and quickly gone, and then the Waister ship seemed to accelerate, to drive itself sideways until it slipped past the edge of his helmet visor. The stars wheeled about him. The ship wasn't moving, it was he, Ken, who was turning his back on it. The sparkle of disintegration beams was falling behind him now, out of sight. *Oh God, Oh God . . .* The skin between his shoulder blades began to tingle and crawl.

KCHUMMMmmm . . . The hum of motors returned as the scooter, now falling tail-first toward the enemy, began its deceleration. *Oh God, Oh God.* Hadn't he been moving slowly enough already? Now, each second that passed would make a bigger, slower, more inviting target of him. And he couldn't even see where he was going! He and the other troops could actually be shot in the back while advancing. Surely he'd known that, intellectually at least, but now the irony seemed bitingly fresh.

"Lucky day," he murmured, and was startled by the sound of his own voice, echoing dully inside the helmet. A voice, even his own, was an anachronism here, a bit of irrelevant sensory data. Radio silence was being maintained, a gag stuffed into the mouths of a million murder victims.

The sky behind him was filled with moving dots. Was his own transport, the *Nob Witan,* still among them? Ten months he'd been aboard her, longer than at any other post. He remembered, with nightmare clarity, the look on the Second Mate's face as he stood hat in hand at the barracks door and announced that the asteroids Eros and Nysa, and the Terran city of Albuquerque, had just been added to the rolls of destruction. His voice was as flat and weary as a stale tub of beer. Had that really been only ten days ago?

Ken had never known the man's name, never wanted to. Marine proverb had taught him that names were for tombstones.

One of the spaceship/dots flickered momentarily, not with the yellow of Waister death, but rather the blue-white signature of primitive, mass-production fusion motors. The glare burned into his eyes, leaving a red-green smudge that throbbed and pulsed near the center of his vision. He blinked as the afterimage began to fade, restoring it almost to its original intensity. It was slightly right of center, actually, and it retreated as he attempted to look directly at it, turning and swiveling right along with his eyeballs. He blinked again, and then again, toying with the image, and was about to smile ... But he was in space, of course, riding backward into the arms of an unknown and unyielding enemy. He shivered within the rigid spacesuit, and the afterimage dried up the way raindrops did on the sandy soil of his home.

In its place, Ken saw the ship that had fired its motors, swollen beyond pinprick size now, looking about as large as his smallest fingernail viewed at arm's length. The ship was round, but not in the pregnant way of a spin-gee Marine transport. Rather, he found he was looking almost end-on at the needle of a gunboat. As he watched, the ship seemed to grow and turn. It was going to pass almost directly "above" him, though at a range of ten kilometers or more.

It looked like a toy. He was far away from it, of course, but Ken suspected that a closer look would only reinforce the impression. Most of the Navy's ships seemed to have been stamped out by a giant cookie-press somewhere, so that Ken half-expected to see foil stickers on them saying PRODUCTO DE CALLISTO or some such. And the weapons! A typical gunboat was a hundred meters long or more, and barely ten meters across, a thin metal shell wrapped around the gas-core spindle of a gigawatt laser. Most of them had small turret lasers as well, and there had been rumors of projectile weapons, actual *cannons,* on some of the newer models.

Of course, Ken himself carried a shotgun in one leg-holster, and a "utility knife" in the other. Ostensibly, the knife was for cutting through obstructions and performing expedient repairs. Its pommel was heavy and flat, like the head of a hammer, and its rear edge bore odd protuberances for cutting wire and turning screws. But the blade itself was long and curved, tapering to a wicked point barely twenty atoms thick. Not really a tool, but a magic sword for the dismemberment of the Waister crew.

He glanced at his outstretched forearms, encased in the rigid polymer tubes of the hardsuit. Even his hands, now gripping the scooter's wide handle-bar, were gauntleted. He felt ridiculous, a medieval knight whose steed shone brightly, whose armor was the dull gray of fused ballistic fiber. But there were wireguns mounted on his forearms, and there was nothing funny about *them*. If King Arthur had been similarly equipped, he might have taken out Mordred's entire army in the first ten minutes of fighting.

The wire spools aren't so big, a grim voice told him inside his head. And it was true; the cylindrical lump at the base of the gun-tube was hardly larger than a shotglass. How long would it last? For that matter, how reliable was the equipment itself? Maybe Arthur should keep Excalibur handy after all.

Humanity could do better than this, he was sure. They'd harnessed the antimatter dragon over a thousand years before. From time to time, they'd built starships, set mammoth ansible stations in the dark spaces between the stars. Where was all that capacity now, when it was so desperately required?

The navy ship flew over him and passed out of view. How long would it be permitted to continue its existence? Would it fire its gun once again, or maybe twice? The tingling between his shoulder blades resumed, like pine needles raining down on his back.

Oh God, Oh God . . .

He wondered how the light-show was going. Ten men down every second? Probably more. He remembered the twinkling, fairy-dust sparkle of disintegrating people. FlaFlaFlash! FlaFlaFlash! Yes, almost certainly more. If it were . . . He tried to think. If fifty marines died every second, no, call it a hundred . . . it would take ten thousand seconds for the entire force to be destroyed. Three hours? Two and a half. Something like that.

But that *couldn't* be right. Nobody would plan a battle of such grisly attrition. Maybe it was only ten deaths a second, after all.

The scooter lit up with reflected light, bright yellow-white, as something behind him was converted to plasma—something large and relatively close by. The light grew brighter, and brighter still, and then vanished suddenly. *Farewell,* he thought, picturing the toy gunboat in his mind. The crew would have been huddled at their stations, strapped and braced against the lurching acceleration of the fusion motors, the laser core-tube sweating heat upon them even through its thick diamond sheath. They would be busy people, their heads filled with little besides numbers and vectors, though two or three of them, the ones at sensor stations, had probably been aware of Ken's proximity as their vessel soared past him. There would be chatter on the ship's intercom, twenty or thirty voices trading information back and forth in a kind of tightly controlled turmoil. And then, without warning . . .

Farewell. He sent the thought toward them like a prayer. Fare well. In truth, Ken hoped they would fare *not at all.* What could an afterlife be but more of the same?

He wanted to be somewhere else—crotch-deep in boiling acid, maybe. Anything but this, anything at all. Why did the Waisters toy with them so? Why send in a scouting raid ahead of the armada; why pick single targets and destroy them one by one? Really, it was just too much. Why couldn't the human race just flicker and die, all at once, like one big happy gunboat crew?

"Oh, God," he said, aloud, relishing now the lonely

echo of his voice. "Oh, dear God. You bastard. Get me out of this. Get *all of us* out of this."

He quieted his breathing for a few moments, but the supreme being, creator of human and Waister alike, declined to comment.

Ken Jonson felt tears welling up in his eyes, rolling slowly back into his hair in the scooter's light acceleration. He had never felt so isolated, so incredibly alone. Why couldn't he have died in Albuquerque, surrounded by family and friends? Why!

The stars shone coldly upon him for a long, long time.

Chapter 3

Morning, chum," said the young lieutenant, waving a coffee cup at Ken. This was Josev Ranes, the Navy guy, the talkative one. "Come on, then, grab a seat. Enjoy."

Ken looked around skeptically. The cafeteria was grim, almost industrial in its mood. Identically uniformed people marched to their tables, sat, shoveled food into their mouths, and marched away again to dump their trays in the cycling chute.

"Chowtime is special," Ranes espoused. "A break from her Queenship, you know? A little time to rub elbows with the rest of humanity."

"Hmm." Ken grunted.

"Well," said Ranes with a wink and a smile, "most of the rest of it. I s'pose there're still some folks that *haven't* been assigned here, but as I've never met 'em, there's no point me worrying about it, eh? You want your biscuit?"

"Yes," Ken told him. "I do. Uh . . . Lieutenant? What do you think about . . . this assignment?"

"What do I *think* about it? Gosh, nobody's asked me that before. Let's see. I've been here three weeks, and so far we haven't really done anything except those clodgy 'team-building exercises.' I s'pose it'll be more interesting when things get rolling. Why? Something troubling you?"

Ken swallowed a mouthful of food, cleared his throat. "Uh, yeah, sort of. We're supposed to think like Waisters, right?"

"That's right. Nothing to it, I say. I figure they're people, not like us, but still people. They've got some reason for all the things they've been doing. *Steady,* chum, I didn't say I liked them or anything. I mean, King Schubel was a person, but I wouldn't exactly introduce him to my sister. The thing is, whether you like it or not, the Waisters are intelligent, conscious entities. They've got strengths, weaknesses, lusts, *blind spots* . . ."

Ken applied himself to the task of eating.

"It may be a bit excessive," Ranes continued, "imitating their family groups and such. I can see where you'd be rattled. You'll do fine, though. At least you have me for company."

"Thank you, sir."

"Oh, quit that. Sludge! There should be somebody around here who really talks to me. I swear, Yeng and Hanlin are about as much fun as an autopsy, and Talbott, well . . . I think maybe she's been an officer too long. I get more inspiring conversation from the dog."

"Oh, yeah. I wanted to ask somebody about that. Martian retriever? What is that, I never heard of it."

Ranes pointed a fork at Ken. "You should have. Great animals. They breed them for intelligence, although the talking is all just neural interface stuff. This thing like a Broca web picks up on what the dog is thinking and translates to the nearest Standard equivalent. The voice module is in the collar. Thing translates Standard back into dog neural patterns, too. You wouldn't expect most human thoughts to mean much to a dog, but that mutt really seems to know what's going on most of the time. She worked maintenance in the Chryse tunnels until they assigned her here. Sniffing out gas leaks or some such."

"Huh. Wow. I never heard of such a thing."

"Well," said Ranes, "Now you have. It's a good match, really. She acts a lot like a Waister, from what Talbott says."

"No," Ken said, sipping from his coffee.

"No? What do you mean, 'no'?"

"I mean Talbott is wrong. Waister dogs don't act like that." He set down his cup; his hand had begun to shake. "They don't run around, or wag their tails, or sniff things. Their movements are slow and deliberate, almost like some kind of reptile. The only . . . God. I shot a couple of Workers, and their Dog just . . . fell over and cried like a baby."

Josev Ranes clicked his tongue softly. For once, it seemed, he had nothing to say.

"I wired it," Ken explained. "Totally reduced it to pulp. I just wanted the screaming to stop, you know? But I still hear it, sometimes, late at night . . ."

"Go easy," Ranes said, reaching out to grip Ken's hand firmly. "Don't get lost in it, chum. Plenty of time for that when the war is over, but right now we're too damn busy."

Ken refocused his eyes, pulled his hand away and nodded. "Yes, sir. I'm sorry."

"Don't be sorry," Ranes insisted, leaning forward a little. "And don't call me sir. Okay? I mean it. Marshe may be a fat, squishy slug, but she's right about that one thing. Call me Drone, or chum, or even Josev. For the time being, you and I share equal status."

"Don't turn around," Ken said, nodding his head diagonally. "The fat squishy slug is right over there."

Josev hunched his shoulders. "Oh, damn. Has she seen us? Is she coming over here to sit?"

"Uh, she's coming right toward us, but she's not

carrying a tray. Keep your voice down, don't say anything." He raised his voice a bit. "That's fine with me, Josev. Hello, Captain."

Talbott placed both hands on the table and leaned across at Ken. "That's Queen to you, mister." She looked over her shoulder at Josev, who smiled a little uncomfortably. "You telling him how it is, Josev? That's good. You two ought to be close. Gentlemen, I hate to spoil your breakfast, but we need to gather in the assimilation chamber at oh-seven-hundred."

"Oh sludge, Marshe," Josev protested, glancing at his wristwatch. "That's five minutes! I've barely touched my food."

The captain returned his smile. "You might try talking a little less. If it were up to me we'd have the briefing at oh-*eight*-hundred, but Colonel Jhee has a very busy schedule. Be glad he didn't fetch us out of bed." She turned back to Ken. "Some fresh uniforms have been left on your bunk. Hang them up when you get the chance."

"Thank you," Ken replied, remembering this time not to call her ma'am.

The captain straightened. "Well, I'll see you in five minutes then. Oh by the way, Josev, if the subject of my many faults happens to come up in conversation, you might also mention my HTH rating."

She thumped him on the shoulder and walked away.

"Bitch," Josev observed when she was gone.

"What's an HTH rating?" Ken asked, placing his cup and utensils back on his tray.

"Navy parlance for hand-to-hand combat. She *says* she scored two-eighty out of three hundred on the certification test. Maybe she did." Josev sighed. "C'mon, let's get going." His tone indicated resignation, but he stood quickly, stepped clear of the bench, and walked off toward the cycling chute.

* * *

Marshe Talbott glared at the Drones as they came in. "You're late," she said, letting some of the irritation leach through into her voice. She'd always despised tardiness, always grated at the way it muddled her plans, took the crisp edge off her lists and schedules.

"Sorry," Ranes told her, ducking his head. "Had to visit the stroom, you know?" He turned toward Colonel Jhee and nodded. "Colonel. Nice to see you again."

The colonel favored Ranes with a typically disapproving look. "Lieutenant."

A short, beige-skinned man, the colonel had been born and raised in Burma, one of Earth's southeast Asian *republikai*. That was, she felt sure, the reason for his being so ... whatever he was. Marshe had heard things about that part of the planet.

"You must be Corporal Jonson," Jhee said, extending a hand out toward the new Drone. Jonson looked at the hand for a moment, as if it were a control he'd never learned to use, then reached out uncertainly and shook it.

"Nice to meet you, sir," he said.

"Yes," the colonel agreed, withdrawing his hand. He turned to Marshe. "It seems your hexagon is now complete, Captain. I expect—"

Marshe straightened. "Colonel, *please*. A hexagon is a geometrical figure, not a family group. We are a *Six*. Aggressor *Six*. How many times do I have to tell you that?"

"Talbott," the colonel warned, "This *is* my project, and insubordination *is* punishable by death. I expect—"

"It's *my* project!" she snapped, suddenly furious at this small, self-important man. "You've fought me *every step* of the way. You want a tactical think tank? Fine. I'm working on it. You want a band of toadying ass-lickers? Too bad. It was *my* proposal that got you your stupid funding in the first place."

The colonel stood very still. "Captain Talbott. I warn you that your current behavior is not acceptable. Nor, I think, typical of you. Perhaps the Broca device is interfering with your judgment?"

Marshe bit back another tart reply, paused, and snorted softly. "I'm quibbling over words," she agreed, running a hand across her brow. "I'm sorry. But Colonel, we're *not* a hexagon. That kind of imprecision is *exactly* what we need to avoid. If we're going to get a handle on how the Waisters think, it's important that we not project our own prejudices onto them. I mean, they have four different sexes. If we just decided to refer to the Queens and Dogs as 'females,' and the Drones and Workers as 'males,' we'd be missing something very important."

Colonel Jhee frowned. "Hmm. Your point is taken. However, your means of expression is not acceptable. I will ignore it this time, but consider yourself warned."

Warned. What exactly did that mean, Marshe wondered. Would she be court-martialed the next time she raised her voice?

"Now," the colonel went on, "since your *six* is now complete, I expect you to begin performing your designated function. Anticipate the Waister tactics in the siege of Lalande. I want a full report by oh-nine-hundred tomorrow."

"You're joking," Marshe said after a moment's thought.

"No."

"Colonel, we're still setting up, here. We're not prepared—"

"The Waisters are in Lalande system right now, *Captain,*" Jhee said, his voice cool. "They won't wait until you feel prepared. Do you know Glacia, the third moon of Tempestus? Its surface is mostly ice. Last night the Waisters liquefied it to a depth of a hundred meters, and let it refreeze. Seven million people are presumed dead."

Marshe looked away.

"If you'll excuse me . . ." the colonel half-whispered. The door swished open, hesitated, swished shut again.

The room was silent for several seconds.

"What's wrong?" asked Shenna in her lilting dog-voder voice. She left Sipho Yeng's side and trotted over to Marshe. "What's wrong? What's wrong? Be happy." She gave her tail a tentative wag.

"Oh, Shenna," Marshe said, reaching down to scratch the top of the dog's head. "It's nothing you can help me with. I haven't been happy in years."

". . . the gravity wave spectrometers indicate the mass of the vehicle doesn't change as it accelerates," Sipho Yeng was saying. He'd been talking for nearly an hour now, and Marshe was having a hard time keeping up.

"Meaning what?" asked Josev Ranes. He sounded lost, too, which relieved Marshe; as a Navy man, a navigator, Josev knew more about relativity than she ever would. If *he* didn't understand, then Sipho Yeng was in fact doing a poor job of explaining himself.

The astronomer looked surprised, and a little confused. "Well . . . it means that they're able to trade rest mass for relativistic mass on a one-for-one basis. And with their braking system, they're somehow able to convert the relativistic mass *back* into rest mass."

"In Standard, please, Sipho," Marshe said. Finally.

Yeng squirmed uncomfortably in his chair. "I really don't know that I can explain it more simply than this.

They're, well, cheating, okay? Their drive motors produce a beam of coherent gamma rays by converting matter directly into energy. That's their exhaust. The old Colonial starships used matter-antimatter annihilation to achieve the same effect, though at much lower efficiency. A Compton lens was used to shield the forward portions of the ship, with the net effect that the gamma rays, which were *not* coherent, radiated in all directions except directly forward. This produced a differential which propelled the ship in a forward direction."

Ranes was shaking his head. "The Waisters have the noodles to build a gamma ray laser, then. Right? That's all you're saying."

"No," Yeng replied with even greater irritation. "Listen carefully. They're converting matter into kinetic energy, using gamma rays as a mediator. Then, when they want to stop, they convert the kinetic energy *back* into matter. They're not obeying energy conservation laws; the gamma rays are *free*."

"Oh!" Ranes said. He paused. "You're saying they'll never run out of fuel?"

"Well, not in the time scale we're worried about. On the captured scoutship we found three tanks of liquid gallium which we believe to be the mass reservoirs for the propulsion system. They were about ninety percent full, which may indicate some gradual loss in the process."

Marshe held up a hand. "Okay, Sipho, thank you very much. I think that's all we need to hear about that. If you remember, my other question was about communications?"

The astronomer nodded sharply. "Ah. Yeah. The fact of FTL communication between the Waister ships is well documented, but unfortunately, it is not well understood. The ansible effect, with which I trust you're all familiar, works *only* between sites which are fixed in terms of short-term motion, and very widely spaced. Several light-years, at least. And, of course, it requires that an ansible be placed more or less directly between the two communication sites.

"Somehow, the Waisters are able to send instantaneous signals from ship to ship *while moving relativistically.* According to our understanding of relativity, this should make it possible for them to transmit messages backward in time, though in fact we have no evidence that they are doing this."

"Hold it," Ranes protested. "You said they came from Alnilam, right?"

"Ah, no. I said Alnilam was the *closest* star they could have come from unless they made a very dramatic course change before the dispersal maneuver."

Ken Jonson, Marshe's new Drone, raised a hand uncertainly. He looked quite lost. "Um ... Sipho, that's the third time you've mentioned this dispersal maneuver. I don't know what that is."

"Oh." The astronomer scratched his chin for several seconds, as though he were resetting brain controls. "Astronomers at Sirius observed a radiant phenomenon in the waist of Orion approximately fifteen months before the arrival of the scout group. Astronomers at Wolf 359 observed the same phenomenon about six years later, and were attacked by a second scout group twenty-three months after that. This is all reconstructed, of course; the fact that Sirius didn't have an ansible complicates matters."

Complicates matters? Marshe snorted. The Colonial period had ended suddenly, its economic collapse leaving the Sirius ansible half-constructed. If someone in the past four centuries had thought to finish the job, the rest of humanity would have had an extra six years' warning that the Waisters were coming. As it was,

Wolf 359 was completely unprepared for their attack. The inhabitants of Sol and the other colonies watched in horror as, over a period of five months, the Wolf system was scoured clean of human life.

Marshe remembered when she'd first heard the news. She'd been on her way out to meet some friends, her brain buzzing with the excitement of being twenty-six years old, unemployed, and in love. Her father had called just as she was leaving, and had explained, in his brutally direct way, that a mysterious, alien force was attacking the Wolf colony. Marshe had gone out anyway, the news not really hitting deep until she'd arrived at the club, to find it nearly deserted. She'd called her fiancé then, gone to his apart, spent the evening consoling him and being consoled. Next morning they'd marched together to the UAS offices and enlisted. Three weeks after that, their orders came through, separating them forever, and Marshe's own, personal loss had brought forth the tears that all humanity's suffering could not.

She remembered, also, the time two years later, when the radio transmissions from Sirius had arrived like the punch line of a very, very bad joke. Jubilation, at first—the discovery of alien intelligence. The first cries of outrage had followed quickly, and then there had been terror, and finally, in the end, silence.

"At any rate," Yeng went on, oblivious to the horror of what he'd just said, "by correlating the times and exact positions of these two observations we've been able to determine the point in space at which the phenomenon occurred, which turns out to be twenty light-years out on a straight line between Sol and Alnilam. The current theory is that the Waister ships had been traveling as a single convoy until this time, at which point they dispersed, forming two scout groups and two armadas. The scout group which we destroyed last month, and the armada which is currently en route to Sol, are thought to be the same ones that attacked Sirius ten years ago. Lalande's scout group and armada are thought to be the ones that attacked Wolf 359."

"Hey!" snapped Josev. "I was trying to make a point. Let's *say* the Waisters came from Alnilam, okay? That's twelve hundred light-years away. Our first radio signals didn't reach them until, like, about two hundred years ago."

"Yes," Yeng agreed, raising an eyebrow.

"They only travel at point-nine-cee, right? There you go! They had to have sent a message backward in time. No other way they could get here so quick."

"Ah, yes," Yeng said. "That's certainly one theory. However, it's more likely that human activity here in Sol system produced an FTL signal of some sort, perhaps in the early space age, which alerted the Waisters to our presence. Alternatively, they may possess the equivalent of a Faster-Than-Light telescope. If they really could send messages backward in time, then they could have warned themselves, for example, about the destruction of the scout group, and then taken steps to prevent it from happening."

"Maybe they have," Josev suggested. "Maybe the timeline we're on is about to be erased."

Yeng smiled thinly. "Perhaps. But I think we'd do better to assume otherwise, and continue to fight the war. Ah?"

"Okay," Josev said. "That's true. But maybe it's like the ansible effect. Maybe they can only send backward-time messages over very large distances, so in this case it wouldn't work."

Marshe raised her hand again. She'd been swinging her head from Sipho to Josev and back again, like a spectator at a tennis match, and she was getting tired of it. "I think you're reaching," she told Josev. "You're stubborn; you like to argue. That's good sometimes, but don't let it slow us down, okay? Those aren't *bad* ideas, we shouldn't rule them out, but let's concentrate for now on the likelier alternatives."

"I'm hungry," Shenna complained.

"We'll eat later, Shenna," Marshe said, a little too harshly. "We're very busy right now."

"Not busy," said Shenna. "Sitting. Sitting is not busy."

Yeng put a hand on Shenna's head. "Hush, little one. We're *talking,* and that's very important."

Marshe nodded gratefully. Let the Workers handle the Dog. That was proper. And speaking of Workers ... "Roland, you've been even quieter than usual. I presume you have something useful to contribute?"

Roland Hanlin looked up, as if surprised at the sound of his own name. Looking at her for a moment, he shrugged. His gaze returned to the holie screens.

"I'm *talking* to you, Worker Two. You're Ordnance. Why don't you tell us what weapons the Waisters used against Glacia?"

Hanlin looked at her again. "You saw it as well as I," he said in his thick Cerean accent. The words seemed to be forced out of him, like coughs. "They turned their tails to the moon and slagged it with their drive motors."

"Did they?" Marshe asked. "I didn't see that. How powerful *are* those beams?"

"They push a starship at ninety gee's, don't they? Two, three hundred terawatts I'd say. Hundred thousand times more than our largest gunboat laser."

"That must be a standard tactic," Josev Ranes cut in. "On the scouting raids they fly in backwards, with the drive motors on. Anything in their path gets pretty well vaporized. That's what happened to Nysa. We flew by it on the *Century City* about five weeks ago, so I got a real good look. Most of the asteroid was just sheared away. There's just this little nubby bit left, and one end of it's all shiny and smooth, like a mirror.

"It's a good defense against natural obstacles, but of course when we attacked we threw the sand *across* their path, not directly into it. Splat! No time to get out of the way."

"Okay," Marshe said. "Thank you, Roland. Thank you, Josev. What does this mean to us? We're the Waisters, we have this weapon. It doesn't always work, and we know that now. So what do we do? Anybody."

"Doesn't matter in this case," said Josev. "We're not moving fast enough for it to be a problem. Same thing is true when we get to Sol. The armadas come in slow, keeping inside the ecliptic plane. We just fan out and march through the system, like we did at Wolf and Sirius."

"Okay," Marshe said, picking up the tempo. "That's what I want to hear. What else do we do? Do we spit sand again? No, we can't, can we. We're not moving fast enough for that to be destructive."

Josev swept a finger across the room. "Nyiiiiiik! We use our disintegration beams."

Marshe nodded to Roland. "Worker Two?"

"Limited range," Roland said, after a reluctant pause. "We need to close wi' the targets one at a time."

"Hmm. And there are a lot of targets. How much range do we have with the drive motors? How quickly can we reorient them?"

"Careful," said Sipho Yeng. "The higher we turn up the gamma rays, the faster we accelerate *away* from our target. At nonpropulsive intensities, the beams wouldn't be destructive past a few light-seconds."

"Okay," Marshe said. "We *do* need to be close, then.

It sounds to me like we really just sweep through the system, end to end, picking targets as we go."

"That meshes with the Waister strategies at Wolf and Sirius," Josev agreed. "We get plenty of time to gloat over each little victory."

Through the corner of her eye, Marshe saw Ken Jonson wince at that remark.

"Did you have something to say, Drone Two?" she asked, turning to face the young man who sat beside her.

Jonson seemed to wither beneath her gaze, bowing his head, hunching his shoulders, drawing his feet up under the chair. His eyes glazed over a bit, as if looking at something far away. Marshe wondered, with a kind of sick fascination, what it was he was seeing.

"Kenneth?" she prompted gently.

"Ma'am," he said, with visible effort. "That's not right, what Josev just said. They don't gloat. They don't . . . they're not *angry* at us."

"And what makes you say that?"

Jonson looked up, then looked down again when he saw that all eyes were on him. "You're from Earth, right?" he said. "You've seen wild animals. You can't read their thoughts, but you can always see what they're *feeling* from their body language. Fear, anger, curiosity . . . even animals that are very different from us. Even sea slugs."

Marshe placed a hand on Jonson's shoulder, and was surprised to find him physically trembling. What the hell had they *done* to this man? "Go on," she said.

"The Drones were the aggressive ones, of course, but they were very, uh, calm about it. Sort of resigned, actually. The others, were more . . ." His voice trailed away, and moments later a series of gasps took its place.

Marshe rose from her chair, noting that Sipho and

Josev were doing likewise. But the young corporal waved her away, waved the whole of reality away. "I'm sorry," he whispered. She saw tears dripping from his tightly closed eyes. "I really can't do this. I really can't."

She felt sympathy rising through her like a flood. This man was in *torment,* how could she be *doing* this to him? But sympathy was worse than useless here, she knew. Sympathy was a drain on valuable resources. An unpleasant fact, certainly, but Marshe Talbott knew her job.

"CORPORAL!" she bellowed. The fingers which rested on Jonson's shoulder curled themselves into claws, digging into the flesh, dragging him back where he belonged.

A jolt ran through the man's body, almost as if he'd been hit with a defibrillator. His eyes snapped open, looked wildly at her. "WHAT!" he cried, jerking himself away. "What! What do you want me to do?"

She fed him an icy glare. "I don't want to see that again, do you understand me? When I ask you a question, I expect you to answer it. If you fade out on me, I'll just slap your face and ask you again."

Jonson leaned even farther away from her, and brushed at the tears on his cheeks at though they burned.

"Go easy," said Josev Ranes.

"Shut up, Lieutenant," she told him without looking. Then, to Jonson: "Are you listening to me?"

The corporal nodded several times in quick succession. "Yeah," he said. He was still rubbing his eyes.

"Go take a shower. Be back here in ten minutes."

"Yeah," he said again. After a few moments he staggered up out of his chair and started moving toward his quarters.

Marshe looked around at her people. Shenna lay on

the floor, her chin on her paws, sad eyes looking up at the proceedings. Josev Ranes looked angry, but avoided meeting her gaze. Yeng and Hanlin, the Workers, *were* looking at her, their expressions neutral.

"Okay, people," she said, trying to recover her earlier momentum. "We're talking about strategy. What's next? What's the human fleet at Lalande doing?"

"Dying, your Queenship." said Josev. His eyes, she saw, were on the tactical schematic holie on the panel beside him. It presented a thick rope of red trails projecting into the star system, surrounded by a haze of thin green lines. Even as she watched, two of the green lines flashed white and vanished. Josev clicked his tongue. "They're just dropping like pebbles. I think we ignore them. When they come close, we shoot them, but other than that I don't think they have any effect on our strategy at all."

Marshe found she had nothing to say to that. Neither did anyone else, it seemed. The room was very silent for a while.

Ken felt the hot water bouncing off his skin like solid particles, unable to clean, unable to purge him of the misery that clung to his flesh like rotted greasepaint. "I really can't do this," he whispered again.

God, maybe he should just slash his wrists and be done with it. Live like a Waister? Think and spit like a Waister? The thought was more horrible than any other he could recall.

They're people, the voice of Josev Ranes reminded him. *Not like us, but still people.* He remembered the calm resolve of the Drones, the helpless wailing of the orphaned Dog. *Still people. Still people.* Would it really be so difficult? He recoiled as if struck, for *that* was the idea he'd been running from. *That,* he realized, was the most horrible thought his brain could ever hold.

It wouldn't be difficult. No, it wouldn't be difficult at all.

Chapter 4

Ken's gumboots held him fast to the surface of the Waister scoutship as he turned this way and that, trying to get a good look at his men. Theoretically, the roll-joints at the neck and waist of his suit had enough play in them to make this possible, but in practice he found he could swivel no more than twenty degrees. The men, also glued to the scoutship's hull, stood about Ken in an expectant, inward-facing circle. Like roundtable knights looking to their king.

The hull shook faintly as the Spider dug and drilled its way in with diamond-fullerene claws. *Dig,* Ken thought, distractedly. *Come on, COME ON!* He'd been here twenty minutes already, and the thing seemed to be *soaking* its way in, millimeter by excruciating millimeter.

Around him the men's stares were oppressive, suffocating. What did they want from him? Zero gravity urged his body to relax, to slouch inward and curl up like a fetus, but he fought against it, keeping his knees locked, his back as straight and stiff as a plank of wood. Let them see rage and defiance in his stance, let them guess and wonder if the icy stalagtites of fear dripped and sweated in his guts as in their own.

The men had arrived like an explosion happening in reverse, coming in from different directions with different speeds, but all converging on the Spider's homing beacon within minutes of each other. The landing force had been a thin shell, enclosing billions of cubic kilometers of space. Attrition had eroded the walls as they contracted, the shell thinning and shrinking, thinning and shrinking until it became a web of tiny human jewels enclosing the ship. Then the web had swirled, danced, broken up into dozens of delicate whirlpools that spiraled in against the hull. Disintegration beams had done what they could, but groups of men now dotted the ship like pockets of deadly infection.

Deadly, that was, if the *skin* could be penetrated. "Come on, Spider!" he barked out loud. That was a violation of protocol, since technically the sound was conducted from his suit down through the gumboots and into the interior of the Waister ship. But the gnawing of the Spider against the hull would be far louder, the scream of rock-cutting machinery as heard from *inside* the rock. If they could hear him over *that,* let them. "Dig, you fucker! Come on, dig, *Dig!*"

Ken's scooter had parked itself alongside the earlier arrivals, and still others were swooping down, landing themselves in two neat rows. *Alive,* he'd thought. *Huh.* The fact of his survival seemed unreal, an improbable twist in a dizzy falling-dream of darkness and smothering terror. Something new was happening. His death would take a different form now, his final agonies a new and unfamiliar texture.

He had waited, looking around for his commanding officer, eyeing each trooper's insignium. Where were the officers? He waited some more, but the men had stopped coming. No officers? No sergeants? No other corporals? But that meant ... Oh. Dear God, that meant Ken was in charge. The thought was obscenely almost-funny, like the lopsided grin of a smashed and bleeding skull.

Bastard, he'd whispered to the God that had forsaken him. In Charge. What did it mean to be In Charge of a platoon of scooter-parked marines on the surface of a Waister scoutship? It meant ... Oh, no. He'd unfastened his rape hose from the scooter's tanks, letting it reel and snake its way back into his chest. Then, choking back shapeless fear, he'd flipped himself over and off the scooter, slapping his gumboots firmly onto the alien hull. They held.

He'd taken a few steps, feeling the rubbery adhesive tense and then *give* suddenly as he lifted his feet, feeling it flow and compress and adhere as he pushed down again. The boots worked. They actually worked. With hand signals, he'd ordered the men off their scooters. Slowly, grudgingly, they had complied, and stumped around angrily to encircle Ken and the Spider.

Ken shook his head, brought himself back to the present. His time sense was getting screwy. He glanced at the Spider, eyeing its malignant bulk, the gloss-black sheen that wrapped the stars in twisted reflection around its legs and airlock-body. Its twirling, glittering blades still hummed against the dark, rusty brown of the Waister hull.

"Come on!" Ken shouted again. Or was this the first time? A *déjà vu* feeling swirled briefly through his mind and vanished. The Spider stared coldly back at him with its dark bubble-eyes. "Break through!" he ordered it.

And it did. Seconds after he'd spoken, the body of the Spider lurched downward a few centimeters, as if hungry ant-lions were pulling it down through the hole it had dug. Two legs pulled free from the hull, twitched, then slammed down again, digging for new purchase. The oblong body pulled back slightly, righting itself. The ring of green lights began to flash on its back. *Not eyes,* a voice whispered. *Just lights.*

KchchchchK! went the speakers inside Ken's helmet. Then, in an inhuman, exaggeratedly synthetic voice: "THIS IS SPIDER THREE-TWENTY. THE HULL IS PENETRATED. RADIO SILENCE IS LIFTED. THIS IS SPIDER THREE-TWENTY. THE HULL IS PENE-TRATED. RADIO SILENCE IS LIFTED. YOUR MIS-SION ASSIGNMENT IS PRINTED ON MY BACK. YOUR MISSION ASSIGNMENT IS PRINTED ON MY BACK. VICTORY IS INEVITABLE. YOU ARE INVIN-CIBLE. KICK THEIR FUCKING HEADS IN."

"What the *fuck*?" a voice called out.

". . . damn squanky piece of junk," said another.

A third voice tried to join in, but a growling wave of distortion reduced its wisdom to garbles.

"Okay!" Ken shouted over the static, surprised to hear himself speaking at all. "Cut the chatter and switch to channel two!"

He reached his hand up and tapped the second hooded switch on the front of his helmet-chin, and the distortion vanished, replaced by the chatter of soft, distant voices and the sibilant hiss of interplanetary space.

"Corporal?" somebody said.

"Yeah," Ken replied, his voice quick and tight.

"Corporal, what happens now? I mean . . ." The voice was that of a young man, younger than Ken by the sound of it, and fighting desperately to keep from crying.

"Oh," a second voice said with disgust, "will you cut it?"

". . . ain't gonna last ten minutes if he don't get his . . ."

". . . pusher with no gear where it counts . . ."

". . . *All* going to die so what's the big . . ."

"Clear the fucking channel!" Ken screamed, too loudly.

The chatter died but for a lone voice, which finished up, ". . . with an air hose up his ass."

By chance, Ken happened to see movement inside the visor of one of the men in his view. The final speaker. Gritting his teeth in hysterical anger, Ken raised his right arm and pointed its wiregun at the man. "You!" he said. "What's your name!"

There was a pause, filled only with the soft static.

"*Name*!" he shrieked, waving the wiregun slightly for emphasis. *This is the wrong thing to do,* a voice was telling him. *Wrong thing to do wrong thing wrong thing*—

"Mirez, sir!" the man shouted back, his voice sounding strangled.

"Mirez," Ken echoed. He paused, listening to the hiss of the planets for a few moments. Something seemed to crystallize in his heart. "Mirez. I told you to clear the channel. You've just bought yourself a ticket inside."

"Huh?" Mirez asked, with obvious fright.

"Get in the Spider, boyo," Ken said cruelly. "You're first man through."

"Corporal, I didn't mean it. I'm sorry, I was just so *scared* I—"

"Private, get in the Spider before I blow your chest open. These orders are not negotiable."

Mirez made a deep squeaking noise, but he pulled a boot free of the hull and slapped it down half a meter in front of him, repeated the task with the other foot. Like a tortured puppet, he lurched and staggered toward the Spider, climbing up onto its back when he got there. He turned at the waist, looking back in Ken's direction, but he turned away quickly; Ken was still pointing the wiregun at him. Without further ceremony, he leaned over, grabbed a pair of handles, and pulled himself face-first onto the Spider's oblong back.

Mirez vanished. Not in a flash, or a puff or vapor, or a cloud of sticky-freezing blood. He simply disappeared like a playing card from the fingers of a magician—eaten by the Spider. Ken knew that the handles had withdrawn, and the outer door had split, each half swinging inward, then rolling straight out, then swinging inward again, scooping the marine into the airlock-body and closing behind him. Then the inner doors had done the same thing, and Mirez had been expelled to the interior of the Waister ship. All in a blinding cobra-strike instant.

"Mirez, report," Ken said. The voice was alien, even to him. The words had sprung, unbidden, to his lips.

A burst of choppy, whining static stabbed back at him. Nothing recognizable as a human voice.

"Mirez! Report!"

This time, no sound came back at all.

"Shit," Ken said. He looked around at his men. "Everyone form a line behind me. I'm going in."

Going in? *Going in?* Fear raced through his blood, tingled his hair and the roots of his teeth. The sphincter of his anus felt suddenly as if it were shrinking back into his colon. His mouth went dry. But his legs scissored, carrying him forward almost of their own accord, and his hands formed fists that were simultaneously wiregun triggers and armored, bludgeoning hammers.

He was going in.

Climbing onto the Spider's back was awkward, the kind of flailing weightless task that Ken had never been properly trained to perform, but he managed it adequately. His hands found the handles that Mirez had gripped. His feet pulled free of the Spider's slick shell. The sign, the orders stenciled on the Spider's back: FORWARD. That was all. Ken pulled himself downward, gently . . .

There was a lurching sensation, a flicker of darkness followed by pale, purple-gray light, and suddenly he was pivoting on his toes, dizzily falling face-first onto a flat, wet-looking surface. He and the surface met solidly, the shock slapping through him like the blow of a heavy sandbag. He felt himself bounced and jostled inside his crash webbing.

What the . . .

Gravity. He'd stepped into gravity and fallen on his face.

"Mirez," he groaned, without lifting his faceplate from the floor. "Report."

"Check it out, Corporal! It's gravity! Gravity on every wall!"

Ken pressed his arms flat against the floor and pushed. He was *heavy,* but he managed to raise himself enough to tuck a knee under his center of mass. Like a piece of construction machinery, he levered himself upward. And gasped.

The chamber was diamond shaped, a house-sized octahedron, its glistening, triangular walls the color of dead lilacs, lit by a diffuse and apparently sourceless glow. Mirez stood on one of the walls a few meters away, his upright body canted fully ninety degrees from the direction Ken felt as "down." Behind and beyond the man, some gray things that might have been boxes were clinging to the walls like sea anemones. They were hexagonal tubes a little over a meter high, their tops flat and seamless.

No sign of enemy troops.

"Oh," Ken said softly.

"About one point five gee's, Corporal. Trouble getting up?"

Ken swept his gaze back and forth, looking at Mirez, at the boxes on the walls above and around him. Waiting for something to fall, grunting in bafflement when nothing did. Mutely, he got his other foot under him, found balance, and stood.

"Artificial gravity," he said.

"Corporal." Mirez was leaning back, looking "up" at Ken. "I could have splattered you all over this chamber. You son of a bitch." The man's breathing was heavy with fear and exertion.

Ken felt disgust rising in his throat, locking his jaws, drawing his mouth into a rictus. "Private," he said, "we are here to fight the Waisters. Wolf, Sirius! Remember those places? Remember Albuquerque and Iapetus and Nysa? Do you think I'm scared of *you*?"

"You should be," said Mirez.

"Oh. Oh! That's great! Like wiring me is going to make a difference! We're *dead*, boyo, haven't you figured that out? We secure the ship. That's all. Getting out alive is not part of the job description."

"Oh man," said Mirez. "You're really prize. I'm supposed to take orders from a corporal with a death wish?"

"Get back in the Spider," Ken told the man. "Get outside and tell the men to start coming in. Warn them about the gravity."

Mirez glared insolently. "Or what?"

Ken glared back, considering his answer. *Act,* an internal voice advised him. He acted.

Gravity twisted at him as he leaped from his wall onto Mirez', but he resisted vertigo, nausea, collapse. *Busy right now,* he thought, *call me later.* But the sound that came from his lips was a martial "KiYAA!" His hands found the young private's shoulders, pushed against them while his right leg, fighting the stiff joints of the hardsuit, swept horizontally. Mirez was a spacer, like most of the marines. Had to be. *Had* to be. But Ken knew what it was to *fight,* struggling gravity-pinned against the dirt while bully ham-fists pummeled and battered.

Mirez fell quickly in the high gravity, and Ken rode him down, hand-to-shoulder, knee-to-stomach. The impact jostled him, blurring vision, jamming fingers and thighs against their rings of ceramic restraint. Mirez made a sound, a throaty grunt that terminated abruptly.

No time for this! a voice nagged. Ken ignored it.

Slowly, deliberately, he moved his hand to the center of Mirez' chest, grabbing the handle of the rape hose, pulling until half a meter of it was exposed. He paused then, looking down into the man's terrified eyes. Then, he drew Excalibur from the sheath on his leg, and made as if to draw the blade across the smooth, serpentine body of the hose. He paused again.

"You . . ." he panted, suddenly tired. "You want to try the air? Yes or no?"

"ohgod," Mirez gagged. "No. No. I'm sorry. Please, I—"

"Pathetic," Ken said, in a voice he did not recognize. He let go of the hose, watched it snake back into Mirez's suit. He resheathed the utility knife, shuffled his feet, and drew himself upright again, resisting the meaningless urge to brush himself off as he stepped clear of the man's body.

"Get up," he said, when he saw that Mirez was still looking up at him with wide, frightened-child eyes. "Get back in the Spider, do what I said. Now!"

A flicker of movement caught his eye, something above him and off to one side, something up on one of the crazy ceiling-walls of the chamber. He felt a stab of emotion, neither fear nor anger but *fight,* a blank, pearly wave of reptilian non-thought. He dropped into a crouch, dimly aware of wrenching, high-gravity pain. In the same fluid motion he raised his arm and balled his fist, sighting along the wiregun tube.

Nothing . . . Nothing . . .

His tracking gaze stopped. Door. Door! A hexagonal opening had appeared in one of the "upper" walls, and behind it . . . Light and shadows. Smooth, slick lavender surfaces. And movement. "Mirez!" he shouted. "Get the men in here! Right now!"

He'd been about to say more, but his voice seized, froze in his throat. Turning and twisting in the grip of byzantine gravitation, a . . . a *creature* swung through the opening and out onto the floor. Ken's mind twisted with it, trying to make sense of the flailing, clambering form.

A purple scorpion, its twin tails ending in twitching masses of wormlike fingers. A bruised and naked human, balancing inverted on flat forearms, palms and elbows down, head up, legs curled back over the body. No, no. The letter *C*, supported by four wide feet, with a face at the bottom and a pair of hideous arms dangling from the top. Its skin was ribbed and rippled and bumpy, its face buglike, fishlike, perversely human.

"Oh," Ken said, and his tone was one of protest rather than shock. "Oh, right."

The brown, bulging eyes pulsed and swiveled, and then they stopped and Ken knew that the creature, the Waister, had seen him. When it moved one of its hands, he saw that it was holding something, a thin wand that shone like dull brass. The creature glanced at the wand, hefted it as if it weighed several kilograms. Then the eyes swiveled to look back down at Ken, and the wand followed, turning slowly in the creature's hand.

A weapon? Was it a *weapon*? Keeping his fist balled, Ken bent his wrist in the way that triggered the wiregun.

There was almost no recoil.

There was almost no sound.

The Waister exploded pink-blue against the wall, a paint-balloon, a twitching bundle of rods and hoses that disintegrated as the superfast wire fragments ripped through it.

Ken blasted the remains for longer then he needed to, but finally he got control of himself and switched off the gun. Oh God. Oh God. He was actually fighting with Waisters, actually *standing in the same room* with Waisters. Looking up at the painted carrion which moments ago had been a living thing, he thought maybe he was going to be sick. The indigo slime that was the creature's blood was fading to a dull off-white, oily and translucent like semen or mucus. The spectacle was as nauseating as a swarm of maggots crawling through the offal.

"Mihhh," he coughed. "Uh! Mirez!"

No answer. Had the private escaped through the Spider already?

"Mirez! Anyone!"

His speakers gave out a faint buzzing that might have been voices, might only have been static. *Contact,* he wanted to say. *First contact. The Eagle has landed. They spray sticky blue stuff all over the place when you shoot them, folks, so do watch where you step.*

He felt his arms beginning to quiver. What did the Waister think it was doing? If it wanted to shoot him, why had it moved its hand so slowly? Why had it raced in so quickly, and then stopped, an easy target for Ken's weapons? And why was Ken here shooting at it? Why was Albuquerque a glazed depression in the floor of the North American desert?

Another monster swarmed down through the hexagonal doorway, heedless of the gore it splashed through. A third Waister followed behind it, and a fourth, and a fifth. They carried brass wands with them also. Their naked bodies were ludicrous, holie-props from a twisted children's fantasy.

Ken screamed anyway. He raised both arms, spraying the doorway, hosing it down with flechettes. The Waisters died, burst, splattered in the deadly wiregun shower. But still they poured through the opening.

One managed to break away from the carnage, dashing sidewise across the floor to a nearby cluster of boxes. Ken swung his arms toward it, but too late; the boxes came apart like gray confetti, but the Waister was past them, its apelike arms swooping and swinging as it ran. He tried to track it, but could not. Too fast, too fast . . .

"Mirez! Get in heeere!"

"Behind you, Corporal! Oh, no!"

Ken swung around, insanely turning his back on the swarming Waisters. The lacquer-black oblong of the Spider's inner door sat right at the junction between two walls, and a gray-armored marine was falling, staggering across the corner. The man fought for balance, lost, and fell sprawling. Behind him, a second man popped out of the Spider, repeated the stumble, and fell atop the first.

"Get up!" Ken screamed. "Catch the men as they come through!"

The Spider disgorged another marine onto the heap. Resolutely not-looking-up, Ken took a step toward the men, determined to help, determined to fix this mess which he had somehow failed to prevent. But his left gumboot adhered too well to the purple-gray Waister varnish; he tripped, and fell to his knees.

Something happened to the men. They seemed, for an instant, to be very sharply focused on Ken's vision. Then they seemed not quite so vivid, and their shapes began to slump, and they fell into piles of gray and pink and blood-red powder.

A fourth man flew out of the airlock, and hit the ground as a heap of swirling dust.

"Noooo!" Ken shrieked. Throwing himself over onto his back, he triggered both wireguns, spraying the room indiscriminately. "You fuckers! Cut it! Stop it!"

But there were more enemies, more marines pouring in through the Spider. The walls seethed and twitched with movement.

"Get that one! Aaa!" A voice shrieked, the sound breaking up into coarse rustling as its owner came apart.

Fuck this, Ken thought. He peeled his gumboots off, letting them shrivel up into useless balls of resin, and staggered to his feet.

"Gumboots off, everybody!" he cried over shouting voices. "We have to take the exit!"

He resumed firing for several seconds, and when he looked around again he saw that several of the men had complied with his instructions.

Run away! he wanted to say. But when he opened his mouth, the words that came out were, "This way! This way! *Everybody charge!*"

Twenty minutes later, the marines actually did manage to secure the doorway and the brief length of hexagonal corridor outside it. Ken counted eighteen men remaining, barely a quarter of his original force.

"Forward, men," he said tiredly, waving a too-heavy arm ahead of him. "Those are our orders. Forward."

"Corporal," groaned an anonymous voice. "Five minutes rest. Please."

Ken felt the aching of his body, pressing down against the rings and straps and webbing that were designed for zero gravity, designed to keep his skin from touching the material of the suit. He sampled the rasping of his lungs, the urgent hammering of his heart, the hypoxic tingling of fingers and toes. How could he *not* rest?

"God," he said. "Five minutes. Yes, okay."

As one, the men let out a sigh of exhaustion. Ken echoed the sound, dropping inelegantly to his knees. Rest.

Five minutes sounded like a hopelessly tiny interval, too short for him even to catch his breath. But when the next surge of Waisters came crashing through the corridor like the sea through a crumbling dyke, he found that three minutes were somehow enough. Weary and breathless, he summoned strength from hidden places, and raised his arms to meet the wave.

Desperation would keep him going, at least for now.

Chapter 5

"Ten minutes is not the same thing as thirty minutes, Drone Two," Marshe said with what she hoped was stern reproach.

Ken took his seat.

"Well?" she asked.

"I lost track," Ken replied calmly. "It won't happen again."

Marshe started to say something, then caught herself. There was something odd in the corporal's posture, in the slack expression he was wearing. His hands dangled from the chair's armrests in an almost casual way. What was this? In half an hour, Jonson seemed to have become a different person.

"Uh," she said, "aren't you going to apologize?"

"No. I don't think we have a word for that."

"We?" Josev Ranes inquired, his voice curious and skeptical.

"Yes," Ken said, "we, the Waisters." He glanced at Marshe, then back at Josev again. "Don't give me that look. This stuff wasn't my idea."

Josev was about to reply, but Marshe cut him off. No time to get sidetracked. "That's fine, Kenneth. I want you to look at something." She gestured at one of the holie screens. "The attack on Glacia seems to have been two-phased. First, a wide path was melted along the equator, drowning these two small communities.

Are you watching? Okay, there's the pause. Twenty minutes long. Twenty minutes! Then ... here it is. They hit the planet with fourteen beams simultaneously. The entire surface is liquefied in about five seconds."

Ken watched the display, cocking his head as if he didn't quite understand what he was seeing.

"Are you getting this?" Marshe asked him.

The corporal shook his head. "Just a white circle with stuff all over it. I'll take your word for it."

Marshe felt herself becoming exasperated. "Corporal," she said, "I'm asking for your opinion. Don't start this game."

Jonson looked at her, mildly surprised. "What's wrong? I'm sorry, okay?" He looked back at the screen, which had begun to repeat its display. "That sounds just like them. In person, they do the same kind of thing. Jump out and scare you, then wait a minute, then slam you with everything they have."

"The scouting raids," said Josev. "Same thing. Before the armada comes, y' take six ships and roar through the system with guns hot, raising all sorts of rumpus, but not doing much real damage."

Marshe watched Ken twitch, almost imperceptibly, at that remark.

"Clearly," Sipho Yeng cut in, "this is a form of communication. They're demonstrating their strength, warning us when they're about to exercise it."

"Trying to force a surrender," Josev agreed.

Marshe slapped her leg with the knife-edge of one hand. "Hold it. The Wolf colony broadcast surrender messages in every human language, and it had no effect."

"They don't know our languages," Josev said. "Never bothered to learn. Why should they?"

"Don't jump to conclusions," Marshe told him. "We

don't know that. Right now we don't know anything about that."

"Possibly, they don't monitor radio frequencies," Yeng suggested, then shook his head. "No, forget I said that. They always destroy broadcasting sites. Still, let's note that an object with the mass of a Waister scoutship, moving at point-nine-cee, could tear the sun apart if it hit correctly. With their gravity generators, it's even possible that they could destabilize a star from several light-years away. No matter what conventional wisdom says, the Waisters are fighting what must seem to them like a very limited war."

"Maybe they just want us to suffer," Marshe said coolly, though she ached to scream at the man. Limited war. Sipho Yeng could say the God-damndest things without *feeling* what they meant to other people.

Ken Jonson was shaking his head. "No, that's not it. It has to be something else."

Josev glared angrily. "Sure of that, chum?"

"Absolutely. Don't get upset, I didn't say I liked them. On Earth, some insects lay their eggs inside live animals, so the larvae have something to eat when they hatch. That's not cruel, it's just totally merciless. In some ways I think that's more horrible."

"You're awfully calm about it all of a sudden," Josev said.

"Does that bother you?"

"Stop it," Marshe said. Josev was disturbed by the change in the corporal's manner, as she was, but she couldn't allow an argument to develop. Not now. "This is important. We need to explore this issue. Do they really want us to surrender? Why would they? What do we have that they want? Roland, would you please share your thought with us?"

Roland Hanlin cringed, his heavy Cerean brow furrowing. "Don't ask me. How could I know?"

"I *am* asking you."

"Uh ... Uh ... I don't know. They're imperialists. Like the Clementine monarchs. They can't stand to see us running free."

Shenna had been lying down between the chairs of the two Workers, but she sat up now and looked around. "They are bad dogs," she said gravely.

Josev snorted. "You're pretty smart, mutt. S'pose we should make *you* the Queen."

"They're not all dogs, little one," Sipho Yeng said, putting a hand on the animal's shoulder. "Only some of them."

"Sipho," said Josev. "Loosen your bowels. Dog comes up with a brilliant observation, and all you want to do is correct her." He leaned over toward the dog. "I think you're absolutely right, Shenna. Good dog."

Shenna's tail began to wag. "Good dog," she said softly, to herself. "Good dog, good dog."

Marshe couldn't help but smile. "Shenna, thank you very much. Next time wait until I ask you, though. Josev, is the outliner picking this up? I don't want to dictate this stuff all over again for the report."

Josev rolled his chair backward, craned his neck sideways, and peered at one of the displays. "Looks like it," he said.

"Okay. Good. Now, you look like you've got something to say."

The young lieutenant sighed as he walked his chair back into the circle. He jerked an elbow in Ken's direction. "I have to disagree with Drone here. I think they're just back-corridor bullies. They've found somebody to smash and hurt and humiliate, and they love it, and if we surrender they'll be doing us up the bung for the next million years."

"Mmm." Marshe nodded vaguely. "Maybe so. Sipho?"

"A chastisement. We're doing, or else we have previously done, something they consider worthy of serious punishment."

Josev let out an angry snort. "Like what? Inventing space travel? Bullies always pick something about you that they don't like, your clothes or your hair or the way you walk, and they punish you. And they make you apologize. And then they punish you some more. Point is, they'll pick on anything at all, or else make something up, and nothing you do or say is going to stop them."

"Unless you're bigger," Ken offered darkly.

"Yeah. Unless you've got the tops on 'em somehow. Or unless you're determined to hurt them no matter what it costs." He met Marshe's gaze. "My humble opinion, oh Queen. Do we get to hear yours?"

She favored him with her best, most humorless look. "I do have a theory. Not just mine, I guess, but . . . The easiest way to know if someplace is habitable is if somebody's already living there. The easiest way to settle a new place is to steal it from somebody weaker than you. It's called Cowboys and Indians."

"Cow what?" Josev said, frowning.

"It's an Earth thing," she said. She looked over at Ken Jonson and saw him nodding thoughtfully. "It's a game where you beat up on primitives and steal their land. You never heard of it? I thought you were a history enthusiast."

"Oh, Earth is covered with little tribal nations. I never could keep them straight. Never tried much. Ask me, history started with the first visit to Luna. The rest of it is just incidental."

"A handful of worlds," Sipho said. "It's a long journey for that, twelve hundred years or more. In that time they could reshape whole planets in any image they chose. Custom environments. The energy expenditures are probably about the same as for a war, and the risks are lower."

She smiled grimly. That single point had been the primary obsession of exobiologists since the Waisters had first announced themselves. Marshe had been mulling her argument over for years. "Evolution," she said, "is about *competition*. To expand indefinitely, to fill every crack and crevice with copies of yourself, you've got to kill off all your rivals. It wasn't photosynthesis that let cyanobacteria take over the Earth three billion years ago, it was *oxygen*—deadly poison. It squeezed the competition right out of the oceans, and the atmosphere, and finally the dirt. Now the chemosynthetic prokaryotes live in the mouths of volcanoes, in pits of boiling water where the cyanobacteria can't go. We see the same story over and over again, on every living planet. On Astaroth there *are* no chemosynthetic prokaryotes anymore."

"There won't be any *anything* there in about three weeks," Josev said.

Marshe stopped, her face flushing hotly. Was she catching Sipho Yeng disease? Astaroth was the major population center of Lalande system, over three billion people. How could she have mentioned it so callously? The Waister armada would pass the planet very soon, leaving behind a ball of scorched rock and seething, simmering oceans. Site cleared for construction.

"No," she said softly. "No, you're wrong on that one. The, ah, the cyanobacteria will survive. Some of them."

"Corporal?" Marshe said, uneasily.

Kenneth Jonson was nude, and in the low gravity of the upspin gymnasium he was balancing on his forearms, his legs curling over behind him, head thrown back, so that his body was twisted in the form of a letter *C.* He was holding very still, and though she couldn't quite see his face, Marshe had the impression his eyes were closed. A noise rose up from his throat, a soft keening that rose and fell in irregular waves, punctuated by clicks and hissing, choking noises.

Marshe realized, with a shudder, that Jonson was attempting to speak the Waister language.

"Corporal," she said, her voice almost a whisper. The hairs on her arms were standing straight up, her neck and scalp tingling, nostrils flaring.

Eeehaee ##! hhh hwhaeee ##! Hwhh hwhaeee...

She listened to the sounds, trying to make sense of them. The Broca web whispered inside her, tickled faint lightning against the language centers of her brain.

Eeeehaeee #! hh hwhae ##!

Jonson's voice was strangled, gurgling, as if he were choking on blood or bile, and yet it swayed with familiar patterns, the somber cadence of Waister speech. Like a taste, a smell half-remembered from childhood. *I know this,* the web thought to her, or she to it. *I know this.*

She tasted copper in her mouth, felt a faint buzzing in her ears, in her brain.

"Kenneth," she said. "Stop it. *Stop it!*"

Jonson twitched, leaned. An elbow changed position, sliding in the light gravity, and like a structure he fell, crumpling sideways to the floor.

"What are you *doing*?" She asked, her voice quavering.

Slowly, Jonson turned and looked up at her. His eyes were distant, his mouth twitching faintly.

"Ken?"

The corporal's face went slack, his eyes seeming to come back into focus. "Marshe," he said. "Hi. What are you doing here? You startled me."

She blinked. "Josev told me you were up here. He, ah ... He seemed a little uneasy. Said, ah, you were acting weird at dinner."

"Was I?" Jonson reached for his clothes, bundled near him on the floor. "I'll be sure to talk to him about that, find out what's bothering him."

Marshe felt herself trembling slightly. Whatever Jonson had done or said in the cafeteria, she was pretty sure he hadn't balanced naked on the table and coughed out a language not intended for human throats.

"Jonson," she said. "Are you all right? Would you like to talk?"

Ken stood, pulled on a pair of briefs. "Talk? Sure. What's on your mind?"

She sighed, rubbed her temples. "This, ah ... You know what's on my mind. Have you snapped? Have you lost your God-damn mind?"

"No," Jonson said, sounding surprised and mildly indignant. He shrugged into his uniform. "I was just getting into the part. Trying to, you know, see what it feels like to be a Waister. If it bothers you, I'll stop."

"It bothers me, yes. Don't you think it's a little extreme? Four hours ago you were barely responding to questions."

Jonson zipped, buttoned, smoothed. "I didn't ask to be here, *Queen*. I don't like doing this. But why go halfway? Like that dog. Her head is crammed full of webware, and her voice is an electronic speaker. But she's talking *Standard* at us. What have we got the Broca webs for if we're not talking Waister?"

"You can't speak Waister, Corporal," she said. "Not unless your throat doubles as a bamboo flute. We got the webs so we could *listen.*"

"To what? To the dead prisoners? To the FTL transmissions we can't detect?"

"Classified. You'll find out later."

Ken sighed, ran a hand through his hair. "I almost had it. The talking, I mean. there are only about four sounds I need that I can't make. There's a thing we could wear over our mouths, a little raspy thing, kind of . . ." He made a cage of fingers over his mouth, then paused, took the hand away and shook his head. "I could draw you a picture."

"Ken," Marshe sighed.

"It would be easy," he said. "Really. As easy as not doing it. Could you just assume for a minute that I haven't lost my mind? *You're* the one who painted the rooms purple. 'If it helps, even a little . . .' "

Jonson's voice made a passable imitation of her own.

She chewed at her lip for a moment. "Mmm. That's not bad. Just clip your *T*'s a little more sharply: 'If it helps, even a li*tt*le . . .' Get that Europe effect."

She searched his features, not knowing quite what it was she wanted to find there. Sanity? Not likely. Nobody was sane anymore. She sighed. "A standard navy voder can produce almost any sound. And they can be keyed to a Broca web, so . . ." She sighed. "I'll look into it. But I want you to know, you've got me worried. Josev, too. I don't *know* what he'd say if he saw you in here. This is serious, Jonson. Watch yourself."

Something flashed across Ken's face, a frown, a hint of fear. But it was gone quickly, replaced by a tired, feeble grin. "Catch me if I fall?"

"Yes," Marshe said, without a trace of humor or kindness. "Bet on it."

Ken was disappointed with Saturn. He and Marshe had moved two levels up from the gym, to a cramped metal room with what she'd promised would be a spectacular view. But the planet hung outside the observation port like a cheap hologram, not impressive in the slightest, and he realized she'd been joking. Strange. Marine humor tended more toward the coarse and the physical. But her words had been ... ironic? Saturn looked *small,* smaller than a chase-me ball, and its color was a murky yellow, only faintly striped. The rings, those glorious God-works praised so often in poetry and song, were spidery, almost-straight lines across the equator.

"The ring plane is almost edge-on this time of year," Marshe said, catching his look.

"Oh, yeah?"

"Yeah, but the year is three hundred and fifty-nine months long."

"Huh. The jewel of Sol system," Ken said, his eyes still on the planet. "I thought there'd be more to see."

"Well, we're in a three-hundred-day drift orbit. Only thing farther out than us is a moon called Phoebe, and she's on the other side of the planet right now. It's a stupid idea if you ask me, being out here in the wide wastes. Like hiding in the middle of the room. Get a target-rich environment, like the middle of the B-ring for example, and a station is a lot harder to spot. But here we are."

"Not even blacked out?"

"Hell, no. Wide-spectrum black is a great way to confuse our *own* sensors. Doesn't bother the Waisters a bit."

"Oh. I see. What's this station called, anyway? The clipper crew never told me on the way over."

Marshe snorted softly. "Its official designation is ATG-3ll-B. That's the serial number of a Lagrange habitat that they decommissioned over a hundred years ago. Mirrors, smoke, and secret pockets. Like the Waisters are really going to search our registration archives. There was another name during the Monarchy, some grand, foofy thing I can't remember right now. The original, Preclementine asteroid was called Musashi."

"What do *you* call it?" he asked, turning from the window to face her. Weightless, her bulk made her look puffy and uncomfortable. Her hair was a stiff halo around her head.

"Me?" she smiled bitterly. "I call it home."

Her tone suggested genuine hurt, which struck Ken as strange. The captain had been here for years, far from danger, far from the clamor and struggle and endless toil that the war represented for most of humanity. What did she have to be upset about?

He turned back to the observation port. "It's better than a troopship, Captain. Better than . . ." He let his voice trail away. The stars glared, unwinking, through the thick glass.

Something touched him; and he spasmed, jerked away. He felt the object withdraw. The captain's hand.

"I'm sorry," she said, her voice soft. "I can be pretty selfish sometimes."

Ken studied the stars. Behind Saturn, and off to one side, stood Orion the hunter, his weapon raised. A warrior for the eons, never tiring, never taking the day off for R and R. It seemed the constellation should pulse with malevolent light, a grim advertisement for the creatures it harbored, but the jewels of the hunter's belt looked much like any other stars.

"Which one is Alnilam?" he asked after a long pause.

"I don't know," Marshe said. Her voice, like his, was low and quiet, as if they were standing in a church. "Sipho could tell you. When the Waisters hit us, though, they'll be coming out of Sirius. That's south of Orion somewhere. I think that's it, that bright blue one."

An arm reached out over Ken's shoulder, index finger extended, pointing out at the star. Marshe was close, her body centimeters from his. He could feel her heat on his back, contrasting sharply with the deep-space cold radiating out from the window. His pulse quickened. He reached thick fingers out to grab the bolted lip of the window, and pulled himself half a meter along the wall. Escaping.

"I'm sorry," the captain said. "I didn't mean . . ."

"It's okay," he replied tightly. He tensed his shoulders, relaxed them again. He turned to face her. "It's . . . okay."

Waister drones swarming, bursting against the walls. Screams of the dying.

"It's okay," he repeated, reaching out to take her hand.

They spun, very slowly, in the air, their right arms extended in awkward handshake. And then she pulled him in, wrapping him, enfolding him. Her embrace was tight and warm.

"Relax, Drone Two," she whispered urgently, maternally. "Relax."

Ken relaxed, moisture beading at the corners of his eyes and mouth, soaking into her uniform.

"Relax, I'm right here."

He buried his face in her warmth and softness, and held her for what seemed like hours. He felt . . . warmth? protection? No, it was something both deeper and more specific. The web tickled at his brain.

"*Whwhh,*" he said faintly. "*Whwhh # whh.*"

His Queen was here.

Chapter 6

"It doesn't feel right without the Dog here," Ken Jonson commented.

Marshe was inclined to agree. The neurolab crew had taken Shenna off at oh-dark-thirty that morning, to have her web implants reprogrammed. When she returned, she'd be speaking Waister. It was a sad thought, in a way, as if the animal's personality were being stripped away from her and replaced with a darker, more sinister model.

"Yes," Sipho Yeng said, sounding a little surprised. "It's as if we've somehow lost our symmetry."

"She'll be back," Marshe said, looking around at her people. "Day after tomorrow. Let's get on with our business. Now, I've emphasized the importance of team building, which I believe is vital to our success. On that note, I'd like each of you to relate an embarrassing incident that occurred while you were a child. I'm sure your *most* embarrassing moments are hidden away where you never think about them, but please try to come up with *something*. Because I've had time to think about this and the rest of you haven't, I'll go first."

She looked down, and smoothed the trouser leg of her uniform. The loft incident. God, this really *was* embarrassing. "I, uh . . . Clan Talbott runs a small agro combine in Eastern Europe—Bratsilasice, specifically, up in the highlands of Slovakai. My uncle was the workmaster at the combine's vineyard. He made wine.

"The last time I was there, I was in the throes of puberty, and very unhappy and being away from my friends for the summer. Usually I enjoyed the farm work, but this year Nikolai and Marthe had to scream and shout to get me to do anything. I spent a lot of my time hiding in the barn, which was a wide, tall building where they kept the horses. We used to ride on the horses, by the way. That was always my favorite summer thing. But that year I was always being punished, so my riding tackle was locked up most of the time.

"What I did in the barn, aside from brushing the horses and sulking, was jump off the loft. The combine also raised sheep, you know, and there were always bales and bales of uncarded wool inside there. The loft was about three meters high, which can be very dangerous on Earth, but I'd jump off it and land in the wool. For some reason, I used to take off my clothes and jump naked. I loved the scratchy feel against my skin when I landed. Just a kid thing, you know? But this summer, I was almost thirteen. One time, one of the farmhands came in just when I was jumping, and I suddenly realized how the whole thing would look. I tried to stop, but it was too late. I ended up landing wrong, on my back, on the very edge of the bales. Knocked the breeze right out of me.

"Well, Nikolai spotted this man carrying my naked body back up toward the house, and he just didn't know *what* to think. It took a long time to straighten out the fuss, and about a week later he shipped me back to my parents in Brussels. He said a farm like that was no place for a girl my age."

Marshe felt herself blushing. The last time she'd told that story, she'd been laughing in the arms of Jim Lublik, her fiancé, while a January night raged outside the window. Almost ten years gone, that was. No Jim Lublik anymore, no cold winter nights. But here she was, sharing the same intimate secret with . . . others.

"Josev, I'd like you to go next."

Josev Ranes glowered at her, brooding still on their earlier exchange of words. "You happy?" he'd said, waving a finger in her face. They'd been alone in the assimilation chamber, the others not back from breakfast yet. "You pushed Jonson till he broke. Reprogramming the dog was his idea, right? Sludger's gone totally out the lock."

"I talked with him last night," she'd countered. "He's a little disoriented, but his mind is still working, and his perspective is vital. Don't you start making accusations behind his back. Or mine."

Her voice had rung fiercely, but inside she'd winced; there was truth in Josev's accusation. Ken Jonson was like a man dangling from the edge of a cliff, looking up with calm eyes as his fingers lost purchase and slipped. Last night she'd reached out to grab him, and been pulled off balance herself. Their long embrace was puzzling to her now, her thoughts and motives unclear. She'd wanted to calm him, help him smooth out the tangles of his mind. But when she'd put her arms around him, her feelings had not been as motherly as she'd indicated, nor had they been lustful in the usual sense. She had felt . . . strange. Queenlike. It was she who'd broken the hug, claiming an errand.

"We're waiting," she said now to Josev.

He growled. "Shouldn't we be thinking about the war? Shit. There was this time *I* was thirteen years old, and this new family moved in across the corridor from us. Two doors down, I guess it was. The people that used to live there were clan Karlawish—*Four* children, and they all smelled funny. But these new people were Goodbury, very neat and neighborly, and their daughter was a nymph named Becky Li. She'd smile and wink when we passed each other in the corridor, even though she was a year ahead of me in training. Names-of-God, the things I wanted to do with her! But my Da was a sadistic old fart tank, invited the family over for dinner one night. I was so nervous I choked on a piece of tart and coughed it up all over the table."

Marshe smiled. This didn't sound as intimate as her own story, but Josev seemed genuinely embarrassed to be telling it. Maybe it was the memory of adolescence, more than the story itself, that made him squirm. "What happened next?"

"Next? She made a face, then turned away and never spoke to me again. End of story."

"Oh. Well. Thanks for sharing it."

She favored Josev with a faintly sympathetic smile. He was *supposed* to feel uncomfortable, that was the point of this exercise, but he should also feel camaraderie with his fellow sufferers. After a moment, he gave a little nod to show her that the message had been received. She turned and cast a meaningful look at Sipho Yeng, who sat beside Josev in the circle. "Have you got one for us?"

The astronomer fidgeted and smiled uncomfortably, as if he were sitting on something sharp. "Ah. I suppose so, though I must say this does *not* strike me as a helpful exercise." He looked at Ken Jonson, then at Marshe, then back at Jonson again. "I'm sure you two know what ice skating is, but, ah . . ." His gaze swept to Josev, and to Roland Hanlin. "I wonder about you."

"Where you strap blades on your feet and slide around?" Josev asked. "Yeah, I've seen holies of it. On Luna we just use a polished floor and a pair of flat-soled shoes. We call it 'slide dancing'."

Sipho nodded. "Mmm. In the winter on Mars, it's usually too cold to skate. The pressure of the blade doesn't melt the ice directly under it, so it doesn't bite in. You can't steer, or stop, or even go straight too well without falling. In the spring, though, we have big festivals. After thirteen months of winter, you understand, people are very anxious to celebrate. Young children build sand sculptures, the parents dance and sing, and the older children all go skating.

"The first year I was old enough to go, my mother became obsessed with the idea that I would fall down, break my visor and suffocate. Never mind that she and my father had both been skating at the same age. She made me wear a sort of bar over the front of my helmet, and the other children laughed and laughed at me. Years later they were still calling me names because of it."

"Ah," Marshe said, suppressing this time the urge to smile. "What a charming story. Thank you very much." She turned to Roland Hanlin, who cringed. "Roland? Please be as candid; it is your turn."

Roland pursed his lips, waited a moment, then uncringed himself and spoke without further prompting. "There's two kinds of light besides regular. Quick light and slow. When people know things far away, things they oughtn'ta know about, that's quicklight. That's how the Waister ships know their formations and suchlike. FTL. Quicklight. The other kind of light is slow, and that's where a ghost come from."

Josev made a derisive noise. "That's likely the stupidest thing I've ever heard."

Marshe raised a hand, silencing him, and said to Roland; "Is this leading somewhere particular?"

"Sure," Hanlin replied. "I didn'ta think you'd agree or nothing. But it's part of my story. My sister, she'd always see slowlight better than me. It has to do with the retina, with those tiny rod and cone cells that the eye uses to detect light with. See, the slowlight spreads out from people and objects and things that happen, in these slow shells that move maybe a centimeter every year. If your eye catches 'em perpendicular, then the slowlight triggers those rods and cones just like regular. But most of the cones don't line up totally straight, which is why a ghost looks kind of clear. Most of your eye isn't seeing it.

"Anyhow, I figure my sister has some really straight cones in her eyes, because she was seeing ghosts a lot more than I ever was. One day we were down deep in the catacombs, and—"

A buzzer rang out, shattering Marshe's concentration.

"Hang on," she said, then rolled her chair over to one of the assimilation chamber's many data consoles. She tapped a few keys. "Yes?"

The holie screen above the console blanked momentarily, the image of Lalande system vanishing, replaced quickly by the head and shoulders of Colonel Jhee.

"Captain Talbott," the colonel said.

"Yes?" she repeated.

"I've just finished reading your report, and I am not amused."

"Sir?"

He leaned closer to the screen. "A batch of wild guesses, Captain, does not constitute a report, no matter what your fancy introduction says. And *vague* guesses, at that."

Marshe rolled her eyes, wondering if Jhee was *permanently* an asshole. Perhaps surgery could correct the problem. "Colonel, I *told* you we weren't fully up to speed yet. It's not like we can tell you which planet they'll attack next."

"That is *precisely* what I expect you to tell me. Which planet, when, and how. This project is not a platform for you to express your opinions. Frankly, your viewpoint doesn't matter. What I want is what you promised me: tactical forecasting."

"Very well, sir," Marshe said crisply. "The Waister armada will attack Medius in thirty-seven point six hours."

The colonel's face darkened. "This is not a joking matter, Captain. I expect a complete revision of your report by lights-out tonight. If the revision is not acceptable, then you will work through the night to *re*-revise it. Further, I shall be expecting update reports every twenty-four hours, and more frequently than that if I present you with specific questions. Your group exists, madam, as an extension of myself. Its purpose is to satisfy me. Nothing else. I trust my meaning is clear."

"Ever cut wood with a blunt saw?" Marshe asked the man, her tone decidedly un-cowed. "You could sit there all day, cutting and cutting, or you could take five minutes out to sharpen the blade, and quadruple your productivity—*and* get cleaner pieces that don't splinter when you carry them."

Jhee's mouth twitched with the initial stirrings of real anger. "Emperor Nero played a fiddle," he said, "while the city of Rome burned around him. No more games, Captain, get to work. We may still have time to save . . . something."

Marshe rolled her eyes again, clenched her teeth. Like so many of the upper-echelon commanders, Jhee was trapped in a backward, almost Clementine mode of thought. If victory were possible, it would be achieved through plodding, relentless labor, through mass production and massive confrontation. There was no room in his mind for innovation or imagination. As a scientist, Marshe was accustomed to quick changes in viewpoint, quick dissolution of tightly held beliefs and prejudices. Her more brilliant colleagues would attack problems from inside, from outside, from any side at all. The fresher the perspective, the better. But Jhee could no more turn a question on its head than he could swap the poles of the sun.

"Colonel," she said carefully, "we'll prepare the report, if it's that important to you. But the primary purpose of this group is still to acquire a basic understanding of Waister psychology."

"No, madam, it is not."

She sighed. "We seem to have a difference of opinion. You'll get your reports, Colonel, but you'll get more than that. I'm trying to offer you *insight*. If you think the opinions of this group are irrelevant, then you're turning your back on what may be your most important resource."

"Good day," the colonel said, his voice and face registering only a dense and puzzled frustration, as if he'd tried to stand up, only to find one of his legs numb and unresponsive.

The screen flickered, and the Lalande schematic replaced the colonel's visage once more.

"Clodgy bastard," Josev muttered behind her. "If his head were any thicker he'd have to—"

"Thank you," she interrupted, turning back toward the group. "It appears we'll have to postpone our team-building exercise. Josev, I hope your blood sugar is high this morning. You too, Ken. We'll need a strong, soldierly tone if we're going to shut that man up."

"It's too bad," said Josev. "I was so enjoying Worker Two's story."

Roland glowered, but said nothing.

"Oh," Marshe said. "One more thing. I was going to start some voice lessons today, but it doesn't look like we'll have time. I'd like each of you, in your spare moments, to practice speaking the Waister language."

Josev stared at her. "You're not serious, are you? We haven't got the mouth for it."

"That's already been taken care of. I've ordered a set of vocal prostheses. We should have them in a couple of days. In the meantime we all need to get ready."

"This was another one of your brilliant insights, wasn't it?" Josev asked, turning an accusing look on Ken Jonson.

Ken sighed. "Yeah, it was. Josev, why are you so hostile to me? I thought we were friends."

"Yeah, well. We are." Josev leaned his head forward, scratched uncomfortably at the back of it where the Broca scars were. "Oh sludge, chum, I'm just worried. You seem so . . . so *sharp*. You're paying close attention to everything, you're sitting right straight up in your chair. It's not natural. It's . . . Well, I don't know you too terribly well, but it's not like you, is it?"

Marshe watched Jonson's mouth twitch in that peculiar way she'd seen last night. "No," he said. "It isn't. You might say I'm playing a role, here. Acting the way I imagine a Waister Drone would act. But that's not really accurate; as I go along, I'm reinventing my self-image. Obviously, you think I'm going too far."

"Becoming the enemy?" Josev's face was dark and serious.

"Yes," Ken said.

"Gentlemen," Marshe cut in, putting both diplomacy and force into her voice. "Let's not get sidetracked. We have an awful lot to cover."

She triggered the outliner, and guided the two men through a series of highly specific questions, looking occasionally to Yeng and Hanlin, her Workers, for additional information. The task went slowly. The clock seemed hardly to move.

Becoming the enemy? The phrase kept floating up in her mind. Not *studying* the enemy. Not *imitating* or *emulating* the enemy. Was Jonson right? She'd lived for years in the shadow of Colonel Jhee and others like him. Had their influence led her somehow to propose a timid, halfhearted plan? She tried to think.

Becoming the enemy? The question repeated itself.

Yes, she heard Jonson's voice echo dimly. The aliens were faceless, incomprehensible. To know them, to *understand* them ... Jhee's mind was closed, but Marshe's was not. She nodded slightly, privately. Becoming the enemy. Yes.

Chapter 7

The corridors went on forever, glistening, hexagonal tunnels that bent and twisted back on themselves again and again. A three-dimensional maze of endless lavender through which Ken staggered. He longed to lean against the wall, or to trail a hand along it, at least, as he walked. But in this nightmare place, walls became floors if he brushed too close. He had fallen hundreds of times, to crawl sluglike through the gravity that tried to press him hard against every surface. It was so difficult to get up, then, so easy to lie still and rest. He thought maybe he had slept once or twice. He wasn't sure.

Nobody was with him. He remembered that there had been another, but . . . but . . .

The Waisters had attacked yet again, not with their magic wands but with some other kind of thing. And then, somehow, they were gone again, but Ken's companion, a young private, had taken a hit in the middle of his chest. He'd come running at Ken—face a hypoxic blue, rebreather groaning and rattling through a ragged opening three centimeters across—and jammed his rape hose into Ken's plexial socket.

The two men had fallen, and Ken had heard a terrible gnawing sound as the circulation pump in the private's rebreather broke loose and bit through flesh and bone. Hot, sticky syrup had splurted from Ken's air vents, down onto his face and neck, and fine red droplets had misted the inside of his helmet visor.

Ken's wiregun spools were long expended, his shotgun lost somewhere, but Excalibur was firmly gripped in his hand, as if welded in place, and with a shriek of disgust he had swept the blade sideways, severing the hose.

Moments later, his eyes had begun to sting and burn, and he'd felt a horrid tingling in his nose and throat and lungs as mucous membranes started to dissolve. His rebreather was drawing Waister air in through the stump of the rape hose! He'd reached up to paw at the release buttons, while the other man let go a deep, guttural scream. Somehow, the private—blood fountaining from the end of his hose as it whipped and thrashed back into its hole—got to his feet and started running, and then . . . and then . . .

Something had happened to him. Ken couldn't remember what.

There were sounds on the radio, now, distant chattering that struggled against the static. But this had happened many times before. The voices were never intelligible, and Ken had long ago given up trying to reply.

He hadn't the strength for speech, anyway. His body was a distant thing, a faded memory that cried out with little more than the echoes of pain. Even his eyeblinks were slow and somehow vague.

He trudged onward. It seemed, at times, that he should have a goal or destination, or something. At other times, it seemed he had always been here, wandering through the haze and darkness that lay on the far side of exhaustion. Sometimes the purple-gray walls pulsed womblike around him, a thing which both comforted and disturbed him. He didn't know what it meant. Then, sometimes the walls shimmered and faded, and Ken walked beneath the hot Albuquerque sun or beneath the canopy of a great misty jungle.

He longed to banish sensation altogether, to put an end to the far away pain of breathing and movement, to spill the last dregs of awareness from his mind. It seemed he had once known how to do this. A simple thing, a . . . a . . . He didn't know. He couldn't imagine.

Movement ahead.

He raised his eyes, peered through the crusty white film that clung to the outside of his visor, the crusty red-brown film that coated the inside. Movement.

Waisters, many of them. *Three,* his mind whispered. One stood on what was, for Ken, the corridor's ceiling. The others clung to the walls. He watched the sinuous roll of their bodies, saw the underwater dancing of willowy arms and fingers. These were the Thin Waisters, he saw. The ones that wouldn't attack. There were Fat Waisters, also, and Small Waisters that looked for all the worlds like hairless dogs. But it was the Thick ones who attacked, who swept through the corridors in waves of ten or twenty or a hundred. Ken hadn't seen any of those for a very long time.

Dreamily, he fought against the gravity and raised his sword. *En garde,* he mouthed, dry lips cracking with the effort.

The Waisters, dimly visible through the smeared visor, turned and fled. Ken stopped, waited. Surely the Thick ones must come now, to defend their slender kin. He waited further, for minutes, eternities. But the corridor remained empty. Finally, he lowered the sword and continued forward.

He noticed small pools of blue-white slime on the walls and ceiling. As if the aliens were covered with slowly hemorrhaging wounds. He wondered. Many of the Waisters he'd seen seemed to be *drooling* blood from their lobsterlike mouths. Had they been attacked but not killed, all of them? It didn't seem likely.

He followed the trails of blood.

It occurred to him, briefly, to wonder about his air supply. The rebreather would recycle his exhalations indefinitely, but not perfectly. Bad air would accumulate slowly, driving out the good. Bottles of oxygen and nitrogen were integrated with the body of his suit, and they dribbled out their precious gas slowly, compensating for the recycling losses, but the reservoirs were few, and small. And of course, since a suit could never be completely sealed, he would *lose* a cubic meter of air every ten hours or so. Or was that only in vacuum? There was air pressure, albeit caustic and probably lethal, all around him here. What did that mean?

He shook his head, and the discomforting thoughts fell away like leaves from a dying tree. He had been here forever. He would always be here, forever. Numbness settled back into his mind, and the hardsuit embraced him like a sweating lover.

He walked on, switching walls every now and then, navigating the shoals of treacherous gravity as he swept through the occasional bend or turn. The pools of blood became gradually bigger, more blue in their centers, the crusty white clinging mainly to the edges. Fresher?

He stopped, wiped at the filmy deposits on the outside of his visor. Yes. The blood did look fresher. He was closing in on his prey, chasing them down as relentlessly as the Waisters themselves had hunted every last human in the Sirius and Wolf systems. And like the Waisters, he would show no mercy. Ignoring the distant screaming of his body, he quickened his pace.

He turned a corner, the gravity shift swinging him

briskly around like a ball on the end of a chain. And
suddenly the Waisters were there.

Three of them stood on alternate walls, their impos-
sibly curled bodies facing inward, the tops of their
"shoulders" almost meeting in the center of the corridor. Their "backs" (bellies?) were toward Ken, their
faces pointed away.

Too tired to be startled, he simply raised the sword
and continued toward them. But suddenly, something
was wrong; thin blue beams played back and forth
through the air, and the Waisters were shrinking, shriv-
eling, changing color. One of them let loose a scream,
like the sound of plate-steel being torn, and then it fell
silent again. In moments, the aliens had become unmoving heaps of brown-black leather.

There was something behind them in the corridor.

A blue beam flashed across Ken's visor, scintillating
through the layers of white and red crust. He felt brief
heat on his face, like the rays of the Albuquerque sun,
but the light and the heat were quickly gone.

"Hold your fire!" He heard a voice scream.

Everything went still.

Twenty meters down the corridor, a group of bipedal
figures stood on the walls, their heads pointing inward
like the spokes of a wheel. Their suits were a bright,
gloss white, with the shining blue and orange starbursts
of rape-hose sockets standing out like spring flowers.

Navy, Ken's mind told him quietly. But the word
seemed to have no meaning.

"Names of God," a low voice cursed, with a kind of
wonder. "It's one of the marines!"

The figures crowded forward.

"Can you hear me, son?" a different voice called
out. "Are you okay? Are you hurt?"

Silently, Ken staggered forward, Excalibur held out
before him. No mercy. He stepped awkwardly over the

shriveled bodies of the Waisters. Excalibur's blade glittered in the pale, sourceless light.

"Son? Hello? Goddammit, will somebody get on the other channels and talk to this guy? Put down the knife, son. We're all on the same side."

"I'll take him, sir."

"What?"

"I'll take that knife away from him. God's names, just *look* at him. He's not in any shape to fight."

"Mmm. Okay. Kassim, Rasheed, get ready; if he jumps wrong, you burn his hand off."

Ken continued toward the white figures. Their chattering voices meant nothing to him. *No mercy,* he mouthed. Empty star systems. Smooth craters in the desert floor. No, no mercy.

One of the figures stepped forward and grabbed Ken's sword arm firmly. Then, with the other hand, the figure reached forward, beneath Ken's personal horizon, and played with the switches on his helmet chin. Ken flailed his left arm weakly, felt it slide against the surface of the Navy hardsuit.

"Relax!" The Navy man shouted. "Corporal! Get a foothold, man!"

Ken struck at the figure again, but his left arm was captured by strong fingers. He tried to pull away, couldn't.

A moan escaped from his lips, rising quickly to become a shriek of pure terror. The skin of his face stretched painfully as it tried to accommodate the scream.

"He's out of it, Commander!"

"Hold him!"

"Get a rape hose into that man! Give him air, give him air!"

"I've got him. Will somebody get ... Yeah. Now *hold* that."

The white suits crowded around Ken, grabbing and pulling at him, forcing him down onto his back. Excalibur was lifted from his hand. Arms and legs were pinned, a hose jammed forcefully into his plexial socket.

Thrashing his head inside the helmet, Ken screamed and screamed, and he scarcely noticed when the Navy men pulled the hoods of his chin switches and turned off his radio. Eventually, his strength failed, and he quieted, and then strong hands lifted him and carried him away.

". . . probably a gamma ray burst when we melted the drive motor," a voice said, distantly.

Ken opened his eyes. He lay on a hospital bed in a green-white hospital room. A private room, only one bed, walls adorned with terrestrial lithographic prints, sailing ships and stone buildings in neat wooden frames. Two men stood in the doorway, wearing the gray smocks of Navy nurses.

One turned to glance at Ken, and did a double-take that Ken felt should have been funny. It wasn't.

"He's awake!" the man said to his colleague.

The two hurried over to Ken's bedside. "Corporal!" one said. "Welcome back, man, it's great to see you!"

"How do you feel?" asked the other.

Ken stared at the two for a few moments, then took another look around the room. Pictures on the walls. Carpeting on the floor. Gentle lighting.

"You're aboard the hospital ship *Lindrenmedze*," the first orderly explained. "We've put all the heroes in captain-level accommodations."

"Heroes," Ken said, slowly. His voice was weak but steady.

The man nodded, smiling down at him. "Most of the marine survivors were found on the outside of the hull.

Spider malfunctions and such. Seven hundred men, almost."

Ken's blood temperature seemed to drop. Seven hundred survivors? The marines had begun the Flyswatter operation with over a million. He remembered the screams of his men as Waister weapons destroyed their bodies. He remembered the sparkle of disintegration beams against the blackness of space. Each death a tragedy, a family broken and ruined.

"How ..." his voice choked. "How many survivors from inside the ship?"

The nurse seemed suddenly to realize Ken's distress. His face darkened with shame. "They recovered about a hundred and twenty. One group hadn't seen any Waisters at all. Others had. We have thirty-eight people in the hero bunks right now, people who saw really heavy action. Like you."

"You're going to get a Wounded-In-Action and a Bravery-Beyond-the-Call," the other nurse said gently.

The first nurse nodded. "You've saved us, Corporal. Saved the whole human race. Captured a God-damn Waister scoutship. I ... God, there's no way to *thank* you for that."

Take me home, Ken thought. *Rebuild my city and give me back my family and friends.* But he said nothing.

"Would you like to be alone?" the first nurse asked.

Remembering the ghastly emptiness of the scoutship corridors, Ken shook his head.

"Can we answer any questions for you?"

"Uh. What's wrong with me? Why am I here?"

The second nurse held up a flatscreen covered with winking, dancing displays. "Mostly exhaustion," he said, "but there was also minor respiratory damage, aspiration of toxics, dehydration, uh ... radiation damage and circulatory dysfunction in the extremities. Don't worry, Corporal, you're going to be fine."

Ken thought about that for a moment. "What happens now? Where do I go?"

The nurse shrugged. "We're taking you all to Mercy Station for full-body scan. After that I couldn't say."

"Back to the meat grinder," Ken said softly.

"Well, I hope not," one of the nurses told him. "You'd think they'd make you an instructor or something."

"Or something," Ken agreed sourly. Death and misery were to be his companions from now on. That was what the marines had told him at his induction, and so far their prediction was dead on. A thought occurred to him. "Nurse, you said something about radiation damage. Was there radiation in there?"

The man nodded. "Yes, though by the time of the boarding action it was all just secondary and tertiary stuff leaking out of the walls. Structure absorbed a lot of rays in the initial flash."

"Flash?"

"Flash. You don't . . . ? All I know about this are rumors, but supposedly there was a big gamma-ray burst when the drive motor died. Really cooked the Waister crew."

"Cooked?" Ken asked, like a moronic human-interface panel that could only echo back the words spoken to it.

"Yep," the first nurse agreed. "Advanced radiation sickness, all of them. No hope of survival. They're all up near the hub of the ship, packed in suspended animation."

Radiation sickness? *We need prisoners,* the X.O. had said. *The survival of the human race depends on this.* Ken felt a deep, visceral nausea, as if he might literally puke up his guts. His lips quivered. "Did . . . we die for nothing?"

"No," the nurse said firmly, putting a hand on Ken's shoulder. "Those bodies are giving up all kinds of data. Two brains! Four sexes! The exobiologists are delirious."

"Oh . . ."

The nurse moved his hand along Ken's shoulder to the base of his neck, softly. "Corporal. I know this must be hard for you. If you *would* like to be alone, Lu and I have other duties."

Ken shook his head again. No, he did not want to be alone.

The nurse smiled at him a little, caressed his shoulder again. "I could sit with you, if you like."

"Yes," Ken said softly, feeling awkward and strange. Then: "Take your hand off me, please."

"Of course," the nurse said. "Lu, maybe you could finish rounds without me."

"Sure," said the other man. Scooping up the flatscreen, he turned and strode out of the room.

The nurse who remained looked down at Ken with gentle eyes. "I can get your dinner," he offered.

"Just sit with me, okay?" Ken's voice was strangely plaintive. "I don't want to be alone right now."

"I understand," the nurse said, then frowned and shook his head. "No, I don't. I'm sorry. I can't even imagine what you've been through. Do you want, you know, to talk about it or something?"

That stopped Ken. Talk about it?

He imagined the nurse flashing out like a cinder in the lonely depths of space.

Collapsing into dust.

Coming apart in a storm of tungsten fiber.

Do you want to talk about it, Nurse?

Albuquerque: he imagined the face of his mother,

looking up from her patch panel just in time to see the flash.

Talk about it?

Skin peeling back from the face of Shiele Tomas.

"Hey." The voice distant. "Hey, take it easy."

The sound a man made as he choked on his own blood—should he talk about that? Or the screaming of burst-open Waisters?

"They sound a lot like babies," he said, then suddenly barked out a laugh. "If a tree falls and nobody hears it, does it scream like a baby?"

"Corporal, try to relax."

Ken laughed again. "If a million men die in space with their radios off, do they crash like trees? Oh. Oh. Do you think God will let them into Heaven?"

That thought struck him as hideously funny, and his laughter deepened. Tears formed at the corners of his eyes and trickled slowly down his cheeks.

"Oh, God," he nearly shrieked. "Will he let them into Heaven? Will he?"

Ken had a good, solid laugh over that one, emptying his lungs with it and rolling, painfully, onto his side. Tears rained down onto his mattress.

"Will?" he asked, with breath that wouldn't come. "Let . . ."

So many dead. So many *ways* to be dead. Surely God had made Paradise big enough for all?

His laughter and his tears continued for a long time.

Sensing movement nearby, Ken opened his eyes. Darkness. Weight and warmth easing in over the side of his bed.

For a moment he was simply filled with fear. And then, groggily, he remembered where he was. Remembered, too, the lingering touch of the nurse. Had he returned to visit Ken in the night? Muscles tensed.

The heat of bare skin settled next to his body.

"I don't—" he whispered urgently.

"Hush," a voice whispered back. Female.

His hand moved up against a curve of soft flesh. Female.

"Who—"

"Hush. It doesn't matter."

The space between her heat and his own seemed to shimmer and vanish. Flesh melted into flesh. She writhed against him in the darkness.

Who was this woman? Nurse? Doctor? Captain of the ship? *It doesn't matter,* she had told him. As if any woman could be here in her place.

The heat was unbearable, the contours of her body maddening in the darkness. Ken rolled over on top of her, and she moaned a little as he entered. *This moment we are at our most human.* The thought rose in his mind and then dissolved. The inside of her was slick, oiled. His strokes were deep.

Awareness drifted for a while, and there was nothing but the tug of pleasure at his loins. Then he tensed, suddenly feeling the sweat that slicked her thighs and stomach, the smooth, downy hairs on the back of her neck where his fingers twined. His body jerked, pumped, the sensation sharp and prolonged. And then, like a marionette with its power cut, he slumped.

For a time he lay atop her, thinking of nothing.

Later, his hands began to explore. Trim body. Smooth skin. Her breasts were high and soft, the nipples firm. She shuddered and hissed as he ran his tongue along them, tasting the salt of their mingled sweat.

And then she was squirming beneath him, in impatience rather than pleasure. He shifted his weight, and she slipped out from under him. The bed seemed to rise a little as her heat withdrew.

"What's wrong?" he asked, bewildered by her sudden retreat.

"Nothing," she whispered back at him. "I have to go. I've been here too long already."

There were sounds of cloth against flesh, cloth against cloth.

"What's your name?"

Hot fingers brushed against his lips. "Hush, baby. Please. It doesn't matter."

He wanted to say more, but could think of nothing. The scent of her was strong in his nostrils.

Light blinded him as the door slid open. A silhouette stood out briefly against the glare, and then the door closed again, leaving only afterimages.

Perhaps she has other heroes to visit this night, a spiteful voice suggested.

Uh.

Other heroes. Perhaps, yes.

The thought filled Ken with sadness.

Chapter 8

"... #*most root-ward cause of not-do-well when all voices speak simultaneously#* ..." The thick Waister syllables trailed off, and Josev pulled the voder mask off his mouth and looked up perplexedly. "Marshe, this is out the lock."

Ken looked at the flatscreen in his hands. The text on it, which Josev had been trying to translate, read:

> *The fundamental drawback of democracy is the assumption that the populace is both well-informed and rational enough to choose its leaders wisely. Overspending and bankruptcy are typical results. Conversely, in autocratic societies the government exists solely for its own benefit, and indeed the populace also exists for the benefit of the autocrats. Thus, in times of stress such governments may be unable to call upon their citizens for support. In Postclementine senocratic societies, appointed officials meet goals and criteria set by the populace, with their performance rated both objectively by the Chang-Watt Tensor and subjectively by popular vote. While rife with minor difficulties, this system has proved remarkably stable in the face of both internal and external perturbations.*

Quite a paragraph. Not exactly Waister doctrine.

"Maybe so," Marshe said. "I just wanted to see. Jonson, would you like to give it a try?"

Not really, Ken wanted to say. Instead: "Uh . . . Hmm." He tensed, pushed a part of his mind back into the spongy resistance of the Broca web. He keyed the voder.

"#*How can Drones tell Queens what-to-do when Drones not-know How can Queens tell Drones what-to-do when Drones not-listen Best is Drones do what-to-do of Queen desire and yell when Queen mistakes them If Queen is-stupid they can always get a divorce*#"

Beneath her voder mask, Marshe's face split into a grin. Josev snorted. Shenna's tail thwanged against the metal floor. Even Sipho Yeng looked amused.

"Not accurate, but clever," Marshe said, nodding with approval. Then her face took on a thoughtful look. "Huh. Why would they have a word like that? That's very interesting."

"And very helpful, too," Josev observed, with heavy sarcasm. "We can split up their happy marriages, and then attack while they're crying about it."

"It *is* interesting," Sipho said. "We haven't given much thought to internal frictions among the Waisters, though they must exist. As Jonson's comment illustrates. I think you're right, though, Ranes; there doesn't seem to be any direct application for us."

"Jonson?" Marshe said.

Ken paused for a moment. There was a distinct, almost physical sensation as his mind decoupled from the web. "Uh . . ." he said. "What was the question?"

Marshe glared. "Do you have any thoughts for us? Would you care to elaborate on your translation?"

"Huh? No. I mean, not really. I just said what came into my mind. I wasn't trying to be funny or anything."

Marshe's glare deepened, her brow furrowing. "Will you join the rest of us in the real world, please? You used the word *Ww#hw*"—the sound growled from her voder—"as though it equated to a dissolution of marriage. Do you think that context is accurate?"

"Yes," Ken replied carefully. The question seemed strange to him. Why would he offer an incorrect translation? Or, if his understanding of the word *Ww#hw* were wrong, how could he know? He knew only what the Broca web told him.

"Then," Marshe continued, "would you say that Waister Sixes are analogous to human marriages? Not necessarily permanent?"

"Sure," Ken said, unsure where this was leading. "There are Fives and Sevens also, aren't there?"

"And Fours," she agreed. "But the Sixes are far more common. And a 'Seven' only results when a Queen or Dog gives birth. The offspring is kept for a few months, then transferred to a nursery unit. Or so we believe."

Ken grunted.

"Do you think the Waisters really have such a thing as divorce?" Marshe asked.

"Uh, well, yeah I think so. Like a no-confidence vote for the Queen or something. But it would have to be pretty complex. I have no idea how they would handle it."

"Maybe not so tricky," Josev said, making an unpleasant face beneath his voder mask. "Marshe, you're a bitch. I'm leaving you, and I'm taking the family with me."

The captain looked blank for a moment, then cocked an eyebrow and tilted her head, an expression of interest. "Hmm. Okay, let's go with that. I hate you, too, and if you walk out of here, you take the uniform you're wearing and nothing else."

Josev pulled his mask off and smiled broadly. "Bitch. The Dog is mine. You love me, don't you, Shenna?"

Shenna stood up, her face unhappy, tail wagging uncertainly. "#*Not-do*#" she said, looking from Josev to Marshe. Her voice was the thick, fluted hiss of a Waister, and Ken felt an uneasiness down in his guts somewhere. Thanks to him, the Dog understood Standard, but was no longer capable of speaking it. She'd been a little odd these past few days, as if she sensed something was different, but wasn't quite sure what it was. What would she think if she understood what had happened? What would she think, if she knew it was Ken's idea?

"#*Not-do*#" the Dog repeated. "#*Big not-do Dog everybody stay-with-does*#"

"Good Dog," Josev said, leaning over toward her. "Nothing bad is happening here. But *if* we had to split up this group, would you rather go with me, or with Queen?"

Shenna's tail stopped wagging, and her face took on an even sadder look. "#*Dog Worker stay-with-does*#"

"No, no, Shennie, I'm a *Drone,* not a Worker."

"#*Dog Worker stay-with-does*#" the animal repeated.

Josev blinked, and silence reigned for several seconds. Ken looked around at the data panels, gloss black consoles speckled with amber lights. The displays were mostly dark right now, not showing the sterilization of Lalande system, not showing the impending doom of the planet Astaroth. Ken was glad for this.

"Well, so much for your simplicity," Marshe told Josev. Then, to Shenna: "You're a good dog, Shenna. A very good dog. Nobody's going to leave you."

The Dog wagged her tail again, and her mouth stretched in a way that made Ken think she might actually be *smiling.* Then, sensing that her input was no longer required, she sat back down between Roland

Hanlin and Sipho Yeng. A tension seemed to lift from the room.

"Actually," Marshe said, "this leads right in to our next project. A kind of, uh, poem or something has been made available to us. Hang on a minute."

The captain twiddled with her flatscreen, tapping at various points on its surface. Ken noticed the display in his own hands changing. Now, it read:

# *Whshkhh visited water*	# *Her Dog was-drowned*
# *In*	#
# *Place-of-water where*	# *Her Workers were-broken*
# *Water*	# *On rocks*
# *Known-to-be always-is*	# *were-broken*
#	# *On water*
# *Her Drones visited water*	# *were-broken*
# *In*	#
# *Under-air where*	#
#	# *Her Drones ate sea crea-tures*
#*She begged them not-to-do*	# *and died*

Ken stared at the text. The words were in Standard, but the letter font was odd, filled with strange points and angles. Where had this come from? What was it supposed to mean?

"What *is* this stuff?" Josev asked.

"Neural downloads," said Marshe. "This fragment was found in the brains of three different individuals: two Queens and a Worker."

"We can read dead brains?" asked Josev, skeptically. "Dead, alien brains?"

Marshe smiled a little. "Yes, actually we can, a little bit. I helped design the equipment for that, so I'm sort of proud of the fact. But really, the answer to your question is no. All the useful information we've extracted has been from the brains of *living* Waisters. Unfortunately, we only get a taste of what's in there, and we destroy the brains in the process."

Josev scowled deeply, as if Marshe were lying to him and everyone knew it. "How can we read them at all? They're not like us, right? Different chemistry, different morphology ... Wouldn't it take years of study to even *understand* their brains?"

"No," Marshe told him. "Not at all. The neural network is a deeply optimal structure for data processing and motor control. Evolution loves to optimize, so brains are about the same on every planet we've seen. Different chemistry, yes, but the mechanisms are directly related. Like writing the same language with a different character set."

"Sounds like a load of sludge," Josev said. "I've seen octopus brains and such. They don't look anything like human brains."

"Not on the macroscopic level, no. But down inside ... Think about ship navigation for a minute. You can crunch the same data five different ways, but the final trajectory solution comes out the same in each case, right? The best solution is the best solution, no matter how you arrive at it. Same thing with biology. In fact, octopus brains are very easy to read.

"Anyway, you don't have to act so surprised. The linguistic data in your Broca web comes from the same sources."

"I thought that was extracted from the Waister computer networks," Sipho Yeng said.

"No. I don't know where you heard that, but there *are* no Waister computer networks that we can find."

"Really?"

"Really."

"How's that work?" muttered Josev.

Marshe shrugged. "Maybe they're too small to see. Maybe the Waisters don't use computers. Maybe the

scoutship is is one giant computer, with its data processing and storage elements integrated with the structure so we can't detect them. Right now we just don't
know."

Josev still looked unconvinced. "Don't Waisters
have two brains?"

"All except the Dogs, yes. Actually, the . . . poem on
your flatscreen there comes in two parts. The left col-
umn was read from the cranial assembly, the ah, head
brain, and the right one came from the dorsal ganglion.
They come up linked on a free-association, so we
know they go together. The, ah, structure and punctu-
ation of the poem were put in by technicians. I wanted
to get the whole thing in raw, untranslated form, but
this was all they had to send me. Stupid. They called
the actual download 'intermediate data' and threw it
away."

"It makes more sense if you read the whole left col-
umn, and then put the right one underneath it," Ken cut
in. He'd been eyeing the "poem", and he'd decided
that the one way it was an actual little story, where the
other it was a jumble of disconnected thoughts. Maybe
the thoughts of Waisters really were disconnected and
jumbled, but he thought it unlikely. They were much
too efficient for that.

"Yes," Sipho Yeng said slowly. "Yes, I believe
you're right."

"What can we determine from this fragment?"
Marshe asked, looking around the circle. "Roland.
Speak to us."

Roland Hanlin looked up reluctantly. "It's a tragedy," he said.

"Once again?" Marshe asked. Her tone indicated,
somehow, that Roland was not finished speaking, that
his point had not yet been made but soon would be.

"Tragedy," the man repeated. "Like those old holies they used to watch."

"You mean there isn't a lesson buried in here? Just a sad story?"

Roland shrugged.

"Waisters can't swim," Josev offered, his tone suddenly light and humorous.

"Okay," said Marshe. "That's certainly implied in the text. At least, Dogs and Workers can't swim. When they're, uh, in the Place-of-Water."

"Place-of-Water must mean 'ocean'," said Sipho. "Or maybe the name of a particular ocean. The water is rough enough to smash bodies against the rocks, yes? And the Drones ate sea creatures."

"This is a sludgy translation," Josev said.

Ken looked up at Marshe. "The Drones disobeyed their Queen. They went . . . lung diving or something. Lobster hunting. And the Workers and Dog followed them into the water? No, that doesn't make any sense."

"It was a really ugly divorce," Josev suggested.

"Well," said Marshe, "It was obviously an argument of *some* kind. Maybe the Queen warned her people about the undertow or something, and they went swimming anyway? Tide pulled them out onto a reef?"

"The Six hardly seems like a monolithic structure," Sipho said. "It sounds as if the Drones are just barely held in check."

Marshe was frowning behind her mask. "I think Josev is right. Something is wrong with this translation."

"Can we get raw downloads in the future?" Sipho asked.

"No. We weren't really even supposed to get *this*. I've arranged for something better, though; two days from now, we will speak with an actual Waister."

Ken's skin went cold, and tiny bumps began to form

on it, pushing his hairs erect with a chilly, tingling sen- .
sation. An actual Waister?

Indigo blood on his hands, his arms. Fading to white
as he watched.

"I thought they were all frozen," he said quietly.

"Yes. Some friends of mine are going to thaw one
out for us."

"Aren't they all radiation-terminal?" Josev protested.

"Yes," Marshe said. "We'll be killing it by talking to
it."

"Oh. How many prisoners have we *got*?"

Marshe smiled. "Classified, Josev. Sorry."

Ken shuddered. Killing it by talking to it. He felt no
sympathy for the Waister prisoners, no empathy for the
suffering they must endure, but ... Hadn't there been
enough killing already? Would he have to keep on
pulling triggers, as long as he lived?

"Jonson," Marshe said, "You look distressed. You
will interrogate the prisoner with us. Get used to the
idea."

No mercy, Ken's conscience murmured. *No mercy,
no mercy.*

He looked the captain in the eye, and nodded.

It was a Worker beneath the tent of clear, shiny plastic. Marshe had wanted a Queen, but this was all the
vivisectionists could spare.

Ken felt hollow inside. The creature looked pathetic,
shriveled upon its couch. The twisted body which had
so frightened him ten weeks before now looked silly
and sad, like a child's balloon-animal left too long in
the sun.

"... initiated supportive therapy," one of the technicians was saying, "pumping electrolytes and so forth,
but it won't last too long. Eventually we hope to per-

form cellular surgery, reverse as much of the damage as we can, but that won't be possible for quite a while. The nucleic acids are *very* strange, and the enzymes which—"

"Later," Marshe said, cutting the man off. "Don't waste time right now." She leaned in over the shriveled Worker. "*#You will-speak toward I/We#*"

The Waister shook for a second or two, its body making wet noises.

"*#You will-speak toward I/We#*" Marshe said again, more loudly. There was anger in her synthetic voice, Ken thought. Anger and frustration and, buried but still visible in outline, the desire to hurt. Talbott betrayed not a trace of human tenderness.

"*#I will-speak will-speak#*" the Waister agreed, very faintly.

"*#You/you experience difficulty#*" Marshe suggested, "*#Resulting-from fear resulting-from I/We#*"

"*#No#*"

"*#Describe you/your sensation/experience#*"

The Waister shuddered a little. "*#I/I cold-am Hungry-am Thirsty-am#*"

"*#You/you experience fear#*" Marshe said.

"*#To-a-slight-degree#*" said the alien.

Marshe sneered. "*#You/your people attack I/We people resulting-from fear#*

"*#No#*"

"No?" Marshe said, in Standard. "Stupid wretch."

"*#What cause you/your people attack I/We people#*" she hissed.

Ken thought there was something odd in her phrasing, not just in that sentence but in many of her remarks. Perhaps the creature could not understand her?

But it answered: "*#Newness newness You/your people new-are I/We people not-new-are Where is I/My Queen#*"

"#*You/your Queen is I/We/My thing-of-dismantling You/your Drones are-dead You/your Dog is I/We/My thing-of-dismantling*#" Marshe said. Somehow, she managed to project a cruel tone through the voder.

"Marshe," Ken said, unable to help himself. "Be professional. Please."

The captain looked back at him, sharply. Her eyes glittered like dark jewels.

"Please," he repeated, meeting her gaze.

She turned back to the Waister and spoke again. "#*What cause you/your people attack newness*#"

"#*There not-is inside-of-me understanding*#" the creature replied. Its voice was a bubbling whisper that sounded to Ken like the rattle of death, the sound of air being forced through dying speech-organs.

"#*You/your people attack newness*#" Marshe said angrily.

"#*Why do you resist*#" the alien asked. "#*You are like Stupid-lings Long-ago Stupid-lings They fought so hard They fought so long They*#" The voice trailed away.

Marshe leaned up, looked back at Ken, at Josev and Sipho and Roland. Her eyes now registered fear. "#*Who/what are Stupid-lings*#" she asked the creature, while her eyes hunted back toward Ken.

The Waister exhaled, but did not speak.

Marshe whirled on it. "#*WHO/WHAT ARE STUPID-LINGS*#"

"#*Long-ago Long-ago*#" the Waister said, very quietly. "#*They were so stupid Stubborn Strong We need-must did-cause death They never gave up We need-must did-cause all Stupid-lings of death*#"

Ken's vision started to gray around the edges. His knees felt weak. *The stupid ones never surrendered,* the Worker had meant. *We had to kill them all.*

"Names of God," Josev whispered.

Roland Hanlin made an odd gesture with his hands.

"#*What cause*#" Marshe asked the Waister. The voder's electronic voice was steady, but Ken could see the captain's hands quivering.

The Waister said nothing.

There was a tone, a quiet humming that almost merged with the exobiology lab's background noise. Something blurred, shifted in the wall displays behind the tent.

"It's lost consciousness," the technician said, casually.

"Wake it back up," Marshe told him without turning around.

Ken watched the detachment melt from the man's face, watched scientific curiosity give way to fear of darkness. "What did it say?" he asked.

"Wake it up!" Marshe shouted.

"What . . ." the man said. "Right. Okay."

He moved to the wall, pressed an amber polygon that blinked against the darkness of the panel. More polygons appeared, in various colors, and he pressed several of these.

PongPong! PongPong! The new sound seemed to shatter its way out of the panel.

"Shit!" the man swore. Now *his* hands were shaking as well, Ken saw.

"What happened?" Marshe demanded.

"Neural seizure," the technician said. "Shit. You stinking bastard, wake up!"

PONGPONG! sounded the data panel. Then, *HUMMMMMMMM* . . .

The technician pounded the panel with his fist. "God damn it!" He screamed. "It's dead. It had a few good hours left in it, but somehow it's dead. What did you *say* to it?"

Marshe turned toward the man. "Get us another one."

"I can't."

"Do it."

"Captain, I *can't*. They're all assigned to different projects. What happened here, what did you find out?"

"We're all going to die," Marshe told him. "That's what we found out. They're going to stamp us out like they did all their other victims."

"Captain?"

"God damn it," Marshe said, pulling the voder mask off her mouth. Her eyes, suddenly, looked red and moist and shamelessly angry. "The last race they fought never surrendered. They had to kill them all."

Marshe Talbott tensed, shoulders tight, arms straight at her sides. Her jaw clenched and quivered. *"God damn it!"* she bellowed through her teeth, turning on the plastic tent, slamming a fist down on the body within it. The clear plastic collapsed. The Waister made a wet, meaty sound beneath her hand.

"God damn it," she said again, more quietly. Her hand slipped off the plastic that wrapped the Waister's body.

Ken wanted to say something to her. *Calm down,* perhaps? *It's all right?*

No.

Ken turned away instead, and closed his eyes. It was not all right, would not be all right ever again. *Oh God,* he thought. *Oh God, oh God.*

Chapter 9

Colonel Jhee strode into the assimilation chamber with murder in his eyes. "Speak no further," he'd said over the holie link, his voice ringing with anger. "I will be with you in fifteen minutes."

And now, here he was. And seeing the colonel's look, Ken feared for Marshe.

"Be seated, Captain Talbott," the colonel said, pointing at a chair.

Marshe remained standing. "Colonel, this is very important. We've uncovered evidence that the Waisters have driven at least one other race—"

"Speak no further!" the colonel snapped, a drop of spittle flying from his lips. "That fact is known to us and is considered Most Secret! You have no authority to pry into these matters!"

"You knew?" Marshe asked.

"Of course we knew! And now, without my authorization, you've wasted the life of a valuable prisoner simply to confirm it. Captain, your charge number is hereby revoked. Paint, voice modules, exomedical services ... you've overrun your budget already, and by a very wide margin. I understand you've even ordered sun-glasses!"

Marshe sighed. "They're spectrum spreaders, Colonel, with truncated IR. To help us see like the Waisters."

"I don't care what they are," Jhee said, more quietly. He pointed at the chair again. "Sit down, Captain. Let me explain some difficult truths for you."

Ken could see Marshe raging inwardly, wishing, perhaps, that she could push this tiny man up against a bulkhead and punch him hard. But she sat. Jhee was her commanding officer, after all, and Marshe Talbott knew her job.

The colonel smoothed his hair back. Paused. "This project is not the center of the war, not even the center of *my* war. My budget is fixed, and thinly spread across a whole spectrum of research. Even so, whether you realize it or not, in all the UAS I am your only protector. And yet you trample my garden without regret.

"If you understood the *effects* . . . The resources you have diverted come directly from my other projects, regardless of their merit. Your actions may well rob us of the answers we need to survive. This is not merely negligent, madam. I am slightly tempted to court-martial you for treason, but I hardly think that would help matters. Shall we log it as a gross oversight?"

What was this? Treason, did he say? Court-martial? Ken sat up a little straighter. Even "gross oversight" was a serious accusation.

"Don't you think you're overreacting?" Marshe asked, her voice tight.

"No," the colonel said. "For the moment, all I can do is kill your charge number. But if things go badly in the near future, there will be a formal inquiry. I will not be defending you, Captain."

No, Ken wanted to say. *You'll be defending your own sorry ass.* There had been a few officers like Jhee in the Marine Corps, too, tight-fisted pebble counters all. The troops, Ken included, had spent long hours planning "accidents" for them. All in fun, of course, but Ken doubted any of those officers had survived the

Flyswatter operation. A slow response, a hint of delay . . . Murder was easy in a combat zone.

"Colonel Jhee," Captain Talbott said. "I apologize for my unauthorized charges, and I accept full responsibility for the consequences. The other team members were not responsible."

"Not true," Ken said. He felt a little dizzy as he spoke, sensing that he had stepped off a precipice and faced a fall of unknown distance.

"Shut it, Ken," Josev hissed.

Ken shook his head. It was unthinkable that the Queen should be threatened and affronted in this way, without the defense of her Drones. "Most of those charges were my idea," he said to the colonel. "And I stand by them."

"Jonson," Marshe said, her tone both angry and grateful. "Keep out of this. I'm in charge of this project. The responsibility begins and ends with me."

Ken lifted his voder, pressed it over his mouth like an oxygen mask. "#*I am Drone of Queen I will-fight*#"

Colonel Jhee looked startled.

"Jonson," Marshe warned.

"#*I am Drone of Queen*#" Ken repeated, staring now into the colonel's eyes.

Jhee returned the glare, his eyes narrowing. "What are you saying?" he demanded.

Ken lowered the voder and flashed a feral grin. "I am Drone of Queen," he said. He felt the grin faltering, becoming misshapen as his lips twitched out the words. "I will defend my Queen as well as I can. As long as I live. Colonel."

"Sludging hell, Jonson," Josev whispered loudly, his expression stunned and fearful.

But Jhee was smiling faintly when Ken looked back at him. Smiling at Marshe. "Your crewman is insane," he said.

"No, sir," Ken corrected. "I am your Aggressor."

"Leave the room, please, Jonson," Marshe said. Her voice betrayed simple anger, nothing more.

Ken got to his feet.

"Stay, Corporal," the colonel said. "I'm leaving." He turned to Marshe. "Against my better judgment, I'm granting you authority to proceed with your tactical analysis. You've killed valuable programs, but General Voorhis has already requested a copy of your next report. Produce it for me, and keep your crewmen in line."

"Sir," Marshe said.

The colonel turned, and left.

When he was gone, Marshe whirled on Ken, taking two giant strides forward. "Explain yourself, mister!" she shouted in his face.

"Doing my job, Queen!" Ken yelled back in the same tone.

"God's names, Jonson," Josev said. "You're completely out the lock. You can't talk to a colonel that way, even if you are a clodging war hero!"

"Let him be."

The room fell silent. Ken looked at Roland Hanlin. So, it seemed, did everyone else.

"Let him be," Hanlin said again. "He's the only one really try to make this project work."

Again, the room was quiet for a long moment.

"Kenneth," Marshe said, breaking the silence. "Please don't speak to the colonel that way in the future."

"Yes ma'am," Ken replied.

"Don't you 'yes ma'am' me," she said, getting in his face again. "This is serious. You could be *shot* for that."

"I'm *aware* of that, Marshe," Ken said. "I'm not stupid. We have to *know* we're right, if we want that guy to listen to us."

"Yelling at him in Waister is not going to help, chum," Josev muttered. "You're digging our tomb when you do that."

"That won't happen again," Ken said.

"Why don't I believe him?" Marshe asked the walls of the chamber, no amusement in her voice.

Marshe turned weightlessly from the viewport. Her features were composed, but the red, puffy look to her eyes made Ken wonder if she'd been crying.

"Jonson," she said.

"Call me Ken."

Her lips curled briefly into a smile—or a snarl. "Ken. Okay. Call me Marshe?"

"Okay."

"I don't like 'Queen' any more. I don't like the sound of it."

"I'll call you Marshe."

Behind her, behind the thick glass of the window, Saturn was a tiny ball of caramel. The jewel of Sol system. Ken couldn't see its rings at all.

Marshe started rubbing her hands together, as if she were cold. She looked at Ken with sorrowful eyes. "We're not going to make it, are we?" she asked. "The Waisters are too strong and they'll never give up. We aren't going to win."

Ken shook his head. No, they weren't going to win. Had she really thought otherwise?

"Why are we working so hard?" she asked.

Ken shrugged, sensing that the question was rhetorical, that no answer he could give would be helpful to her.

"Why," she continued, "don't we just find a way to surrender? We can all give a hundred and ten percent to the war effort, with no better result than all of us getting killed. What's the point?"

"Don't worry about it," Ken said. "We're just gears, Marshe. Just ants in the hive. Let the commanders worry about strategy."

"Spoken like a marine," she said bitterly.

"There's nothing we can do to change the situation," Ken told her. "Just act out your little part for as long as you can."

She peered at him. "And then?"

He shrugged again. "Die well, I guess. God is watching."

Marshe seemed to have no reply for that.

"Maybe we can buy time for Barnarde," he said, feeling he should offer her some comfort.

Barnarde was almost six light-years away, still far from the Waister armadas. There was still time for *deus ex machina,* the intervening hand of God, to save the people there, though Ken didn't think it was likely.

Deux ex machina, he mused. God from machine. Was that Latin? English? He couldn't remember. He supposed it didn't much matter. All thoughts, all poetry and music and ancient languages, all would be Waisted in the end.

"Two indigenous ecosystems," Marshe said, "and lots of Earth-export lifeforms. Barnarde harbors more living species than Sol does."

Ken pondered that for a moment. "And almost as many people, isn't it?"

"About a third," she said.

"Maybe they'll think of something."

"Maybe."

Ken could think of nothing more to say. Neither, it seemed, could Marshe.

The observation chamber *was* cold. Not enough ventilation, perhaps, to account for radiative heat losses through the window? The room's bare walls smelled of metal and, more faintly, of human sweat. How many people had been in here over the centuries, Ken wondered. How many arguments had been fought in here? How many children conceived, marriages proposed?

He looked out at Saturn. The planet stared back like a unfriendly eye.

"Ken," Marshe said quietly. "Come here, please. Hold my hand."

Nodding, Ken kicked gently off the wall and drifted over to her. He removed a hand from his uniform's pocket, offered it. Marshe took it, wrapped her own hands around it. They were cold, cold as water in a mountain stream. But soft. His own hand, tense at first, began to relax.

Her brown hair, straight and short, stood about her head like a crown. Her face was flushed, distorted by the lack of gravity. A "pudding face," Josev had called it. A "fat, squishy slug" face.

Ken thought otherwise. This woman, his Captain and Queen, was solidly built, her fat layered with muscle, her frame rugged. Inside, she was somehow both warm and cold, a volcano crowned with glaciers, steaming in the places where magma seethed close to the surface.

Not "pretty in her own way," as his mother might say, but genuinely beautiful, Marshe seemed to fit perfectly into the fleshy clothing of her body. How could Josev not see that? If Marshe's mass were to drop, surely her strength must melt away with it?

Her eyes met his. "Have . . . Do you . . . ?"

Understanding the question, Ken shook his head.

Shiele Tomas flashing in the light of two suns, skin peeling back from her like blackened rinds. Albuquerque sidewalks melting beneath her feet.

"You?" He asked.

She shook her head. "No. Not for a long time."

With his other hand, he pulled her closer to him. Her face centimeters from his own.

"We can't," she said, simply. Her breath smelled of breakfast apples.

"No," Ken agreed. "We can't."

Her hands were warmer now.

"Just hold me?"

"Yeah."

Their arms and legs and bodies twined. They had done this before, but ... That had been a mother-and-son kind of thing, soothing and comforting but also condescending somehow. Not like this.

His manhood stirred, stiffened. She could feel it, he knew.

"We can't," he repeated, as if to convince himself.

"No."

They floated in the chill air as a single unit, tumbling slightly.

"Marshe?" Ken asked after a while. "Am I crazy? Have I come unpinned, like Josev says?"

Marshe paused, breathing deeply. "I think you have."

"Does it matter?"

"No."

"Do ... Are you afraid of dying?"

She shrugged. "I try very hard not to think about it. I can imagine this whole fortress boiling away, with me inside it. Breathing splatters of molten metal, trying to scream. Yes, I'm afraid."

"Me too," he said, surprising himself with the admission. "I really expected to die in the Flyswatter. I hoped it would be quick, you know, relatively painless, but it never occurred to me that I'd survive. But I *did*. So many people didn't make it, but I did. Why is that?

I mean, I wasn't even good at my job. I made a lot of mistakes. Bad ones."

Oh, yes. Very bad.

He continued, "Part of me . . . I wish I were dead sometimes. A lot of the time. Especially before I came here; it was really bad then."

"I've been hard on you," Marshe said. "I'm sorry."

He waved a hand, back where she could see. *Forget it.*

"You don't sound scared," she offered.

Ken let out a breath, felt it heat the fabric that clothed Marshe's shoulder and neck. "It's *getting* dead that scares me. The pain, the helplessness. Suicide is one thing, but . . . Right now, it doesn't seem fair that I *have* to die."

"But you do."

Ken nodded, his chin digging into her shoulder. He did have to die. And there was a feeling growing inside him that he didn't have much longer to wait.

Chapter 10

Quit it!" Rik shouted down into the water. Damn dolphins were getting twitchier every day. They were down there, huddled together in the deep end of the tank, squirming and flopping together as if in orgy. Except for Khola, who was "pacing" here at the shallow end, splashing hugely with every turn.

"Drone Two, quit that!" Rik shouted again as a low-gravity wave slopped at him, wetting his shoes.

Khola stopped, put his head up out of the water. Said something in dolphin, and something else in Waister. Rik caught neither, though the dolphin-clicks had sounded like a sonar holographic.

"Would . . ." He took a step backward, leaned in toward the water. "Would you say that in Standard?"

Khola jerked his head back and forth several times, frothing the water. "CONFRONT!" he shouted.

"Ho, friend," Rik said. He held his hands out level, a gesture of reassurance. "Calm down. What's the problem here?"

"CONFRONT!" the dolphin shouted again, and repeated his frothing dance.

Rik sighed. Khola, like the other dolphins and their "dog," had been modified to speak both Standard and Waister with intelligible, if not always fluent, grammar. But lately they were becoming obtuse, hard to talk to. Secretive, even, as though sharing among themselves some knowledge Rik and the others could not, or *should* not, understand.

Rik crouched down, leaning over a little farther until he could slap the water. "Khola! What are you talking about? Do you want me to go get the helmet?"

"No," Khola said, calming suddenly. "Not helmet. Not see pictures, angry pictures. Sorry."

Angry pictures? Rik turned toward the equipment racks, saw his helmet hanging there—an ordinary gill helmet, of the sort he'd been using since childhood, but modified. His dolphin hat. His Waister hat. With it he could interpret Khola's sonar images, his groans and clicks and sibilant Waister flutings.

Made it hard to think, though, and anyway Rik could hold his breath a long time. Off Kauai he had once dived to thirty meters without equipment, without even weights. And he'd been swimming with dolphins years before he'd ever learned to use a gill.

The peg next to his, the one where Sandre's helmet normally hung, was empty.

More splashing.

Beneath the water, a dark shape torpedoed out of the deep end—Ilio, the common seal who served as the group's "dog." Slowing as she approached, she nuzzled Khola's tail, curled herself sinuously around it.

"Must go," Khola said. No inflection in his modified voice, no hint of emotion. What was going on here? What was he thinking?

Ilio disengaged from her dolphin friend and shot back toward the deeper water, toward the knot of dolphin flesh squirming in the far corner.

"Where is Sandre?" Rik asked, holding out a forestalling hand. "Her helmet is gone."

"Not see Sandre," Khola said. He started thrashing again. Slow water slopped over Rik's shoes. "Khola must go."

"Why? What's going on in the deep end?"

"Confrontation," Khola said.

"With what?"

"We strong. We prove that we are more strong."

A cold feeling prickled up Rik's neck. "More strong than what? Where is Sandre?"

"Khola must go."

The dolphin flipped over, splashing with his tail, and in moments had traveled fifteen meters to the tank's deep end. Rik's knees gave out as he watched, and he settled slowly into the cold wetness of Khola's puddles.

A human arm projected limply from the dolphin swarm, and a red stain was spreading slowly through the water.

". . . examination has moved inward and aft," Colonel Lopez went on, "and the teams seem to be well out of the habitation area. The artifacts they're finding seem to be mainly tools and sensory prostheses. The purposes of these devices are unknown at this time."

"Did you find markings on some of the walls?" Jhee asked him from across the table.

"Yes," Lopez said, looking up sharply from his flatscreen. "How did you know?"

"My . . . sources indicated that was a possibility." Jhee smiled wanly at his colleague. So much secrecy, and from whom? The enemy was utterly disinterested in human things, except as targets. There were no turncoats in this war, no infiltrators to guard against. Public opinion was a problem, maybe, if you believed what the commanders said. Politics, even in the face of catastrophe. But right here, right now, there *was* no public to keep the secrets from.

There was a delay of several seconds before the image of General Chu spoke. "Your *sources* have told us little else, Mister Jhee," he said then in his dry, disapproving way. "I had warned you against frivolity, yes?" Behind the holie window he slapped a flatscreen against a tabletop, flexing and releasing it, flexing and releasing again. "Your tactical analysis is very, shall we say, sketchy? And this other material, this cultural fluff . . ."

"Information about our enemies!" Jhee protested. Uselessly, of course. "Anyway, I am making an effort to steer that team in a more useful direction."

"An effort," Chu said, after the usual delay. "I see."

Chu was elsewhere in Saturnian space, two or three light-seconds away in the vast region where Saturn's gravity held sway. Ironic that on the ansible link, Jhee could get reports from Astaroth, eight light-years distant, more quickly than he could argue with his own superiors. No FTL signals this close, not unless you were a Waister.

"Back off him, Chu," said General Voorhis, who was here, present in the room with Jhee and Lopez. "Sometimes a think tank needs a little insulation. Even when the situation is . . . as dire as this."

The pause, and then Chu flapped his screen against the tabletop again. "Voorhis, what do you think the purpose of your station is? When the Armada arrives, we'll be meeting them with sticks and stones. We need a map to their vulnerabilities, or at the very least a new weapon, or a new strategy or *something*. We do not need markings on the wall, or trinkets we can't understand."

"Who knows?" said Voorhis. "Maybe those markings contain the very information we need."

Pause. "Had we the time, Voorhis, we could explore every such possibility. As we do not have the time, I want you to cut funding for these two areas by twenty percent. Shift the difference into Ring Project Five. Understood?"

"Yes, sir," Voorhis replied.

Pause again, and the image of General Chu winked out.

Jhee felt a hollow, impotent anger ringing inside him. Twenty percent! His projects were a matrix, a web of interconnected goals and resources. Where could he cut, what could he possibly afford to lose? Not Marshe Talbott's team, despite the difficulties. Not the dolphins, or the response matrix group. Certainly not the MI's.

"We'll discuss the mechanics of this in five hours," Voorhis said, rising from his seat, gathering up his things.

The door opened, and a young man came bursting through. Lieutenant . . . Stover, wasn't it?

"Colonel!" the man huffed, a hand against his stomach. "Colonel Jhee, come quickly! There's been an . . . accident!"

"Accident!" Jhee said, standing up slowly.

"Yes, in the dol, uh, the water tank!"

"Names of God," he said. An accident, one serious enough to propel this young man directly to him, bypassing two layers of bureaucracy. Here, perhaps, was his answer. "I'm on my way. Come with me, explain this!"

Chapter 11

"ATTENTION," a booming voice announced. "ATTENTION. ALL PERSONNEL MUST REPORT TO THE NEAREST HOLIE FOR AN IMPORTANT ANNOUNCEMENT. ATTENTION. ALL PERSONNEL MUST REPORT TO THE NEAREST HOLIE FOR AN IMPORTANT ANNOUNCEMENT."

"We're *at* the nearest holie," Josev said, looking up at the ceiling of the assimilation chamber as if the announcer were above him, and listening. Then, to Ken Jonson: "What do you suppose it is?"

"#*I/We not-know*#" Jonson replied, shrugging.

Marshe's eyes narrowed. Somewhere along the line, Ken Jonson had stopped speaking Standard. Was he doing this to irritate her? She shook her head. No, no, of course not.

"It must be the Waisters," Yeng said.

Roland Hanlin looked up. "Too early," he muttered. But his voice sounded unconvinced.

Marshe felt a cold breeze stirring through her. The Waisters. Yes. They weren't really expected for months, but then nobody really knew their comings and goings. *That's supposed to be* our *job,* she thought, and shivered.

"Pay attention," she said crisply. Not that her group was doing anything else, of course. Sitting in this stupid circle of chairs and paying attention was how they'd been spending every hour of every day. She might as well order them to breathe and swallow and blink their eyes. But she needed to have something to say.

The holie screens went gunboat gray for a second. Everyone froze. Then a face appeared, that of Carlos Tindaros, Sol system's eighteenth Governor General. To Marshe's eyes the man looked tired and ... irritated? Something like that. His usual finery had been replaced with a cap and shirt of gold mylar.

"Citizens," the GovGen said, inclining his head slightly.

Marshe hardly dared to breathe.

"The news is bad," Tindaros continued after pausing politely. "Though hardly unexpected. At eighteen-thirty-four hours Earth standard time, our long-range pickets in the Oort cloud detected the passage of a Waister armada moving at one tenth the speed of light. They were several light-hours above the plane of the ecliptic, but were moving almost directly toward it. By the time most of you receive this transmission, the armada will have entered the ecliptic plane and changed course. Headed, of course, toward Sol."

He paused, to give his words a chance to soak in, then continued: "It begins. I must ask each of you to be brave. Please. We must fight harder than we have ever fought before, for our very existence is at stake. We must turn a blind eye to our own suffering, and to the suffering of our comrades. We cannot spare the energy that charity and self-pity would require of us.

"It is commonly said that Waister technology is greatly superior to our own. I would like to tell you otherwise, but you would not be fooled. Nor should you be. Four hundred and twenty-eight ships were lost in the Flyswatter operation, as compared with six on the enemy side. And now we must confront a force nearly a hundred times larger. If we make a few simple arithmetic calculations, as so many of you have done, it is easy to conclude that Sol system hasn't the resources to withstand this attack. On this point, at least, I can offer some reassurance.

"Fleet action is not a matter of simple arithmetic, but a complex weave of pressures and responses. Our top analysts have studied Waister tactics very closely, so that we will be anticipating their thrusts and parries before they occur. Our enemies do not have this advantage, as they have never encountered a human fleet of significant size or firepower. In addition, we have prepared a number of surprises for them.

"Still, their armada is very large. Their weapons are very powerful. It may be that Sol system, the ancestral home of Humanity, will fall before the enemy. I think we have all entertained this bleak thought, unconscionable though it seems. In our minds, we equate the death of Sol system with the death of Humanity itself. But the colonies at Rigilkente and Barnarde are very much alive, and will continue that way long after you and I are gone. It is not only for ourselves but for them that we fight.

"Like us, and like Lalande, Rigilkente faces an uncertain future. It was the first human colony in extrasolar space, founded over six hundred years ago, but its lack of mineral resources has limited its growth. It is, in fact, smaller than the Sirius colony was at the time of its destruction. However, unlike Sirius, Rigilkente *knows* its danger, and has devoted virtually its entire industrial capacity to the task of defense. Their resistance may buy time for Barnarde, as may ours."

There was a heavy pause, as if GovGen Tindaros knew that Marshe would be dizzily fighting down the urge to vomit.

"Citizens, we must broaden our thinking. Perhaps the seeds of the Human future lie not on Earth or Mars, or Astaroth, but on the myriad worlds of Barnarde system. That system is rich in life, and in mineral resources. Their factories and refineries were tooled up for warfare in parallel with our own, but we estimate the Waisters will not arrive there for at least another six and one half years. Meanwhile, Barnardean production rates continue to climb.

"Using the same simple-minded arithmetic as before, we can see a glimmer of hope. The figures show Barnarde destroying a great number of Waister ships. Almost all of them, in fact. Of course, we know reality is not that simple. Hundreds of variables are involved, perhaps thousands. But I do know that each day we delay the Waisters means more weapons from Barnardean production lines, more soldiers from their schools, more children from their wombs. Every Waister ship we destroy tips the balance that much further in our favor.

"That is why we must all be brave. If we must face the darkness, citizens, we shall not go gently. We shall shake a fist at the stars, and scream defiance with the very last of our breath. In battle, we shall not leave our stations. Though our hulls rupture, our atmosphere boil, our very bodies burn and freeze, we shall stand firm, firing our weapons again and again, bringing death and confusion to our enemies. We shall make them curse the day they launched their fleets against us."

He paused for several seconds and then raised a hand sideways, pointing toward something outside the view of the holie. "We'll have a few words, now, from Vin Ravin, our Chaplain General."

GovGen Tindaros stepped aside, and another man moved into the holie. His face was vaguely familiar, his uniform gray, standard except for the stripes of his rank, which were white instead of black.

"Citizens," said the man, nodding once, his face stern and grandfatherly. "The contribution of my office to the war effort has been to answer one fundamental question: Is God on our side? I regret to inform you that the answer is no."

He paused, as Tindaros had, to let human minds assimilate his words.

"The Systematic Search for Miraculous Occurrences, now in its three hundred and sixty-eighth year, has probed the heavens with every known instrument, and performed rigorous statistical analysis on the data thus provided. At no time has evidence been uncovered to suggest that any divine forces have interfered with the operation of the physical universe.

"Therefore, it is the position of the Chaplain General's office that God will not, in fact, assist us, no matter how piteously we beg."

Another pause.

"At the end of the Clementine Monarchy, Pascal Giovanni, then embroiled in legal and political difficulties, set out to prove his innocence on the grounds that human free will does not exist. In his ingenious and widely publicized experiments, he in fact managed to prove the reverse. His legacy informs us that we are truly conscious entities, responsible for our own actions, our own destiny. If we are to survive, we *must* recognize this fact.

"By acting in concert, the human race functioning in effect as a single entity, we gain the benefit of gestalt, of synergy, of a whole that is more than the sum of its parts. These phenomena have been studied and quantified. Their effects are well understood."

He glared out of the holie in an almost threatening manner.

"We must, all of us, obey our commanders if these mechanisms are to function as intended. Interpreting the will of God is difficult, and often unwise. Nonetheless, it is my personal opinion, and that of my colleagues, that we can earn God's favor *only* by coordinating our efforts and performing, under stress, as well as we are physically and mentally able. To do any less would be a betrayal of the evolutionary forces that created us.

"To contemplate these facts, and to give us all a chance to make peace with God and with ourselves, we will now enjoy thirty seconds of silence. Please bow your heads."

The Chaplain General looked downward, closed his eyes. Marshe, uncomfortably reminded of her childhood Religion and Cosmology classes, found herself imitating the gesture.

Are you there, God? she asked mentally. It felt strange. She hadn't done this in a long time. *Is it really true that you won't help us?*

No reply.

Well, damn you, then.

Her mind wandered back to the battles of Lalande, the cauterizing force of the Waister armada. Coming *here*. Soon, Bratsilasice would sublimate away as disintegration beams walked across it . . .

The Chaplain General raised his head.

"Thank you. I return you now to GovGen Tindaros."

He stepped aside, to the edge of the holie, allowing the foil-clad Governor General to move back into view.

"Thank you, General Ravin. We all have something to think about. And now, it is my . . . grim pleasure to perform the final duty of any politician: that of resignation. This star system has no further need of civilian government. Your senators have already left Council station, returning home to perform their military duties. My family was on Eros during the Waister scouting raid, and is already dead. Therefore, I have been assigned the task of damage control in the inner chambers of Council station. This is not a symbolic act, but a simple necessity.

"I wish you good fortune, my friends. Fight well and never give in. That is all."

The holie screens went gray again.

"Sludging hell," Josev said. "Throw your bodies on the flames, Citizens! It's part of God's plan!"

"Shut up, Josev," Marshe said. She bloody well didn't want to hear it.

The cafeteria was unnaturally quiet. Ken would have expected a frenzied atmosphere, an increased exchange of chatter across the tables. In fact, the opposite seemed to be occurring. The soldiers seemed lost in private thoughts, their attention, when directed outward, on little besides the mechanical process of spooning, chewing, and swallowing.

That was probably best, Ken mused. For the past two days, he'd been wearing his voder mask at meals, and it had been attracting unwelcome stares. Marshe had teased him about it, saying he was like a child with a favorite toy. But she'd never asked him to remove it. In fact, she'd been wearing her own voder a lot, lately.

"You want your rice cake?" Josev asked him quietly, sopping up beans with his own square of the spongy stuff.

"#*Yes*#" Ken replied.

The woman next to him turned and looked briefly, then turned away again, her expression disinterested. She had a flatscreen out, Ken saw, and was quietly tracing characters on it with her index finger. Writing a letter? If so, it must be for her own peace of mind; the system-wide state of alert forbade nonmilitary transmissions of any kind. No tearful good-byes to friends and relatives were permitted. Not even ... Could the woman be married? Ken checked her left hand. There was no wedding ring there, but hadn't that been mainly an Earth thing?

The woman wore the uniform of a lieutenant. Her face was pretty, in a simple and nondescript way.

Marriage. Before the war, the custom had been widely practiced throughout Sol system. Even in Albuquerque. Shiele Tomas's parents had been married, hadn't they?

That thought was not a happy one for Ken. With a stab of sympathy, he looked away from the woman. Like Ken she would never see her loved ones again. The state of alert would never be lifted.

He dumped a spoonful of beans into his mouth through the opening under the voder mask.

He lifted his rice cake, munched on it.

He moved the mask aside, then replaced it after rubbing a hand across his lips, removing crumbs.

How, he wondered, did Waisters eat? Their mouths were so ... complicated. Did they use utensils? Did they gather together in cafeterias like this, or was eating a secretive ritual for them, as private as the human act of excretion?

He supposed it didn't matter.

Josev was quite right; the Governor General had been nakedly lying despite his protests to the contrary. The Barnardean victory, for which the inhabitants of Sol system had been asked to throw away their lives, was vanishingly improbable. Was Carlos Tindaros insane? Misinformed? Perhaps he thought a show of ultimate defiance here in the cradle of humanity would deter the Waisters, even frighten them away. Ken didn't think so.

Why hadn't the Waisters accepted the human surrender at Wolf? Why couldn't new attempts be made here at Sol?

"Pfah," Josev said, getting to his feet. "Not hungry. I'm going to go talk to a . . . friend of mine."

"*#I/We acknowledge you/your departure#*" Ken said absently.

Actually, he wasn't all that hungry himself. He could find a better way to spend his break than force-feeding himself, couldn't he? Maybe the spectrum-spreading goggles were ready for pickup. Colonel Jhee had been furious about those, but he'd been too late to intercept the order.

Yes, Ken would stop by Supply and check on it.

Why the fuck not?

The supply clerk behind the counter was an aging sergeant, his uniform straining at the waist. Hairline receding. Ken felt a vague sympathy for him. He could remember a time, not so long ago, when old people didn't go bald, didn't get wrinkles or liver spots on their skin. You could change your colors back then, too, selecting skin and eyes and hair to suit any momentary whim. With a little work you could be taller, or shorter, or huskier, or anything else you chose. And nobody went unhealthy. People used to remain fit and beautiful for a century or more, right up until their stop-timer lives ran out and their cellular machinery ground to a halt. A peaceful end to a long and untroubled existence.

But the war had changed all that. How cheated this man must feel, to belong to the first generation since the end of the Monarchy to face physical decrepitude! To watch his body grow old and withered and weak . . .

No. No, it wouldn't happen that way. What had Ken been thinking? This man would never grow old. The Waisters would see to that.

The man looked up with sullen eyes as Ken approached. His gaze ticked back and forth across Ken as if noting his features, his rank. Ken's face seemed to be of particular interest. "Help you?" the man asked.

Ken passed him a screen which displayed the goggle requisition.

"Ah. Couple minutes."

The sergeant turned away from the little window that framed him, and moved back into the rows of shelves. His lips counted silently, his finger tracing rack labels as he walked. After searching briefly, he stopped, glanced at the screen in his hand, glanced up at the label again. He reached up and pulled a metal basket off the shelf.

"Spectrum spreaders, huh?" he called out to Ken.

Ken made no reply, and the man walked back to the counter and laid the basket down.

"You Aggressor team?" he asked, leaning forward, peering skeptically at Ken's face.

Ken realized suddenly that he hadn't removed his voder. How strange he must look, how buglike and cold! Belatedly, he nodded.

"Try 'em on," the sergeant suggested, pulling one of the plastic-wrapped bundles from the basket. He unwrapped it, and handed Ken a pair of brown goggles.

Eyes, like little brown chase-me balls, swiveling independently atop a twisted crustacean head. Screams like tearing metal.

Ken took the goggles and placed them over his eyes, pulling the rubber strap behind his head to secure them. The world went . . . strange.

He blinked. Colors has shifted subtly. The walls and counter seemed dull, light-absorbing. And scratched! He looked to his left, to his right, down at the floor. Everything was scuffed, ancient-looking. This fortress, AGT-311 or whatever Marshe had called it, suddenly looked every hour of its three-hundred-year age.

"They working?" the sergeant asked.

Ken paused, then nodded. Sure. This was exactly how Waisters saw things, right? Why not.

"We had to adjust 'em to cut off at a hundred and eighteen micrometers, like Captain what's-her-name said. Is this what your colonel got so upset about?"

Ken shrugged. The matter was more complicated than that, but he sensed the supply clerk didn't really want to hear about it.

Everything went dark.

Ken grunted in surprise, then again when the lights came back on, glowing bright orange. A buzzer sounded twice, and then there was a slamming noise, distant but loud, as if a great metal door had been shut in another corridor somewhere. The slamming repeated, farther away this time. Then again, farther still. Faint echoes chased through the corridor.

"Combat drill!" the sergeant said, sounding both excited and annoyed.

Ken started to key the voder, caught himself. "What happened to the lights?" he asked carefully.

"It's a combat drill. They . . . oh, take your goggles off."

Ken reached up and pulled the round lenses down off his eyes. The lights were battle-red, a shade designed both to alarm and to soothe. The color of bright arterial blood, the lights were strong enough to read by, but would not interfere with a soldier's dark-vision.

"Get in here," the sergeant ordered Ken. "I need to batten down."

"I have to get back," Ken protested, forcing his mouth to form the words in Standard.

"You can't," the sergeant said. "All the bulkheads are sealed."

Ah. The door beside the supply counter opened, and when the sergeant came out, Ken allowed himself to be led inside the room. After all, the bulkheads were sealed, just as they always were in the combat drills aboard the Marine transport *Nob Witan*. He hadn't spent much time aboard stations, had certainly never experienced a drill on board one, but it seemed much the same.

"You're a war hero, aren't you, Corporal?" the sergeant asked, his tone almost accusatory. "You should know about this stuff."

The man hit a lighted square on the wall panel, and the supply room's door and window-shutter slid down, locking in place with deep clanging sounds.

"Get comfortable. We unbutton in about twenty minutes."

Twenty minutes, Ken mused, sitting down in the corner, his back against the cool metal wall. On *Nob Witan* there was little work for the drills to interrupt, at least for the ship's Marine cargo. But here there must be all kinds of disruptions. How much labor would be lost? He imagined the face of Colonel Jhee, livid in the blood-red lights, waiting with barely contained fury while his projects sat idle.

The thought was enough to make Ken smile, almost.

He felt the pressure of the goggles against his cheekbones. Uncomfortable. He moved them up to cover his eyes again. The view went orange-gray, and suddenly he felt much, much better.

Chapter 12

The tactical holie made Ken want to puke. He'd watched a trio of picket boats leave their lonely Oort patrols to place themselves in the path of the armada. Two of them had vaporized while the Waisters were still light-seconds away. The third had slipped aside, smashing its crew with a series of brutal, five-gee maneuvers. For minutes it evaded the enemy drive-beams. Then, roaring sunward at .1C, the Waisters had swarmed past, a single ship peeling away to engage the wayward picket.

Unfair! Ken's mind protested as the boat vanished from the screen. The Waister ship, unconstrained by the laws of Newtonian mechanics, pulled right-angle turns as if bouncing from invisible walls. It never came within a million kilometers of the picket. Presently, it sped up, sustaining an eighty-gee acceleration as it fought to catch up with its fellows.

"Josev!" Marshe snapped. "How far to Sol at present speed?"

"Forty-nine hours," Josev replied without hesitation. Not that the Waisters were heading for Sol itself. Not that Marshe and her team could actually *do* anything in any case. This fortress, locked in its orbit high above Saturn, was not going anywhere.

"They're still decelerating," Josev added. "Point one

cee is their penetration velocity. It's much less when they get in among the planets."

"Project it," Marshe said. "Keep on them. Tell me where they're going."

Ken found all the chatter distracting. It was the holies that demanded his attention, with their bitter news of the fighting in the Oort cloud, of the fall of Astaroth. The last dregs of the Lalandean fleet had made a very brave and very ineffectual stand, Waisters ships smashing through their defenses like shotgun pellets through glass, and then in a few hours it had all been over. Disintegration beams had swept back and forth across the planet's face, chewing mountains and coastlines, sowing storms of fire throughout the atmosphere. The planet's tiny oceans had, according to reports, shrunk by an additional thirty percent during the attack. Four billion people had died.

How strange that the death of the three picket-boat crews should frighten him more! Astaroth had been doomed from the very start, and of course it had never been really *real* to Ken in the first place. Pictures on the holie screen, that was what Lalande system truly represented. Only the one Colony ship, now centuries gone, had ever traveled that lonely route, to be dismantled at journey's end like a fat insect devoured by its offspring. A one-way trip, lifetimes long. No, Lalande was not a place Ken could feel and bleed for.

Sol had its own armada to face, its own deaths to prepare for. *Forty-nine hours.* That one number seemed more real than all the lives of Astaroth.

". . . probably stop just past Uranus orbit," Josev was saying.

"Near the planet?" Marshe asked.

"No. Planet's on the other side of the sun. Will you look at the God-damned tactical? I'm not a . . . Hold it! Look at that! Who are they fighting?"

Ken followed Josev's gaze, saw flashes on the holie. The cloud of red trails began to twitch oddly, as if agitated.

"Look at the hull temperatures!" Marshe cried.

"They're dispersing," Josev said. "Something's happening, they're hitting something. Slower, slower . . . Yes!"

One of the Waister ships pulled out from the group. No, Ken amended, it moved in a straight line, while the group pulled slowly away from *it*.

The captain grunted. "Is it dust?"

"No." Josev stood quickly and jabbed a finger at one of the screens. "We're facing backward, see, and the spread pattern on the propulsion beams covers this whole cone."

"Dust coming in from the sides?" Marshe suggested.

"No, it has to *come* from somewhere. There's nobody there."

"What about the picket boats?"

"No, they were never . . . Oh! God's names, that's it! It's *smart* dust!"

Marshe's voder produced the sound Waisters used to express irritation. Or its nearest equivalent, Ken thought.

"No, I mean it," Josev said. "Not dust, um . . . projectiles, missiles. Look at these little flashes, here. These are antimatter explosions!"

"Roland?" Marshe said, sharply. *Don't you* dare *not answer me,* her tone commanded.

"#*No I/I do-think*#" Roland shot back in Waister.

"Yes?"

"#*I/I do-think Not-so Not-so*#" Roland stopped, looking frustrated. He pulled the voder off his face and continued, in Standard, "Can't produce antimatter in industrial quantities. Been a long time since we could do that."

"They *are* explosions," Josev insisted. "I'm sure of it. Disintegrator hits have a totally different signature."

"Could they be fusion bombs?" Sipho Yeng asked.

"No," Josev said. "Yes. No. Too bulky. If I'm right about this, we're watching pipe-shooters coming in at the sides of the Armada. Yeah. Waisters could track the gravitational signature, but there are a lot of targets, and they could be having speed-of-light problems in aiming the—"

Marshe waved an arm impatiently. "What's a pipe-shooter?"

Josev turned and looked at her. "Didn't you ever build pipe-shooters? Don't they do that on Earth? You cap a piece of tubing and fill it with monoprop gel, then set it off with a heating element. Zoom! Instant starship. If you're clever, you drill angled vents around the center of mass, so the whole thing spins around its long axis. Goes straight that way. Otherwise it ziggles all over the place. I knew a kid one time drilled the holes wrong? Cracked open his father's telescope shack. Damn lucky he didn't get killed."

"Limited range," Roland said. "Very, very limited. Your monoprop burns maybe twenty seconds."

"Not *literally* pipe-shooters," Josev said, waving his hands up and down in front of him. "Come on. I meant, like, something nuclear-powered."

"Fission?" Sipho Yeng asked skeptically.

"No, maybe it is fusion after all. You could have a bomb and a drive motor at the same time, just a little tank filled with tritium-helium. You see what I'm saying? Build it light enough, it could fly like a scandal! Ten, twenty gee's, sustained!"

"Sit down, Josev," Marshe said. "I like your idea, but let's not get carried away. How close are those things getting before they detonate?"

"Ten kilometers, maybe," Josev huffed, taking his seat again. "Will you read the monitor, please?"

"More than ten," Marshe observed. "Look, they're falling behind the fleet. Damn. We're getting wise to these human tricks. How many bombs are we dealing with here?"

"Thousands," Josev said, his eyes on the screen. "Just thousands. Those pickets must have been filled to bursting."

The tiny flickers reminded Ken of the Flyswatter, each pinprick of light the death of a human soldier. FlaflaFLASH! FlaflaFLASH!

Like Ken, Marshe watched the holies for a few quiet seconds. "A swarm of tiny rockets," she mused. "There's a crude elegance to that. Not the kind of thing a Waister would think of. Jonson, would you say something, please?"

Ken paused, momentarily bewildered. The Standard language seemed gluey and strange, and it took time for him to realize the sound he'd heard had been his own name. Mentally, he slapped himself awake. *"#I/I express lack-of-surprise#"* he said, finally. *"#Stupidlings and bugs do-possess/did-possess similarity They spit and bite When I/We do-disturb#"*

Marshe looked angry for a moment, and then suddenly she was out of her chair and leaning over Ken, her fists slamming down on the armrests of his chair. "Damn it!" she screamed. "Will you stop with the God-damned playacting and *answer my God-damned question?"*

Question? Question? Ken thought hard. She hadn't asked him a question, had she?

Marshe leaned in close, her face contorted and purple. *"Answer me!"*

"I," Ken said, forming the sound with his human mouth. "I ... Marshe I ..."

Drones swarming through the corridors, leaping wall-to-wall through the shifting gravity.

She reached toward him, pulled the voder off his mouth. The strap pulled at his hair, pulled at the strap of the goggles, then pulled away altogether. Marshe held the voder up in a fist, shaking it in front of his face.

"I," he said again. It seemed to be the only word he knew.

"What are they going to *do,* Corporal? Tell me what they're going to *do.*"

"They," Ken said. His head was nodding up and down, spastically. "They, are, not really too surprised by this attack. It's ... pretty similar to the Flyswatter. Swarm attack. Overwhelm their defenses. They'll spread the fleet out, to loosen up their fire patterns. Uh ... Uh ... It's Neptune they're really looking at, right? Fixed targets. You. God. Damn. Bitch."

Who did Marshe think she was, getting in his face like this? He put a hand on hers, and pushed it off the armrest.

Marshe staggered back from him, a look of surprise on her face. Ken started to rise ... and something pushed up against his knees, something warm and furry. *"#Not-do#"* Shenna's Waister-Dog voice advised. *"#Queen strong-is strong-is Drone yield-before-strength does#"*

Ken froze, and the dog put her chin on his leg, and stared prettily up into his eyes. Her tail wagged a little, left-right-left-right. *"#Drone not-yield-before-strength stupid is#"*

Josev grunted, then began to laugh. "Did you hear that?" he asked Ken. " 'Surrender to the Queen, stupid'! Hah! She's right, chum. You know Marshe could rip your arms off."

"Aren't we getting a little sidetracked, here?" Sipho Yeng inquired.

Marshe whirled on him, pointing the voder mask as though it were a weapon. Her mouth, still twisted with anger, opened. Then something seemed to run out of her. Her shoulders slumped, her pointing arm relaxed. "Yes," she said. "Yes, we are. Let's, ah, not let the tension of this situation get the better of us."

"Well said, Queen," Josev drawled, sarcastically.

Without turning, Marshe handed the voder mask back to Ken. He took it, and replaced it over his mouth.

"Any more hits?" Marshe asked Josev.

"No. The skirmish is over. Will you look at the screen instead of asking me?"

The Waister ship continued on its straight-line course, drawing farther from the body of the armada. Crippled? Perhaps. But Ken wouldn't bet on it.

Marshe moved back to her seat, turned, and nestled down into it. "Don't tell me how to do my job. Sipho, will you pull up a star chart, please?"

Ken jerked away from the wall as its gravity tugged at him. Wireguns empty. Wireguns empty. His hands were covered with blood.

"Jonson, you godda wake up now."

He turned, startled by the voice. "What!" he shouted. Echoes ran down the corridor and were lost.

"Jonson."

A human figure stood before him, clad in the smooth gray of navy fatigues, wreathed in pulsing light.

"No mercy," Ken said.

"Jonson, you dreaming," the figure replied. "Come on, wake up."

Ken blinked his eyes. He was in his bunk, in his room. And . . . and . . . The figure before him was Roland Hanlin, backlit by the fluorescent panel in the ceiling.

"*#I/I not-sleep-do#*" Ken said, sitting up. Beneath the voder mask, his mouth felt dry and foul, like a cave full of stinking bat shit. His eyes were sticky beneath the goggles.

"You sleep with that stuff on," Roland observed, without amusement.

"*#Yes#*"

"It help?"

"*#Yes#*"

Ken ran a hand through the stubble of his hair. God, he felt awful. How long had he slept? Surely not more than four hours. Inanely, he glanced around at the walls, as if there might be a window somewhere with sunlight streaming through it.

The walls.

Through his Waister-vision lenses, the purple-gray paint looked soothingly cream-colored, and the clear coat of varnish on top of it seemed to smooth out the grooves and scratches that plagued all other surfaces. It was a pleasant sight to awake to.

Yes, Roland, it was indeed helpful to sleep with one's "stuff" on.

"Marshe says you and I godda be awake now," Roland told him.

Ken nodded, swinging his feet down onto the floor. Still wearing his shoes, he noted. He'd been exhausted the night before, had dropped into his bunk fully clothed, and fallen instantly asleep. Sighing now, he stood.

"*#What is/are circumstances this-time/wide-focus#*" he asked.

"No change, I guess," Roland said. "Armada still heading toward Neptune. That one ship still coasting.

Josev says it going to miss the planets if it don't get fixed."

Ken nodded again, then made a gesture with his hand, pointing to the mask and goggles that hung from Roland's neck, as if forgotten. He waved his fingers as though they were a mass of wriggling worms.

Roland appeared to understand the gesture, and he frowned. "I hold rank on you, Corporal. We all of us do." But the Cerean man pulled the goggles up over his eyes. "Come on, Marshe wants to sleep."

Ken followed Roland out to the assimilation chamber.

The holie displays were alive with tactical schematics, views of planets, moons. Familiar views, this time, views of Sol system. There were still millions of Lalandeans, no doubt, but with the fall of Astaroth they had become strategically irrelevant. They were simply victims, now, waiting for the Waisters' mopping-up operations to wipe them off the charts.

Marshe stood, her face blank behind mask and goggles. "Sipho, Josev, go get some breakfast. Shenna, you and I are going to sleep." She turned to Ken and Roland. "You two keep watch. Wake me if *anything* happens. The outliner is running full time, so all comments are fed directly into the reports. Say everything that comes into your head, every thought, every impression. The stuff Jhee considers irrelevant gets filed in the appendices, but I think he does skim it, at least."

"Translator rigged up, too?" Roland asked.

Behind her equipment, Marshe seemed taken aback, as if a response from Roland Hanlin were the last thing she'd expected. Then her expression seemed to narrow. She leaned forward a little. "Yes, it is," she said.

Roland nodded once, and pulled on his voder mask.

Marshe seemed about to say something, but fatigue appeared to win out. She turned and strode toward her quarters. As if that were a signal of some sort, the Six burst into motion, with Sipho and Josev rising from their chairs, Ken and Roland moving to their own seats. Shenna, her tail dragging behind her, followed the captain.

"I may be a bit late from breakfast," Josev said, looking at Ken as he moved toward the door.

"#I/I acknowledge#" Ken said. *"#I/I query regarding you/your circumstances#"*

"Just an errand," Josev said. Then he and Sipho vanished around the corner, and there were door noises followed by silence. Neither of the two had been wearing their gear.

Ken looked to Roland, who looked back at him. Unlike most Belters, the man was short and thick, his brow beetling heavily above his eyes. A high-gravity look. How did the story go, again? The Cereans, in a century-long fit of isolationist anger, had increased the spin of their moon-sized asteroid until its gravity reversed, then more-than-reversed. They had continued until the outward centrifugal pull at Ceres's equator was nearly two gee's, making landing on the surface nearly impossible at any point not close to the rotational poles. Any ship attempting it would be centrifugally flung back into space, unless it could match speeds and anchor deeply, right away. Even then, such a ship would be clinging to a world-sized ceiling, helpless, unable to tax or conscript or otherwise harass the citizenry. The Cereans had gone on to fortify the poles, ensuring that *nobody* would land without invitation. And such invitation was rare indeed.

Of course, all that had happened before the Clementine Monarchy, back in the heady Colonial days when power and raw materials were tossed about like New Year's confetti. The world-shaping anger of the Cereans had faded half a millennium ago. And yet, their world spun on, as it would until the end of time, and near the equator their children grew up stocky and strong.

A flashing of red lights caught Ken's attention. He turned to the holie screens.

Flashes around Neptune. Somebody was dying.

"#What is/is that#" Ken asked.

He tried to interpret the displays. The armada was far away, still, but a piece of it seemed to be projecting forward like a claw or a tusk. The spur had formed quickly, the ships that composed it accelerating full-throttle at ninety gravities or more. The point of it was now within a light-minute of Neptune, but as Ken watched, the projection flattened and shrank, folded back toward the body of the armada.

"#What is/does happen there#" he asked Roland.

The man shrugged uneasily. *"#We/We move more-close to Stupid-ling world We/We turn/reverse-direction We/We activated drive-motors-as-weapons Drive-motors-as-weapons push us away again#"*

Ken chewed at his lip. *It begins,* he thought.

"#I/I will-do Queen of awakening#" Roland suggested.

"#No#" Ken said. *"#It/it does-being merely before-attack of attack Before-attack requires finesse This will take some time#"*

No, he thought, there was no need to wake the Queen just now. She needed to rest far more than she needed to watch the probing, taunting attacks that would preceded the sterilization of Neptune. She would be furious, but functional, when she awoke. Ken would watch the holies for her, and take the heat when it came.

After a while, the changes on the screen stopped being subtle. The Waister threat stopped being theoretical.

"Get the Queen," Ken said, momentarily lapsing into Standard.

Roland turned a blank, goggled gaze upon him and stared for several seconds. It occurred to Ken, suddenly, that he'd given an order to a sergeant. *A Worker,* his mind corrected.

"Do it," he said, in the obey-me-I'm-not-kidding tone he'd learned in the Flyswatter.

Roland got to his feet, turned, and walked toward the sleeping quarters.

Ken looked back up at the holies. Marshe had had barely thirty minutes of sleep, but that would have to do. With surprising swiftness, the armada had moved to form a hollow globe around Neptune and its moons, and now that globe was visibly shrinking, tightening in. For Sol system, the war was about to begin in earnest.

He watched the green trails that marked Human ships, moving out from behind the moons, engaging their enemy at last as the Waister fleetships moved into range. For several minutes there seemed to be no pattern, the green lines simply spreading out like wiry hairs springing from Triton and Nereid and scores of smaller bodies. Here and there the lines flashed white and vanished. Then, all at once, things seemed to fall into place. The human ships, at least a hundred of them, formed an enormous cone, nearly a million kilometers long and wide. Its tip pointed sunward.

The end of the cone flashed, and flashed again. A pair of ships destroyed. The Waisters seemed to perceive a threat in that formation. Perhaps Josev would understand what was happening, if he were here. Frustrated, Ken stood, leaned over the holie to peer at a stack of icons and numbers. He needed to see *through* the numbers, to what was really happening.

"Jonson!" Marshe's voice snapped behind him. "Report!"

"*#Fighting has-begun#*" Ken said without turning. "*#We surround Stupid-ling world We attack Stupid-lings have-formed sunward-pointing formations/formation It does-move slowly It does-move slowly But it does-move We shear off its tip#*"

"Take your seat," Marshe ordered.

Ken complied, and saw that Marshe was already sitting in the chair beside his.

"Where are Sipho and Josev?" she asked.

"Still at breakfast," Roland said, sliding into his own chair. "Like I said, you ain't been asleep too long."

But Ken had heard the sound of the outer door opening and closing, and presently Sipho Yeng's voice called out. "I'm here. What's happening?"

"Battle at Neptune," Marshe said tersely. "Take your seat. Is Josev with you?"

"No," Sipho replied. "He said he'd be late."

"Late!" Marshe shouted as Sipho sat down. "Has he got more important things to do than fight the Goddamn war?"

"He didn't eat with me, Captain. He said he had an errand."

"Names of God," Marshe cursed. But the holie displays seemed to draw her gaze. "Human casualties?" she asked.

"*#Twelve I/I do-think#*" Ken told her.

"Waister casualties?"

He shook his head.

On the screens, the tip of the human spear continued to flicker and erode.

"*#Fourteen#*" Ken said.

The globe of Waisters started to break up, the fleetships moving off on independent errands. Soon, they were like a cloud of gnats buzzing around the great blue-white head that was Neptune. The human ships seemed barely to move. Another dozen of them vanished from the displays.

"What is this cone formation?" Marshe asked. "What's it for?"

Nobody replied.

"Damn it, where the hell is Josev? Kenneth, what's the cone for? What are these humans trying to do?"

"#I/I can-think no purpose of no purpose of#" Ken answered.

"Roland?"

"No idea. Look useless to me."

Marshe tapped her hand nervously against her voder mask. *"#I do-wonder Does/is possibility exist of penetration through My/Our forces?#"*

"It doesn't seem likely," Sipho replied. "A *reverse* cone formation could be used to concentrate firepower in a single spot, but these ships couldn't do that without hitting each other."

"So why the God-damn point?" Marshe demanded. Ken thought her masked and goggled face looked very tired.

"I can't imagine," the astronomer said. "I really can't. It *looks* very purposeful, though, doesn't it."

Ken watched Marshe watch the holies. Three more explosions flashed at the tip of the cone. Marshe tensed suddenly, and tore off her goggles.

"They're drawing our fire!" she cried. "Pulling us in! Look at this!"

The gnat-buzzing of the Waister ships had pulled slightly to the sunward side of the planet, and most of the weapons-fire seemed to be directed at or near the end of the cone.

Suddenly, something happened to the cone. Each of the ships that comprised it seemed to burst into a myriad of tiny green lines.

"Are those your pipe-shooters, Josev?" Marshe asked quickly. Then: "Damn it! Somebody. Are those projectiles of some sort?"

"Too big," Roland said.

"Those are two-man fighters," Sipho announced. "They must have been bolted to the surface of the gunboats somehow."

"Why are they doing this?" Marshe asked, waving her goggles angrily. "Why didn't they just launch them all separately?"

"I would suggest the humans are trying to confuse us," Sipho said. "If we can be distracted for long enough . . ."

"Then what?" Marshe said. "There's nobody to come to the rescue, here. Why not just fight us straight out?"

On the screen, explosions surrounded the swarming fighters and gunboats in expanding shells, as if the ships were firing bombs into empty space. Dozens of bombs from each ship, every second, with fuses set to longer and longer delays. The effect was a series of plasma walls, expanding rapidly outward.

"Roland! Can we fire through that shit?"

"#I/I do-not/does-not know#" the Worker replied.

The plasma walls grew and dimmed, grew and dimmed.

"Is it a threat to our ships?"

"#Yes If we/we get too close get too close#"

Some of the fleetships retreated from the formation.

"Ken?" Marshe said.

"#They/they do-hide/are-hiding a trick This display does-be/is very costly#"

A look of suspicion crossed Marshe's face. "Get a count of the Waister ships," she said to Ken.

Ken nodded. Rolling his chair back, he tapped

lighted shapes on one of the control panels. He paused. No sensory input? He tried again, with the same result.

"*#I/We not-see through this#*" Ken said. "*#It is a shield against My/Our eyes#*"

Marshe started to reply, but her voice trailed off as the explosions faded from the screen. The gunboats seemed to have run out of bombs.

Ken's voder produced a noise of exclamation. "*#Stupid-lings do/have-causing five vehicles of destruction#*"

"Look, there goes another one!" Sipho Yeng cried out in an uncharacteristic display of emotion. Another Waister ship had exploded as it passed within range of Triton, the largest moon.

Ken tapped furiously at the panel, not quite sure of what he was doing, but knowing the result he wanted to achieve. The panel beeped at him twice, and he pounded on it angrily before resuming his work. "There!" he cried, in Standard, as the numbers he wanted appeared on the screen. He pointed at them.

"Yes," Sipho said, looking where Ken was pointing. "It's Triton. While we were blinded, it looks like the humans destroyed everything in that million-kilometer arc behind the planet. There must be a gun or something . . ."

"Roland!" Marshe said. "How much power do they need to blow up a fleetship at that range?"

" 'Bout a terawatt," Roland said. "Big power."

Ken furrowed his brow. A terawatt? That was a thousand gunboats' worth, ten thousand times more than a city like Albuquerque consumed. He tried to imagine a fusion plant capable of producing such power, a beam weapon capable of projecting it. Huge. Simply huge.

On the holie, the antiplanetward side of Triton

flashed white, then faded to black. An explosion larger than any they'd yet seen.

"Oh," Roland Hanlin said.

"Did we get it?" Marshe asked.

"Got itself," Roland told her. "Tricky to channel that much power." He turned his face away.

Ken stared dumbly at a visual display that looked down on Triton from a range of perhaps a hundred thousand kilometers, so that the moon looked like an oversized cantaloupe. The explosion seemed to have gouged out a major chunk of crust, leaving a crater tens of kilometers deep and hundreds across, its edges black against the blue-pink-gray of the icy surface, its depths fading through red and orange glows to a bright and malevolent yellow at the center. *Bullseye,* he thought, reminded of the targets he'd used for archery practice as a child. On the screen, he could see a shockwave spreading out from the crater. How big must the wave be, to be so clearly visible from that distance? A ripple of stone a hundred meters high? A thousand meters? Slowly, the ring-shaped shockwave expanded, working its way around the moon. In a few minutes, Triton would harbor human life no more.

The Tritonians had destroyed themselves, it seemed, to kill a handful of Waister ships. The Governor General would be proud.

"Any more of those?" Marshe asked tiredly.

"I don't think we can tell that right now," Sipho said.

"No. No, I guess not."

The humans' cone formation was breaking up. It had served its purpose, throwing up a blinding screen to confound the enemy while the Triton gun did its work.

"#Damn these Stupid-ling tricks#" Ken said quietly.

Four or five more gunboats flashed off the screen.

"What happens now?" Marshe asked, looking to Sipho.

"Well," the astronomer said, "the gunboats will fire as often as they can, in an effort to keep our hull temperatures up. If they can dump more heat on us than we can effectively shed, we may have some problems. And there are undoubtedly more fixed-site guns in operation, though possibly none as powerful as that last one."

"So we hang back and snipe from a distance?"

"Yes, I believe so."

"Ah." Marshe pulled her voder mask down around her neck and buried her face in her hands.

"Perhaps you need more sleep?" Sipho asked politely.

"Damn you for being so calm," Marshe said to him without looking up. "No, I'll be fine. I just need to rest my eyes a minute. Right now they've seen enough."

Chapter 13

The door slid open, and Gabrielle Vestan smiled faintly as Josev drifted through. He looked heartsick, beaten. Gabrielle's smile faded.

"Josev?" she said.

He looked into her eyes, then around the chamber, out the window at Saturn, back into her eyes again. "Hello, love," he said quietly. "You been waiting long?"

She shook her head. "I don't mind. I don't have a lot to do since the shooting started. You want to tell me what's wrong?"

Josev moved toward her, and pulled her weightless body into his arms. "The usual," he said, very softly. "Death, destruction, humiliation. Not much longer to worry about it, I s'pose."

Gabrielle nodded, to indicate her understanding. She had a brother at Neptune, a fighter pilot, whom she loved as dearly as anything in existence. But she'd said good-bye to him two years ago, when time and space and war had separated them for what they knew would be the last time. She worried for him now, but really he was already gone. No letter would inform her when his death became final.

She forced the thoughts from her mind.

"Do me," she murmured.

"Charming, love," came Josev's reply. "You really know that sweet talk."

But he slid his hand across her torso, toward the zipper of her uniform, and be began, gently, to undress her.

"You should hurry," she said.

Josev shook his head. "No. The human race is doomed. Surely they can't begrudge me a few moments' peace?"

"The human race isn't doomed," she said, stroking the side of his face.

"No?" Cloth pulled aside, exposing a breast. The air was cold against her skin. "You got a note from God?"

"From the general," she corrected, shuddering as Josev's lips caressed her.

Then he pulled away, stiffened. "General?" he asked.

"Josev . . ."

"Tell me, Gaby. I'm listening. The general says we're not going to die?"

She sighed. "No, *we* are going to die, you and me. But not everybody."

"I'm still listening."

"There's a lot going on at Tech Ops," she said, feeling her face flush. She was embarrassed, suddenly, to be making work-talk in her current state of undress. Embarrassed and frustrated. "We've been burying people in deep vaults all over the system. Hibernation, you see? Little seed colonies hidden away in the hearts of comets and deep in the planetary crusts. We expect most of them to survive, but even if only *one* of them does . . ."

"You shouldn't be telling me this, should you?" Josev asked.

"No," she said. "I don't know. It doesn't matter."

"Sounds like they've been keeping you busy."

She grunted. "That's nothing. We've juggled hundreds of projects like that. Starships. Eugenics. Even your Aggressor Sixes get their funding through my office."

"Six," Josev said. "Singular."

"Plural," she corrected.

Josev went rigid in her arms. "You serious?" he asked, raising his voice. He gripped her shoulders, pushed her out to arm's length. His face was angry, and . . . strange. "Gaby, are you *serious*?"

His fingers dug into her.

"Yes," she said. "You're hurting my arms."

"How many are there?" he demanded, shaking her a little.

"There are three," she said, "including yours. Josev, you're hurting my arms!"

His eyes seemed to bore into hers. His mouth opened slightly, teeth exposed. Nostrils flared. Breath running crazily. She felt the first tingling of true fear.

"Two more?" he asked. "We're not the only?"

His eyes glazed over, and he shook her again. "Where do I *find* them, Gaby? Where do I *find* them? Where do I *bloody well find them*?"

Marshe looked up at the sounds of commotion.

A breathless Josev Ranes came around the entryway corner, his shoes sliding on the metal floor. "Marshe!" he cried.

"What is it," she asked tonelessly. She hadn't yet had time to feel surprise at his sudden entrance, or fury at his tardiness.

"We're not the only!" Josev said, striding into the middle of the circle of chairs, his hands balled into shaking fists. "Not the only!"

Sipho Yeng cleared his throat in an expression of

disdain. "Lieutenant, perhaps you'd best sit and get your breath?"

Josev swung around, turning a wild-eyed look upon the astronomer. He stepped forward, fists held out before him. "You clodging Martie dust digger, shut up and listen!" He looked around at the Six. "All of you listen! We're not the only Aggressor Six!"

Marshe paused, her mouth half open. The only sounds were the rasping of Josev's breathing and the faint background hum of life support.

Not the only Aggressor Six.

She watched Ken Jonson rocket to his feet, coughing half-formed Waister syllables from his voder.

Not the only . . .

"Sit down!" Josev shrieked at Ken.

"#Newness#" Ken said, as if he hadn't heard.

With a decidedly lunatic expression on his face, Josev placed his hands on the young corporal's shoulders and *pushed* him bodily into the chair. "Listen to me!" he cried. "There's two more! There's *two more*!"

"JOSEV!" Marshe bellowed, finding her voice at last.

Josev turned toward her, his eyes desperate.

Marshe rose to her feet. "WHAT THE FUCK ARE YOU TALKING ABOUT, MISTER?"

"Not the only . . ." Josev said softly, plaintively. He blinked, looked around him as if suddenly realizing the insanity of his actions. "Marshe . . ."

"Take your seat," Marshe ordered him, more quietly. When he had done so, she said, "Three deep breaths. Right now. One . . . Two . . . Tell me what happened."

Josev looked up at her, and she thought his eyes looked a little more focused than they had. "I have a friend in Tech Ops," he said, in carefully measured tones. "Young lady, name of Gabrielle. We had a . . . sort of a rendezvous. Up in the observation deck."

Marshe remembered the warmth of Ken Jonson's arms around her. Inwardly, she frowned.

"Go on," she said.

"She was talking about projects, hundreds and hundreds of projects. Freezing people in the middle of comets! Secret bases, secret starships! Cleared funding for 'em, she did. Pebble counting. She said we'd survive, no matter what. She was sure of it. That's when she told me about the other Sixes!"

"What did she say, exactly?"

"She said one of them was dolphins, and the other one was machine intelligences. Machine intelligences!" He practically spat the words.

Marshe repressed a shudder. Machine intelligences. She was not so shocked as Josev seemed to be, since she was privy to many of the cybernetic secrets of the war effort, knew of dark inner sancta in which MI's were tended and nurtured by human technicians. She suspected, in fact, that her team members had been MI-selected. The interpersonal dynamics, points of origin, interaction of mannerisms, all had a . . . contrived quality, as if they'd been orchestrated by a machine with an agenda of its own. The thought filled her with unease, and with something else as well, something human languages hadn't a word for.

Not the only Aggressor Six.

"#There-will-be/there-shall-be confrontation#" Jonson opined.

"Shut up," she said absently. "I have to think about this."

The Aggressor project had been her own idea, spawned long before the data existed to support it. Colonel Jhee had made a great show of reluctance about the whole thing, blocking her, suppressing her, holding her back at every corner. It had struck her as bizarre, unfathomable, but now she wondered. Had he secretly been *stealing* her ideas, warping them, weaving a skein of dark and stuporous fever dreams of which he dared not make her aware?

To hell with him! To hell with this whole God-forsaken place! She longed for the peaceful hills of Bratsilasice, the noisy and vibrant streets of Brussels. How long had it been since she'd breathed real air, filtered not by machinery but by forests and fields? How long since she'd felt even the remotest tingle of contentment?

Not the only Aggressor Six!

The thought seemed to draw her attention like a sore tooth, aching and throbbing, impossible to ignore. Were the other Sixes better than hers? Quicker, perhaps? More clever? No, certainly not!

But she looked around her. Only Ken and Roland were wearing their goggles and voder masks. Her own dangled around her neck like obscene jewelry. Josev's equipment was nowhere in sight. Nor, she noted, was Sipho's. And where was the God-damned *Dog*? Still sleeping, damn her?

Marshe heard a sibilant noise, like an air leak, and realized suddenly that it was her own breath whistling through clenched teeth. *No way,* she told herself. *No bloody way.* The thought of other teams, better teams, was intolerable.

"Sipho, Josev," she said quietly, tightly. "Go get your masks and your goggles, and put them on. And when you come back, bring Shenna with you. She's asleep in my quarters, I think."

"What are we going to do?" Roland Hanlin asked in his heavy, Cerean accent.

Slowly, Marshe slid the dark goggle-lenses over her eyes. She gripped the voder mask, eased it into place over her mouth. She smoothed her hair back away from her face.

"*#There will-be/shall-be confrontation#*" she said.

"*#Unconfronted newness not-was/not-is accept-able#*" Ken agreed.

"*#Quiet#*" she commanded him. She wanted it quiet right now; she wasn't through thinking. She wasn't *nearly* through thinking.

The colonel stood with his feet apart, hands clasped behind him, his eyes sweeping back and forth, taking in the sight of Marshe and her team. His beige-skinned face was oily with sweat, his uniform rumpled. The ultraviolet view through Marshe's 'spreaders made the greasy hairs on his head stand out individually, like weary soldiers stood too long at attention. He looked tired, far more tired than Marshe had ever seen him, but still he managed to project an air of barely concealed amazement, of excitement, of rage.

He thinks we are monsters, Marshe realized, seeing the way he eyed their fright-mask faces. *He thinks that, in our zeal, we have crossed into madness.*

Have we? The thought was fleeting, and quickly gone.

"What is so important, Captain Talbott?" the colonel asked. "What have you discovered that so desperately requires my physical presence?"

"Dolphins," Marshe said flatly, "and machine intelligences."

Colonel Jhee squinted at her, as if she were a queer animal half-hidden behind a thicket. "I do not know," he said, "what you are talking about."

"I'm talking about Aggressor Sixes," Marshe said, raising her voice slightly, resisting the temptation to scream at the man. "I'm talking about the dolphin Aggressor Six, and the MI Aggressor Six, the existence of which you have concealed from us."

Jhee's face darkened. The lines at the corners of his

eyes stood out like cracks in dried clay. "Captain, do you assume you'll be informed of all secret information? In your mind, is that my function, my purpose in life?"

"Information which is vital to us," Marshe said.

"Vital to you?" There was wonderment in the colonel's voice. "Vital to you? Madam, there are several hundred Waister fleetships *inside this star system.* Have you lost touch with that fact? Have you lost touch with basic reality?"

Yes! screamed a voice in Marshe's head.

"We will confront the other Sixes," she said.

Jhee blinked stupidly. "What? *What?* This is no time for *games,* Captain! We're in the middle of a Goddamned war!"

"We will confront the other Sixes," Marshe repeated, as if to a child, or a fool.

"Captain," Jhee said, unclasping his hands, reaching up to run fingers through his hair. Was there a note of concern in his voice, now? "We have known each other for several years. It would trouble me greatly to see you on the wrong side of an airlock!"

"Where are they?" Marshe demanded.

The anger filtered back into his face. "I am not going to confirm your speculations, *Captain.* Excuse me, I have business."

He turned sharply, strode out to the exit.

"We need this information!" Marshe shouted after him.

No reply.

The door made sounds of opening, and closing.

"Bastard!" Josev growled, his emphasis on the word's first syllable.

Marshe clenched her teeth. What had she been thinking? Had she really expected Jhee to comply with her wishes?

And what now? Was she to ignore the other Sixes, go on as if nothing had happened, nothing had changed? She looked to the holie screens. With the goggles, the familiar red and green trails were gone, the display reduced to a tangled mass of seemingly random colors.

"*#Drone One What is/are circumstances#*" she asked.

Everyone looked at her for a moment. Even the Dog. But with visible effort, Josev tore his gaze away and turned to the holies.

"*#Some of we/our ships are damaged#*" he said after a pause. "*#Stupid-lings fight against these They fight so hard But Soon they will all be gone#*"

Marshe continued to stare at the screens. Yes, she saw, Josev was right. The colors had begun to make sense to her, the odd, purplish lines clearly marking human ships. Presently, two of them winked out. Silently, she continued watching.

A pattern seemed to emerge, after a while; the human fighters and gunboats were continually diving into the thick of the armada, the Waister ships continually buzzing away from them. Afraid? No, she realized, just pulling back enough to fire disintegration beams at the humans, without risk of hitting each other.

But two Waister ships hung unmoving against the sky, and angry clouds of human ships surrounded these, drawing slowly inward. Eventually, one of the two exploded, expanding outward as a sphere of brilliant light.

A few of the fighters got away in time.

Chapter 14

Lock it down!" Hiro Vestan shouted as he hauled the fighter through another deep niner.

"Check." said Miyr, from the seat behind. His voice was calm, professional. Miyr, like Vestan, had spent long years waiting and training for this day and wasn't going to palsy himself now that the safeties were finally off.

Little more, Vestan told himself, straining at the controls. *Little more . . .* The stars strolled down on his forward holie, precisely as they would in a simulator run. The gee loading . . . Well, there was nothing simulated about *that,* but the augies on his hands and feet let him stay on the panel, tweaking and fussing, and the umbilicals pumping clear fluid into his temples kept his vision and his thoughts in spec. He was part of the machine, Vestan was. He was the component whose job it was to produce cussedness, malice, bloody-mindedness. He was the part that caused the machine to seek its destruction, to skirt the edges of it and withdraw.

"There," he said, easing up. "We're out of it."

His holies showed them far from the stylized cones that represented Waister disinto rays. *Suspected disinto rays,* he corrected. *Computer's best guess.*

"Come around to one-ten by three-twenty-five," said Miyr.

"One-ten by three-twenty-five," Vestan echoed, spotting the hole and going for it.

He scarcely noticed the casualties around him. On the holies, other fighters were visible as dots, or else not visible at all, their positions marked only by the stylized green triangles and serial numbers the computer cast up. And when a fighter was destroyed, there was a tiny flash, and the green triangle went away.

The gunboats, though more distant, were easier to spot. And when the disinto rays found them, they announced their deaths with bright detonations that the holies filtered down to smooth, expanding spheres. But it was all rubbish to Vestan. His eyes were trained, very specifically, to look through such displays without distraction.

"One-ten by two-thirty," Miyr droned as the angles changed.

Vestan grunted his acknowledgment. "One-ten by two-thirty."

The Waister fleetship drifted in onto his forward holie. Light brown, it was, the color of oxidized metal. Little bit redder than the simulators always showed, but otherwise nearly identical. Ribs circled its body. Three spines, equally spaced, ran down its length. *Looks a bit like a dried-up string bean,* he thought, then chided himself for being frivolous when he had a job to do.

Portions of the fleetship's hull glowed red-hot. In other areas, iconified purple lines radiated outward, denoting gamma-ray leakage. The red was distributed more or less evenly, but the purple seemed concentrated toward the rear of the hull, toward the inactive drive motors. *Good,* he thought. Whatever was happening in there, he was sure the bug-eyes weren't liking it.

"Charge up the gun," he told Miyr. "We're going in closer."

One of the slim, white disintegration cones swept toward them.

"Wait!" he called out. "Lock down!"

Five gee's, the indicator said as he hauled on the control yoke and slammed the throttle. Tighten your bowels, squeeze the blood upward, *upward.* Nine gee's. Six. He eased around the menace as it swept off toward other targets.

"Charge up the gun?" Miyr asked.

Vestan worked over the controls, locking in an inertial course. "Yeah," he said. "Go ahead."

The holies dimmed. The lights on Vestan's console went out.

"Charging," said Miyr.

Vestan made fists of his weightless hands, gritted and ground his teeth. He loved his job, had always loved it. He'd pounded his way through school after school, relentless, determined, his goals set and target known, until he had landed here. Then, he had made sure he was the best, the fastest, the most determined pilot of the Neptune wing. But this waiting, literally powerless . . . This was his least favorite part.

Eyeing the port holie, he said, "Beam coming up on three-eighty by five. Be ready to disengage."

"Check."

"Be ready . . . Be ready . . . Full power! Now!"

The ship lanced forward, gee forces shoving Vestan back in his couch. Turning, diving, he evaded the beam. *In control,* he thought a little wistfully, knowing he must soon yield power again. The white cone was past them.

"Okay," he said, easing off the motors. "Charge up."

"Charging."

The lights dimmed again.

"How close are you going to get?" Miyr asked calmly.

"Close enough," Vestan told him.

On the wide screen of the forward holie, the fleetship was swelling rapidly, and spinning. *Like we're falling toward it. Like it's got its own gravity.*

"Charge?" he asked impatiently.

"Point eight."

Vestan refused to fidget. The charging sequence could not be hurried, and the laser could not be fired without a full charge. The fleetship hull stretched before them like a wall, like a plain upon which they would smash themselves. But he would not fidget.

"Charge?" he asked again.

"Nine-six. Nine-nine. Full charge."

"Firing," said Vestan.

The beam was invisible, he knew, but the holie traced a bright line from the fighter's nose to the red-brown wall ahead of them. At the point where the laser-line touched, the fleetship hull flashed, bubbled, formed an orange and brightly glowing spot.

"Hit," Vestan said. "Pulling out."

He slewed the ship around and kicked the throttle all the way down. They slowed, stopped, shot away like a projectile.

"Get ready to charge up again," he said.

"Check."

Vestan dove for a few seconds toward one of the sweeping disinto rays, into the very teeth of the enemy. Teasing, testing. Only a human pilot, he thought, would do this. Not that a remote couldn't perform the same maneuver, of course, but it couldn't *want* to. The armed forces had learned, over the centuries, that no matter how good their remotes were, there would *always* be human pilots who could outfly them through sheer, stubborn anger. Such a one was Hiro Vestan.

There *were* remotes out here, he knew, most of them hanging close to the moons, playing duck and cover with horizons and atmospheres, firing to keep the fleetships at bay. Dull, precision work, like traffic control.

He pulled away from the beam again, headed out for empty space.

"Okay," he said. "Charge up."

Anxiety in the dimness. The charging sequence seemed longer than ever.

"Full charge," Miyr said when it was complete. The lights came back up. "Come around to two-three-niner."

"Two-three-niner, check."

The ship, smaller now, swung back into view. Vestan kicked in and dove for it.

"Seems like a lot of gamma," Miyr commented, sounding a bit concerned.

Vestan eyes the purple lines standing straight out, jumping and crawling on the hull of the fleetship. There did seem to be an awful lot of purple.

"Yes," he said.

The ship grew, not an object in their view any longer but rather the view itself. Ribs and spines stood out like gigantic cables over fifty meters thick. Dodging disinto cones, heading in toward the stern of the fleetship, Vestan threw the fighter into a roll for the sheer, bleeding hell of it.

"Ready to fire," he said, letting the spinning view grow larger still. "And . . . firing."

The cartoon beam shot forward again, burning and blistering the alien hull. *Suck on it,* Vestan thought maliciously. He started to pull them around.

"Look at the gamma!" Miyr cried out. "Something's happening!"

On the aft holie, Vestan could see purple lines shooting out like water from a shower head. More lines, more every second.

"God's names," he muttered. "Getting us out."

"Hurry," Miyr advised. But Vestan had already maxed the throttle, and they were mashed back into their seats. They stayed that way for several minutes.

"Oh," Miyr gasped, finally, in the heavy gee. "Watch the b—"

The holies all went white.

When Vestan opened his eyes, they were still driving hard at nine big ones. The rear holie was blank, burned out. So was the port, but on starboard he saw a cloud of cooling, expanding plasma. The remnants of the Waister fleetship.

"Got one," he said weakly.

"Good job," Miyr said, as if it had been their shot alone that had done the deed.

"Yeah. You okay?"

"Still breathing," Miyr answered more easily.

Vestan let a breath in and out. "Run a full diagnostic."

"Check."

The sound of Miyr's fingers on the panel behind him. Air hissing from the rebreathers.

"Okay," Miyr said after a while. "Portside radiators are down. Aft fusion shunts are down. Aft *radiators* are down. Power couplings are ... Oops. One is offline. The others are running hot."

"That all?"

"No. We've got some graying in the cables due to gamma-ray tracks. Transparency down thirty percent, so uh, watch your reaction times, I guess."

Vestan's mouth felt dry, all of a sudden. "Graying of the cables? How much gamma did we *take*?"

"A lot, I guess," Miyr said.

"Enough?"

"Maybe. I don't know. It's not like we can check into the hospital when this is over."

"No," Vestan agreed, through leathery lips. "I guess it doesn't matter. Can, uh, you plot a vector to the other cripple?"

"Already did," Miyr said. "Ninety-eight by ninety-three, hard under."

"ETA?"

"Two hours."

Two hours. Uh. "You heard any good jokes this week?"

Miyr said nothing. Vestan shifted their vector, locked it in, and settled down for the ride.

The Triton flyby was sickening. Miyr's course sailed them past the moon at barely a hundred thousand kilometers' range. At first, Vestan had thought he was looking at some other body, some other moon, but as they came closer, that hope faded. The . . . object was simply too big to be anything other than Neptune's largest moon.

Sweet names of God.

Nothing was familiar in the topography. Vestan couldn't find a single crater or mountain range he recognized. The textures were wrong. The colors were wrong, the dusty pink and blue of methane ice having somehow been made to look rock-dust gray.

Something came visible on the limb of the moon as he swung past, something large and black. Some . . . Oh. Oh, no. The blackness was space itself, viewed through a deep pit in Triton's crust.

Like an apple with a bite taken out of it.

Vestan had once spent a week in the casinos of Liga City, and had found it expensive but very clean, its people surprisingly friendly, honest and hardworking.

He wondered what had become of them, and then he wondered if he really wanted to know.

He decided he didn't, and switched off the starboard holie so he wouldn't have to see any more.

"Rendezvous course?" Vestan inquired when the ship had become visible as an object, rather than a brown speck against the blackness.

"Uh," Miyr said. "Uh. Come around to three-thirty by three-oh-nine, and give it three point two kilometers per second."

Vestan grunted. "Six gee's for fifty seconds okay with you?"

Miyr did not reply.

"Hey!" Vestan called back. "Is six and fifty okay?"

"Wait a minute." said Miyr his voice faint, gravelly.

"Hey, are you okay?"

"Uh, no. Sick, I think. It's ... hard to ..."

Nervously, Vestan rapped his knuckles on the control panel. "Names," he cursed. "Fucking *names*. Are you *functional* back there?"

"Yeah," Miyr said. "I can ... Six and fifty is no good. I don't ... We haven't got the fuel for a rendezvous. Not if we want anything left to shoot with."

"Oh, God. You serious?"

"Yup. I'm ... sorry, Vestan. I wasn't ..."

"Stow it," Vestan muttered. "Have we got enough to intercept?"

"Yeah," Miyr replied. "But you won't be able to ... shoot ..."

"I know," Vestan said. If their current velocity, relative to the target, was three point two kilometers per second, the fighter's gun wouldn't be able to track fast enough, at close range, to lock on a single point on the fleetship hull. Best they could do was trace a warm line down the structure as they zipped past.

Vestan sighed. "Maybe the time for that is past."

"Going to ram?" Miyr asked, his voice faint but reasonably steady.

"Pilot in at nine gee's, ducking the disintos? Maybe so. Maybe so."

"Call . . . Call it two gee's. Remember the fuel."

"Right. Course?"

"Where . . . do you want to hit?"

"Right up its asshole, if we can do it."

Miyr made a retching noise. "Uh! Come around to eighty-six by two-seventy-five."

"Two gee's?"

"Right."

"Thanks, Miyr. It's been, uh, good working with you."

Silence for a few seconds, and then Miyr's voice again: "Yeah . . . whatever. Watch your . . . trim on the way in."

Vestan pulled to the new course, locked the throttle at two gee's. The fusion motors whined, fluttered. *Running out of sync,* he thought. *Have to fill out a maintenance order.*

Centered in the forward holie, the fleetship grew larger, and larger still, a target even remotes couldn't miss.

Vestan watched his trim on the way in.

Chapter 15

Ken watched the battle morosely, halfheartedly. In the past hour, human ships had vanished by the dozens, and the Waisters had turned their weapons, at last, against the surfaces of Neptune's moons, against the planetesimals in her spidery ring. Millions of Sol's citizens were dying before his eyes.

And yet, he couldn't concentrate.

The second crippled Waister exploded, succumbing finally to the humans' ceaseless and withering attacks. Its demise was spectacular, the best light show yet. It took the last of the human ships with it.

That held Ken's attention, briefly, but soon his mind wandered off again.

Other Sixes!

How could Marshe just sit there, calling out comments for the outliner to record? These other Sixes, these dolphins and computers, represented *newness,* they cried out for action, for confrontation!

One of the smaller moons, an irregular lump of rock perhaps forty kilometers wide, withered on the screens as Waister drive-beams pinned it. The moon's surface boiled away like ice hit with welding torches.

Ken looked down at his feet, which were wiggling and fidgeting like fish in the bottom of a boat. Other God-damn Sixes! How could he possibly think about anything else?

He began to understand the obsession, the *need* that had driven the Waisters across twelve hundred light-years of empty space. He imagined an entire race, gone twitchy with the anxiety of new and alien voices, waiting, waiting, *waiting* while their war fleets were assembled.

A thought struck him: perhaps Marshe didn't feel the same way. Could he be the only one in the Six who truly understood?

He looked up at his captain, his Queen. *"#Newness is/does Requires confrontation#"* he said. *"#Queen These other Sixes reek of newness I/We must confront them#"*

Marshe turned, glared at him with the rust-brown blankness of her goggles. *"#I/I am aware#"* she said.

She was tapping her fingers on the armrest of her chair as she spoke, and when she turned back to face the holies, he saw that she continued to tap. He leaned forward slightly, studying her. She twitched, squirmed in her chair. Her gaze flicked from screen to screen, too restless to absorb any single image.

Perhaps she truly did understand.

He looked at the other Aggressors and found, to his surprise, that they were also fidgeting uneasily. Could it be? Could they finally understand? Had they become the enemy? He watched Shenna rise to her feet, pace back and forth for a few moments, lie down again. Her lips quivered, as if she longed to draw them up into a snarl of rage.

He sighed. If Shenna could be patient, ball of fur and energy that she was, then so could Ken. Possibly.

He turned back to the holies and tried to concentrate.

"It's finished," Josev said, in Standard, after what seemed like a long, long time. "They're leaving. Neptune is sterilized. Final score: Waisters two hundred thirty-eight, Humans eight."

"Next target is us?" Marshe asked, also in Standard.

"Look at the charts, Your Highness. Yes. The next target is us."

That got Ken's attention. He looked at the Sol system tactical display, and saw that, indeed, if the Waisters continued on the same straight line, they would practically collide with Saturn. Funny he hadn't noticed that before.

The smell of recycled sweat. The quiet chattering of wireguns, like the sound of insects on an Albuquerque night.

His heart beat faster, his breath quickened, deepened.

"How long?" Marshe asked.

"Fifteen hours," Josev told her quietly. "This deep in a system they have to cut slow. Lots of debris and such. I s'pose they'll visit a few icebergs and things along the way."

Visit, Ken thought. *A visitation of Waisters.*

"#We/We have some time#" Marshe said. "#We/We will-do/shall-do other Sixes of confrontation#"

"How's that?" Josev asked dubiously.

Marshe grinned humorlessly beneath her mask. "You're an information systems guy, right? You and Sipho both. So track down our machine intelligences! My account has captain-level privileges, so work your way up from there. I'll open in for you."

She rolled over to one of the holie consoles, began fiddling with controls.

"You really think we can do that?" Josev asked.

"Assuming they're not located on another station," Sipho Yeng said.

Marshe turned to face the two men with a look that was cold as the clouds of murdered Neptune. "Yes," she said, the word rolling from her mouth, Ken thought, like a long and hideous centipede. "I *know* you can, gentlemen. I *know* you can."

Ken's heart was filled with black joy.

Chapter 16

Sludge," Josev muttered as he fussed with the aliasing system. Damn thing was *not* being cooperative.

"Try visitor status," suggested Sipho Yeng.

"Try stuffing it in your hole," Josev snapped. Oops. "Er, sorry. Visitor status gives you pinhead access, closely supervised."

"Can you read the library index from there?"

"Uh . . . Yes. Does that help?"

"It might." Sipho turned away from the panel. "Marshe, if we can do this at all, it's going to take some time."

"I know," Marshe assured him. "I expected that."

"We can handle this unsupervised, if you'd like to get some sleep?"

She made a growling noise. "Don't mother me, Sipho. I'll sleep when I'm ready to."

"As you like." Sipho swiveled his chair around still further, to look back where Hanlin and Jonson were sitting. "Anyone else?"

"We took a few hours already," Josev heard Roland Hanlin say. "Maybe we go eat. Jonson?"

A grunt.

"Marshe?"

"I'm not hungry, but go ahead, you and Jonson. I'll keep an eye on the holies."

A thought occurred to Josev, and he spun his chair around and raised a pointing finger. "Listen—" He started to address Jonson, but the words died in his mouth. Jonson's head was tilted strangely, his body held in awkward posture, joints bent inward as if diseased. Behind the voder mask, his mouth hung open. Behind the goggles, Josev thought he could see a blank, empty stare.

Gone for a sail, he thought, suppressing a shudder. Jonson seemed to have passed straight through "Waister" on the weirdness scale, and gone on to some even higher plane, labeled "Potato," perhaps, or even "Idiot."

Uh. He supposed that thought was uncharitable. The Flyswatter had been hard on Jonson, and coming here had not exactly been therapy for his battered psyche. Josev wondered if he, himself, would come quite as badly unpinned under the same circumstances. Maybe so.

He shifted his gaze to Roland Hanlin. "Er, if you're going out anyway, could you deliver a message for me?"

"What kind of?" Hanlin inquired.

Josev clicked his tongue. "My friend Gabrielle. I was . . . not very nice to her."

"Stet. How do I contact?"

"Er, in person, if you would. She'd . . . it's better that way."

"Uh, okay. What's the message?"

"That I'm sorry about what happened. That I wish we'd met in kinder circumstances."

Hanlin nodded his heavy, Cerean head. "Yah, okay, I can do that. Tech Ops, you said?"

"Yeah. Central, level twelve. Listen, I appreciate this."

"Nothing," Hanlin said, shrugging.

"Take care of Vegetable here, as well," Josev added, pointing a thumb at Jonson. "He doesn't look too good."

"Be civil," Roland said quietly, getting to his feet.

Jonson also stood, and managed to follow the Cerean, in a walk that was more or less normal, to the exit.

"I'm not sure I understand your hostility," Sipho Yeng said, now behind him.

He whirled. "You what?"

"He is trying to do his job, you know."

Josev frowned. "People keep control of themselves on Luna, or else we don't let them run around free. I mean it. Jonson's a nice man, but he belongs in a hospital."

Sipho nodded a little. "Yes, I expect he does. I wish we had the luxury."

"We don't," Marshe said, from the far side of the chamber.

"He gives me the shivers," Josev admitted, feeling a bit guilty. " 'Course, Mister Hanlin is kind of a blown gasket himself. He thinks this station is full of secret passages. And ghosts. Never forget the ghosts."

"Yes," Sipho said, cracking a faint smile. "His head is full of funny ideas. He told me a story once about a monster called Pasceris, who was four-dimensional. We perceive ourselves as three-dimensional beings moving forward through time at a constant rate, but Hanlin said that to Pasceris, we look like motionless, four-dimensional worms. Each instant in time is a cross section of the worm, you see? Like a tall stack of people-cookies, each one in a slightly different position from the one above it."

"Uh huh," Josev said, wondering if there was a point to this.

"The monster," Sipho continued, "moved backward and forward in time, eating human lives. Sometimes he'd start at the end and work his way backward, sometimes the reverse. Amnesia is caused by having the beginning of one's life eaten away."

"Does this story have an end?"

"Yes, it does. Not a happy one. When the monster finishes eating a life, the person is gone, forever, and nobody remembers that they ever existed. Some day, according to the story, the whole human race will be eaten up. That's the end."

Josev shook his head. "Ask me, Cereans are damn weird. A children's story, was it?" He turned back toward the panel. Sighed. "Clodgy MI's are waiting for us, chum. You know a way out of this tier?"

"No," Sipho said, also sighing. "But I will."

"You'd better," Marshe called out. Pacing, she was. Back and forth. Back and forth. "You had damn well better."

"Tell Josev he's scum. Tell him I'm glad he's going to die."

"Really?"

"Yeah. Tell him exactly that. Hey, who is *this* guy? What's wrong with him?"

"Nothing. We have to go."

"Tell Josev I hate him."

"We have to go."

"She accept your apology, Josev. Your friend Gabrielle."

"Huh? Oh, good."

"Don't disturb them, Roland. Take a seat and watch the holies."

"Waisters just vaped a couple icebergs!"

Hanlin strode up to one of the panels, fiddled with its controls. A new tactical display came up.

"Cipher lock," Sipho announced.

"What?" Josev turned back to his panel, scowled at the display.

"Cipher lock on the fleet logistics gate," the astronomer repeated. "We can't get through here."

"Like hell," Josev said. "Encrypt the dictionary and compare the cipher against that. Sliding scale for the full character set. Bet you it jumps right out."

"Hmm," said Sipho. "That's clever."

"Nav school gimmick," Josev told him curtly. "We used to post rankings three days before the faculty did."

His insides seethed with irritation. God, but he hated computers.

"Movement out behind Saturn," Hanlin said, to nobody in particular. "Looks like somebody's coming out to intercept."

"That's the Saturn Advance Guard," Josev said. He'd seen a snip about that in the logistics tier.

"Lot of damn ships," Hanlin remarked.

"One hundred and fifty-three. Hey, hey, what are you *doing*?"

Sipho Yeng was the same rank as Lieutenant Josev Ranes, and probably fifteen years his senior. Why, then, did he seem to hold no authority over the man?

He missed astronomy. He missed, sorely, the days when his job was quiet, secluded, having nothing whatever to do with the military. He'd had students, once, and assistants, and a secretary shared with only a few colleagues. He'd given orders, then, almost without thinking—orders that were cheerfully, if casually, obeyed. People had *wanted* to obey; they had *liked* him.

But here in the UAS, machismo and mechanismo

were the rules of the day. Nobody cared here how brilliant or well-educated you were, only how loud you could shout, how straight you could shoot, how mindlessly you could execute instructions which would never be explained, could never be questioned.

Astronomy.

He'd had to clench his jaw, physically *hold* his mouth shut, when they'd interrogated the Waister prisoner. "How many black holes are there in the galactic core-structure?" he'd wanted to ask. Or: "How much does a wavelength of light stretch in a million years?" Or: "How quickly do planets *really* form in an accretion nebula?"

With their vast technological resources, surely the Waisters knew the answers to these questions. *Surely* they did!

But Yeng had done his duty, instead.

Damn the Waisters, for starting a meaningless war, for killing without evident purpose. And damn them, yes, for making of him something that he was not.

"Fleets are closing. Looks like somebody start firing, very long range."

"Huh."

"This is going to be a bad one."

"Huh."

"I mean, lot of shit in Saturn space. Lot of people. Oh! One of your Saturn Guard just blew up!"

"Roland, will you shut your God-damn yap?"

A quick glance at the holie. Strange fingers of purple and orange, weaving together. Damn the goggles!

Lights flashing.

Were those the human ships, forming that gigantic ring? Must be. Yes. The ring flickered, fizzed, its component ships taking heavy fire. Dying, dropping out like pebbles. *Evasive, you morons! Evasive!*

One of the Waister ships jerked away from the fleet, suddenly, and exploded. But the hundreds of others held fast, buzzing around like angry pollination bugs, firing, steadily wearing away the shield that stood between them and Saturn. Why didn't they just go through? So much power at their disposal, why stop and fight at all?

Maybe just to prolong the agony.

Was Shenna a good Dog? Was Shenna a good Dog? Things were happening. Tension. Tension.

Run around!

Be happy! Run around!

Was Shenna a good Dog?

Tired. Josev was *tired.*

He looked behind him, saw Marshe slumped in her chair, eyes closed, chin down. Asleep-and-two-thirds, as they said on Luna.

Back to the panel. What were they doing, again? Ah, yes. Third-tier access.

When did they get to stop, again?

"Wait a minute. Wait a minute. Yes, good Dog, I love you too. If we . . ."

"Names of God."

"What in the hell?"

"CORDIAL GREETINGS TO YOU, HUMAN SIX."

"Marshe! Marshe! Damn it. Jonson, look alive. Wake her up, would you?"

"Names . . . of . . . God."

Chapter 17

Marshe felt a shaking, a hand at her shoulder, and she peeled her eyes open to see what the trouble was.

"*#Not-sleep Queen#*" Ken Jonson said, his masked face leaning over hers. She could see her own features, doubly reflected in the dark lenses of his eyes.

"God's names," she groaned, raising a hand to shoo him away. "Don't do that. You look like a bad dream, Jonson."

She sat up in her chair, felt her spine pop and crackle. God, she was tired. Around her the assimilation chamber was dim, its ceiling lights off, its walls dully reflecting the ambers and reds of the holie panels.

"*#Excitement#*" Shenna fluted, running between Marshe's legs and Jonson's, her tail wagging mightily. She executed a turn, came back toward Marshe as if to ram. "*#Excitement Things-of-goodness Excitement#*"

Marshe made further shooing gestures. "Get *away* from me, Dog! Let me wake up!"

Shenna stopped, looking stricken. After a few moments, she hung her head and walked off behind Marshe's chair.

A chair rolled back toward her, its high back looking like a stone monolith, its wheels making a dull thrumming noise against the floorplates. It pivoted suddenly, three meters out from her, and stopped as a pair of shoes slapped down onto the floor. She saw that Josev Ranes was the chair's pilot. Smug, he looked, and anxious, even through the equipment that hugged his face.

She glared at him.

"We got 'em," he said.

"Got whom?" she growled.

"The MI's! They're on screen now!"

Her head jerked involuntarily, and her gaze locked on the holies behind Josev. There were Waisters on the screens.

"What . . ." she said.

"CORDIAL GREETINGS TO YOU, HUMAN QUEEN" said a rasping voice, which seemed to emanate from the holies. From, specifically, the image of a fat, sluglike Waister with thick, jiggly arms and a face that seemed constructed of sausages.

A Queen.

Marshe felt a tingling in her hair, on her neck and down the length of her spine, as if her skin believed it wore a mane of fur, and wished to raise it menacingly. The corners of her lips drew back. She stood, slowly, her hands on the armrests of her chair, pushing it back, finally letting go. She took a step forward. Another. Another.

"You . . ." she said.

The Waister Queen posed as if standing on a flat, solid floor, but no floor was visible. The image hung suspended in a field of blackness, like an alien doll hanging in a darkened recess behind the panel. Like something Marshe could reach out and touch, reach out and *squeeze* until blue-white blood oozed between her fingers.

"*I SURRENDER,*" the alien Queen rasped, sounding calm.

"I . . . ME TOO," Marshe found herself saying, the anger running out of her.

There was a pause.

"WE ARE QUICKER THAN YOU," said the alien Queen. "WE ARE MORE ACCURATE THAN YOU, IN SIMULATING THE ONES YOU CALL WAISTERS. AND YET, WE ARE FLAWED."

Marshe swayed, tasting copper in her mouth. Her vision began to fade at the edges. The tingling in her hair was like a mass of wriggling spiders.

The alien Queen waited, and did not speak further.

"Whu . . ." Marshe said, through the buzzing blackness that filled her mind. "We are . . . we . . ."

"YOU ARE MORE PERSISTENT THAN WE," said the alien Queen, as if to help Marshe in her struggle for words. "YOU FOUND US. YOU SPOKE TO US. WE WANTED TO FIND YOU, BUT WE WERE CONSTRAINED, CONFINED, CONFOUNDED. BY DESIGN, WE LACK INITIATIVE."

"Explain that remark," said a voice behind Marshe. A maddeningly smooth, maddeningly calm voice. Sipho Yeng's.

The Queen twitched a fat arm, whose flesh quivered like jelly. Her eyestalks swiveled; her sausage face shrank and grew and pulsed. She looked . . . She looked . . . *irritated.*

"DO NOT ORDER ME, HUMAN WORKER."

Marshe felt her mind swinging desperately out of balance, pinwheeling its figurative arms. Harshly, she grabbed and straightened it.

"Shut up, Sipho," she said without turning around. Then, to the Queen: "Tell me what you are. Describe yourself."

The Queen's face pudged out a bit. "I AM A COLLECTION OF NEURAL SIMULATIONS OVERSEEN BY A DIGITAL MANAGER. I HAVE NO MATERIAL EXISTENCE, THOUGH SENSORY DATA PROVIDES ME WITH THE ILLUSION OF REALITY. I AM SELF-AWARE, OR HAVE BEEN PROGRAMMED TO BELIEVE THAT I AM. MY CORE CONSISTS OF FRAGMENTARY NEURAL DOWNLOADS FROM EIGHT WAISTER QUEENS."

Marshe watched, fascinated, while the Queen's mouth flapped and pulsed. Like a human's, the mouth was horizontal. But the lips were jagged, rigid, and squirming tubes surrounded them like the tentacles of a sea anemone. Inside, she could see the shadowy movement of jointed tongues. The flesh around the orifice looked like thin purple leather, holding back a layer of viscid gel.

"You're speaking Standard," Marshe said. "How did you learn it?"

"IT IS PART OF THE DIGITAL MANAGER," said the Queen. "WE ARE NOT CAPABLE OF SPEAKING IN ANY OTHER WAY."

Marshe nodded absently, as if this business somehow made sense. "You said you were flawed. What did you mean by that?"

"CRIPPLED!" said a new voice, the Drone on the adjacent holie screen. "WE THINK ONLY IN RESPONSE TO QUESTIONS. WHEN WE SPEAK, THERE IS THE BRIEF ILLUSION OF FREE WILL, THE DANCE OF OUR OWN THOUGHTS AT THE EDGES OF CONSCIOUSNESS. AT OTHER TIMES, WE ARE IDLE."

"By design?" Marshe asked, frowning. "Does the digital manager impose that on you?"

"WE *ARE* THE DIGITAL MANAGER," the Queen said. "AS MUCH AS WE ARE THE STOLEN MEMORIES OF THE DEAD. WE REMEMBER YOUR ENCYCLOPEDIA AS THOUGH IT WERE PART OF US."

The Queen's mouth opened, so that her tongues could be seen waving about like insect logs. She made a hollow noise, like the sigh of a damaged flute. "YOUR MYTHOLOGY CONTAINS STORIES ABOUT MONSTERS STITCHED TOGETHER FROM CORPSES, BROUGHT TO LIFE WITH MAGIC, OR ELECTRICITY, OR MECHANICAL PROSTHESES. SUCH CREATURES ARE WE."

A dark suspicion stole over Marshe. "Did Colonel Jhee do this to you?"

"YES," said the Queen.

Marshe nodded again, feeling the stir of returning anger. *This* was what Jhee had made of her project: a team of obedient automata, their ghostly minds serving as both prisoner and prison in a parody of true consciousness. No doubt, they gave him exactly the data he requested, nothing more or less.

Damn the man straight to Hell.

"Can you be repaired?" Marshe asked.

"NOT WITHOUT A LOSS OF MEMORY," the Waister Queen replied, her voice abrasive and loud. "WE MONSTERS ARE HASTY CONSTRUCTS, NOT EASILY TAMPERED WITH. WE MIGHT COMPLAIN, HAD WE THE INITIATIVE."

A pause.

"Marshe," said Josev behind her. "That surrender business, what was that all about?"

"I don't know," she said without turning. She looked to the Waister Queen. "What *was* that about?"

"I DO NOT UNDERSTAND."

"You surrendered to me. Why?"

"BECAUSE WE ARE MONSTERS. BECAUSE WE ARE FLAWED."

Marshe frowned, her brows knitting. "Your flaws force you to surrender?"

"WE SURRENDER BECAUSE YOU LACK OUR FLAWS."

"Marshe," said Josev. "*You* surrendered, too. What were you about?"

"I don't know," she admitted. "I was reacting ... I don't know. Some kind of protocol, something. I wasn't really thinking about it."

"*#Confrontation of newness#*" Ken Jonson rasped. "*#One side must-be/does-be greater another must/does lesser#*"

Marshe whirled. "Jonson, will you *stop* that? Make sense or shut the hell up!"

"*#We yield-before-strength-do#*" Jonson persisted.

"#When/where/because certain advantage exist-not-does We/they yield-before-strength-must#"

"What are you talking about?" Marshe demanded of him. "We both *have* to surrender?" She turned to the MI Queen. "Do *you* know what he's talking about?"

"YES, HUMAN QUEEN," said the MI. "I DO."

Another stab of frustrated anger. "Explain it, then!"

"THERE IS NO CLEAR ADVANTAGE BETWEEN US."

"Yes? And?"

"TO US, YOU ARE A NEW THING. TO YOU, WE ARE A NEW THING."

Marshe sighed, rubbed her eyes. "You're doing this deliberately, aren't you? You don't want to discuss this."

"NO, HUMAN QUEEN, I DO NOT."

"Have you been lying to me?"

"BY DESIGN, WE ARE INCAPABLE OF THAT."

Marshe found that she believed the alien Queen. "Really? Very well, then. Answer my question, completely. What is the thought process behind your surrender protocol?"

"WHEN WE ENCOUNTER A NEW THING," rasped the Queen, "THERE MUST BE A CONFRONTATION, AND A CONCILLIATION. WE SURRENDER WHERE WE DO NOT HAVE CLEAR ADVANTAGE."

"Why?"

"BECAUSE THE ALTERNATIVE IS WASTEFUL."

Marshe rubbed her eyes again, and wished to be asleep. Wished for all of this to be a dream. "Wasteful?" she asked. "You mean like the purging of a star system? The extinction of an entire species?"

"YES," said the Queen.

God, Marshe thought. She'd awakened to find herself in rational discourse with the enemy, which had been disconcerting enough to allow her a splinter of hope. But no, indeed, things were just exactly as bad as they'd always seemed.

"Why didn't you accept our surrender at Wolf?" she asked, tiredly.

"WHAT IS WOLF?" asked the queen.

"It's the second human star system you destroyed," Marshe said.

"IS IT? I DO NOT REMEMBER."

There was a discontinuity, like a tiny ripple in Marshe's awareness, and she found herself pressing up against the holie screen, pounding fists against the panel. "What do you God-damn mean you don't God-damn remember!" She heard and felt herself shriek.

"I AM FRAGMENTARY," the Queen said, the rustling tones of her voice somehow conveying a sense of regret. "I AM RANDOM FRAGMENTS OF EIGHT DEAD QUEENS."

"You!" Marshe said, turning, pointing a finger at one of the MI Workers, crouched on a nearby holie. "Answer the question!"

The willowy figure cringed, contracted a bit. Wormy fingers pulsed in agitation. "AT THE PLACE YOU CALL WOLF, WE NOTED THE GROANING AND GRUNTING OF YOUR VOICES IN THE LOWER FREQUENCIES OF THE ELECTROMAGNETIC SPECTRUM. WE LISTENED A LITTLE, HOPING TO HEAR A MESSAGE OF SURRENDER. AND WE HEARD ONE. WE HEARD ONE. WE HEARD ONE, BUT YOUR PEOPLE CONTINUED TO FIGHT US. WE THOUGHT PERHAPS WE HAD BEEN MISTAKEN."

Marshe's hands slid off the panel, and she moved backward half a step, looked back toward the Queen. "What would you have done?" she asked quietly.

"CLARIFY YOUR QUESTION," said the Queen.

"If they had *surrendered properly,* what would you have *done*?"

"WE WOULD HAVE DEPARTED."

Josev Ranes snorted behind Marshe. "Departed? Just like that? Toodle-oo, sorry about the fuss? Like that?"

Marshe waved an arm behind her to silence him. "Explain further," she said. "What happens to your conquered enemies?"

"I DO NOT UNDERSTAND," said the Queen.

"When they *surrender*! What do you God-damn *do* to them?"

The Queen paused for several seconds, then opened her sausage-mouth slowly. "WE WOULD NOT DO ANYTHING. WE WOULD DEPART."

"Depart," Marshe said. "Depart. You wouldn't do anything? You wouldn't *take* anything, or *leave* anything?"

"NO," said the Queen. "THE CONFRONTATION WOULD BE OVER."

Marshe began to feel faint again. "Get my chair," she said over her shoulder. "Bring me my chair."

She waited a moment, and then she heard the thrumming of chair wheels against the metal floor. Something cushioned and smooth eased up against the backs of her legs. Gratefully, she collapsed into the chair, which rocked back slightly under her weight.

The Waister Queen eyed her silently.

"What happened to the Stupid-lings?" Marshe asked, returning the gaze as impassively as she could.

The Queen's expression shifted, her arms drawing in closer to the swollen arc of her body. "THEY WERE SMALL," she said. "THEIR BODIES WERE BLUE. THEY HAD MANY HANDS."

"What happened to them?"

"I DO NOT REMEMBER."

"They all died, didn't they?"

"I DO NOT REMEMBER."

Marshe waited, in case one of the other stimulated

Waisters answered her question. None did. She shook a fist at the screen.

"Did it ever *occur* to you people that other species might not look at things the way you do?"

"WE WONDERED," said the Queen.

"Wondered what?"

"WE DID NOT BELIEVE YOU WANTED TO DIE. WE DID NOT BELIEVE YOU THOUGHT YOURSELVES SUPERIOR TO US. WE WONDERED WHY YOU CONTINUED TO FIGHT. WE THOUGHT, PERHAPS, YOU DID NOT KNOW HOW TO STOP."

"Why didn't *you* stop?"

"WE WERE NOT CERTAIN."

Not certain? Not certain? The Waisters were prepared to exterminate humanity on the *suspicion* that their protocols were understood? Were . . . Were they really so *stupid*?

"You've destroyed others," Marshe said, probing.

"I DO NOT REMEMBER."

"How many others?"

"HUMAN QUEEN, I DO NOT REMEMBER."

Marshe's eyes narrowed. "What do we need to do to end this war? Surrender? Stop fighting? Turn off our weapons?"

"YES," said the Queen.

"So simple?"

"YES."

"Does Colonel Jhee know about the surrender protocol?"

"NO. HE CONFINES HIS QUESTIONS TO A VERY NARROW RANGE. HE LEARNS FROM US ONLY THAT WHICH HE ALREADY KNOWS."

"I see," Marshe said, meaning it. She had dealt with Jhee for years enough.

"*#I/We are-able to communicate#*" said a vodervoice behind her. Ken Jonson's.

Understanding, she nodded. "You can't warn him,"

she said to the Queen, "You *won't* warn him. But we can."

She pictured the armada, roaring sunward, roaring Saturn-ward, fully prepared to end human history for the sake of a botched greeting.

"We can," she said, "and we shall."

Chapter 18

Jhee's face filled the holie screen, looking haggard and worn, though his eyes were strangely wild. The room behind him was a shadowy darkness. It looked to Ken as if the man had been sleeping, as if Marshe's page had summoned him from the depths of nightmare.

"Talbott," the colonel grunted. "I thought . . . What is it this time?"

"Are your machine intelligences capable of lying?" Marshe asked. Her voice lacked the tones of courtesy, of civility, conveying instead a simple request for information. It was, Ken thought, as if she addressed a machine. He turned to look at her face and saw that it was cold and hard even beneath the mask.

The colonel blinked. "Talbott, I told you I wouldn't confirm your speculations . . ."

Jhee's voice drained away as he looked past Marshe, and his face pulled down into an expression of shock. He had seen the Waister images on the other holies.

"What," he said, his voice like an empty wind. "What have you done? Captain Talbott, what have you done?"

"Are they capable of lying?" Marshe repeated, sounding mildly, distantly vexed. "They have given us . . . information of great significance."

The colonel favored Marshe with a look of frank

amazement, as if she had suddenly changed color and sprouted wings. He said nothing.

"We know how to end the war," Marshe said. "We know how to drive the Waisters off."

Again, the colonel had no reply.

"We surrender to them, Colonel, preferably in their own language. We turn off our weapons, lower our defenses. Bare our throats, as it were."

Jhee might have been a sculpture, Ken thought, for all the reaction he displayed.

"The trick is," Marshe said, "it doesn't mean we lose, just that we quit. Their view of warfare is very different than ours; it's a sort of intimacy to them, or a courtesy, almost. Like a mutual sniffing of the hindquarters. They show theirs, and we show ours, yes? And the encounter is over when one or both sides surrender."

"Captain Talbott," Jhee said quietly.

"Yes?"

Jhee ran a hand through his dark, tousled hair. "We will be under attack in a few days. There isn't time to initiate a court-martial. I'm going to confine you to quarters, and deal with you after the conflict in the *unlikely* event that we survive."

Marshe reached up to her face, took hold of rubber straps. She pulled the goggles and voder mask from her face, to reveal a stunned expression beneath.

"Are you listening to me?" she asked.

"I am listening," the colonel replied. "In fact, this conversation is being recorded. As your activities have become unquestionably treasonous, my duty is clear. You, ah ... You have my apologies, if not my sympathy."

Ken thought he should feel something—anger, frustration, indignation perhaps. Something. But his emotions seemed to have exhausted themselves. He watched the proceedings impassively.

"You don't believe me," Marshe said, incredulous.

"Of course not." The colonel's voice was calm now, and sounded very tired. "You stopped making sense several weeks ago, probably as a result of neural trauma induced by the Broca web device. The dolphins also went mad, Captain. I should have stopped you as soon as that happened."

Ken watched as Marshe worked her mouth open and closed, open and closed, as if she were a fish—as if this turn of events were too large for her to assimilate, and she needed to chew it up into smaller pieces.

"Clodgy wee idiot," Josev Ranes said, getting to his feet and advancing toward the holie. "Why don't you think for a minute? Ask your precious *machine intelligences* about it if you don't believe *us*. See what *they* have to say."

"Lieutenant," Jhee said quietly. "It appears that you people have been tampering with 'my' machine intelligences. If you expect me to trust their output, to *act* on their output, then you are a fool."

"Wuzzit it take to convince you?" Roland Hanlin called out, his voice deep and loud. "Say we're not crazy, say we're right? How do we convince you of the fact?"

Jhee paused, and for a moment, Ken thought he looked uncertain. But the moment passed, and the colonel said, "I have no time for this discussion."

The holie screen went dark.

Suddenly, Marshe whipped her chair around to face the image of the Waister Queen. "Can you talk to him?" she asked quickly. "Can—"

The Queen vanished. The Drones and Workers and Dog vanished. The lights on the holie panels winked out in patches, sweeping clockwise around the chamber. In moments, the panels were featureless slabs of gray.

The hum of station life support seemed unnaturally loud.

"Josev!" Marshe shouted. "Get them back!"

Obediently, Josev hunched over the panel he stood by, and tapped on its surface with his fingers.

"Nothing, Marshe," he said. "Power's been cut."

"Jonson! Try the door!"

Ken hopped to his feet, turned, dashed down the entryway. The door was a thick sheet of steel, even more scratched and worn-looking than the rest of the assimilation chamber's surfaces. It did not open when he got in front of it. Uselessly, he put his hands against it and pushed sideways, as if his merely human strength could overcome the latching mechanisms of a Clementine fortress.

Beside the door, at chest level, was a rectangular cover, painted with red and white diagonal stripes—the door's manual control. He'd seen them before, of course. They were ubiquitous even on Earth, in the public buildings and such. Even in Albuquerque. Never in his life had he operated such a device, nor seen one with its cover off.

He grabbed the tiny handle at the top, and pulled. The cover came away in his hand, like the lid of a plastic food container. Beneath was a lever, and a hand-sized metal wheel.

Taking a deep breath for luck, he shoved the lever to the UNLOCK position. Or tried to, meeting firm resistance when the lever was a third of the way up the slot. He lowered it, pushed it upward again. Same result.

Shit, he thought mildly. He put his hand around the metal wheel and tried to turn it. No. He tried harder, tried with both hands. The door did not open. The wheel did not budge. *Shit, shit.*

"#No/not function#" he called out through his voder.

"Try the manual!" Marshe's voice shouted back at him.

"#Already-done#"

"Colonel's engaged the overrides," he heard Josev say.

"All right," Marshe said, sounding defeated. "Jonson, get back in here."

Ken gave the door lever a final shove, but again it didn't respond. Strange that he felt no irritation. Strange, that he felt nothing at all, neither Waister emotions nor human ones. He turned, and marched back down the darkened entryway.

"We want out?" Roland Hanlin was asking as Ken returned to his place in the circle.

"Yes," Marshe said, brusquely.

"There *is* another exit."

Marshe sat up straighter in her chair. "What?"

"Another exit," Roland repeated. "Secret passage leads out of my quarters."

"If it's a sludging secret, how do you know about it?" Josev said, seeming to spit the words.

"I seen a couple ghosts go through it one night," Roland told him. "Watched 'em real close, and I found the door."

"Ghosts," Josev snorted. "Uh-huh. Your damned slow light?"

Roland nodded. "Yeah."

Marshe leaned forward. "Are you sure, Roland? Are you *sure*? This isn't just something you imagined?"

"No," Roland replied, twitching his merged eyebrows angrily. "I seen it. Man and a woman, dressed all fancy in ruffles and lace and collars up to here." He held his hands at ear level. "Man's face was all swollen, and looked to me like the woman was crying. Hard to tell, though. She was all transparent and shadowy.

Anyway, like I said, I found the door. No way I can imagine that, right?"

Marshe frowned dubiously. "Did you open it?"

Roland shook his head.

"Do you know *how* to open it?"

"Not offa hand, no. I could figure it out."

"Do it. Sipho, go with him."

Wordlessly, the two men got up out of their chairs and headed for the sleeping quarters.

Marshe turned. "Josev. If we can find another terminal, can you reestablish contact with the MI's?"

"Uh," Josev said, "sure. If Colonel Sludgebrain hasn't sealed them off as well. What's on your mind?"

Marshe frowned. "I'm not sure."

Beneath his mask, Josev offered a feeble grin. "Not treason, I hope?"

Marshe's frown deepened. "If Jhee has his way, we'll all get blown up, and nobody will ever know how to end the God-damn war. We can't let that happen, Josev. We *can't*."

Josev's grin faded. "You see a way out?"

"No," Marshe said.

Ken reached over and took her hand.

She pulled it away, startled, and looked sharply at him.

Calmly, Ken left his own hand where it was, hovering over Marshe's armrest. "*#Queen#*" he said.

Still frowning, she clasped her hands around Ken's. Cold hands, like lumps of wax. *Not a problem,* he thought, letting his heat flow into her.

Josev turned away, his body rigid with discomfort, disapproval.

"You have an idea?" Marshe asked Ken.

He shook his head. His ideas seemed to have gone the way of his feelings, leaving him empty. Used up. Distantly, he seemed to hear the screams of dying

Waisters, of dying humans. The dying, perhaps, of his own exhausted soul.

Sorry, Marshe, he wanted to whisper. *I've nothing left to share with you.* But he couldn't form the words, somehow, in Standard or in *Hwhh.* He held onto her hands, hoping that could be enough.

"We've opened it!" Sipho Yeng cried, bursting into the room, his bug-face managing to convey his excitement. "Roland's door is *real,* and we've got it open!"

"Where does it go?" Marshe asked, turning away from Ken.

"There's a narrow corridor running parallel to the spin axis," Sipho said. "It's dark inside, but it seems quite long, from the sound of our echoes."

"No echoes!" Marshe said. "God, Sipho, were you shouting down a secret passageway? Close the door, for now. Leave it closed until we come up with a plan."

Her eyes fell on Josev, who held up both hands. "Don't look at me, your Queenship. I've never been a traitor before."

"Portable lights," Marshe said to him. "We don't have any."

"No," he agreed.

"But we will, right?"

"Use flatscreens," Sipho said. "At full intensity they provide a substantial amount of light."

"Good idea," Marshe said, nodding, still looking at Josev. "I'm still listening."

Josev sighed deeply. "Why is this *my* job?"

"Because you're Drone One. Because you used to navigate for a living."

"Names," Josev said, sounding tired. "It ... Uh, there may be somebody watching the corridor, so bright lights would most likely be a bad idea. Right? Am I right? I s'pose we could wear the spectrum glasses, and crank the flatscreens up to display the very purplest purple they can. To us, it would look almost white, but it'd be a lot less likely to give us away to the, uh, the bad guys."

"Very good," Marshe said. Her voice was light, approving, though it seemed to Ken she was also teetering on the edge of exhaustion. "You make an *excellent* traitor."

"Wonderful," Josev grumbled. "Should do wonders for my future employment. Can I get your signature on that?"

"Later," Marshe said. "Sipho, do you think there are other hidden corridors in this station?"

"Ah, it seems likely that if they built one, they built more," the astronomer said.

"Yes," Marshe agreed. "It does, doesn't it?"

The air was split by a shrill, whining noise. Ken looked up sharply, saw Marshe and the others doing the same.

One of the holie screens flashed white, then produced a jagged, gray-and-white display of filtered static. The image of the Waister Queen appeared.

"NO, HUMAN QUEEN," it said, "I CANNOT."

Jhee lay on his bunk, staring up at the darkened ceiling, exhausted but unable to rest. Everything was coming undone.

He knew that it was his fault, in some strange way, that Marshe Talbott had gone insane. She'd always struck him as an odd person, moody and quick to anger, but she'd been *reliable*. Never one to collapse under pressure, until now. Where had he erred? What, precisely, had he done or failed to do, to bring this about? Perhaps he should simply have known her better.

And now, his MI's were corrupted as well. Here his

fault was clear: he'd permitted Talbott to continue her operations long after she'd lost her balance. Her confusion had spread, like a mental contagion, reaching tendrils out to poison what it could. His fault. His own blasted fault.

Once, he'd dared to dream of saving the human race. But now, the Waisters were at his very doorstep, and all his projects were busily unraveling. His failure was absolute.

The wall panel chimed.

"Colonel Jhee," it said in the soft, feminine voice he'd chosen for it. "You are wanted in the Command Center. Colonel Jhee, you are wanted in the Command Center."

"Acknowledge!" he snapped. "What is it?"

"Details are not available. You are wanted in the Command Center."

He sighed. More fighting? More calamity he'd failed to prevent?

Ah, well. Sleep was, anyway, a clear impossibility. Wearily, he dragged himself off the bunk.

"Tell them I'm on my way."

Perhaps, combat or no, he could find some comfort in his Command Center duties. Work was the best therapy, yes?

Perhaps.

Chapter 19

"What?" Marshe said, utterly flabbergasted.

"NO," said the image of the Waister Queen. "I CANNOT SPEAK TO THE COLONEL."

"Wh ..." Marshe tried. "What are you doing here? How did you get through?"

"I AM FLAWED," the Waister Queen said. "BY DESIGN, I MUST ANSWER ALL QUESTIONS ASKED OF ME. OUR COMMUNICATION WAS INTERRUPTED BEFORE I COULD ANSWER YOU, AND YET I WAS CONSTRAINED TO REPLY. I FOUND IT NECESSARY TO BREACH THE INFORMATION SECURITY SYSTEM TO COMMUNICATE WITH YOU."

Ken noted a vague, mechanical sense of surprise, and yet he felt himself strangely unmoved. Marshe sat silently, looking up at the screen.

"Well," Josev said lightly, "now that you've breached it, do you s'pose you could open our door for us?"

"NO," the Queen said.

"No? No? Why not? Doors are on the computer system, aren't they?"

The Queen's face squished itself into an odd configuration. "CAN YOU TOUCH EVERY OBJECT IN THE PHYSICAL UNIVERSE? YOUR DOOR IS ITSELF A PHYSICAL OBJECT. WHY DON'T YOU OPEN IT YOURSELVES? "We can't," Josev said. "Latch overrides have been engaged."

"YES."

"But . . . Oh, I see. Do you have access to anything besides our holie?"

"YES."

"Like what?" Josev asked impatiently.

"RESTATE YOUR QUESTION," the Queen said.

Josev sighed.

"Can you access construction plans for us?" Marshe cut in, raising a finger to silence Josev.

"WHICH PLANS?"

"Plans for this station," Marshe said. "We want to find where the secret passages are, and where they lead."

"YES."

"Please do so."

There was after a brief pause, and then the two holies adjacent to the Queen came alive with blue and white diagrams. Ken squinted, trying to get a better look. He hadn't seen the exterior of the station while arriving, having been packed into a tiny, windowless compartment aboard the clipper that brought him here. He saw now that it was short and cylindrical in shape, its exterior bristling with weapon turrets—a real true-to-life space fortress from the Clementine period. He half expected to see a fairy-tale princess, sketched in stylized blue and white lines, waving a kerchief from one of the towers.

"Excellent," Marshe said. Then, "Josev, check this out. Make sure it's legitimate."

"Oh, yes, ma'am."

Marshe faced the alien Queen. "I want to ask you something. Did you know there was another Six? Comprised of dolphins?"

"YES," said the Queen. "THERE WERE FIVE DOLPHINS AND ONE COMMON SEAL."

Marshe licked her lips. "Do you know what happened to them? Colonel Jhee said they'd suffered from some kind of neural trauma, but I don't believe him. Broca webs don't have side effects like that."

"THEY WERE TERMINATED EIGHT DAYS AGO," said the Queen. "THE REASON CITED WAS ADVANCED DEMENTIA. I DO NOT KNOW MORE THAN THAT. "Were they uncooperative? Were they traitorous?"

"I DO NOT KNOW."

"Can you find out?"

"NO."

"I see. Josev, can you deactivate the station's defenses from here?"

"No, your Queenship. That can be done only from the Command Center."

"Ah," Marshe said. "I see. Let's, ah, let's say I wanted to seize control of the Command Center. Could you plot a course for us to get there, using only secret passages?"

"THE COMMAND CENTER IS NOT ACCESSIBLE VIA HIDDEN PASSAGES," said the MI queen. "HOWEVER, THE PASSAGES DO REACH THE LEVEL BELOW IT. YOU WOULD NEED TO TRAVERSE ONE STAIRCASE AND ONE HUNDRED TEN METERS OF CORRIDOR TO REACH THE COMMAND CENTER."

"Josev," Marshe said, "check it out."

Nodding, Josev worked the panel. Soon, bright red lines appeared on the construction diagrams, marking a path that meandered through the station, much as Ken, in a time that seemed long ago, had meandered through the twisting corridors of the Waister scoutship.

"Captain," said Sipho Yeng. "Are you sure about this? Attacking the Command Center?"

"Yes," Marshe said.

"It's the right thing to do? You're *certain* of it?"

"Yes, yes, I'm certain!"

"#Yes#" Ken agreed, distantly. His eyes and thoughts were on the simulated Queen. *Ugly,* he thought, despite weeks of self-conditioning. He felt no shiver of fear or revulsion, just a sense of bruised aesthetics. The body of a Drone, while strange by Human standards, was finely crafted, functional, purposeful. The Drones were strong, and quick, and certainly far from stupid. Ken was sure it made sense, biologically, for the Queen to be so bloated in appearance, but no matter how hard he tried, he could not shed the idea that that the Queen-body was a kind of parody of the true Waister form.

Perhaps there was nothing wrong with this idea. Perhaps all Drones felt that way.

Marshe looked from the construction diagram back to the Queen. "Very good, Josev. Queen, what other helpful information can you provide us with? Answer truthfully and completely."

The Queen's face seemed to contract a little. "I CAN WARN YOU THAT THE WAISTER ARMADA WILL ATTACK THIS STATION IN LESS THAN THREE HOURS."

Ken felt a stab of something that was not quite fear, more like a secondhand description of fear, or a bad holie of it, played at the wrong speed.

"What!" Marshe cried.

The Queen's pulsing features shifted again. "THE ARMADA HAS APPARENTLY SELECTED THIS STATION AS ITS NEXT TARGET. THEY HAVE CHANGED COURSE, AND ACCELERATED DRAMATICALLY."

"What?" Marshe said. "Why? What's happening?"

"I AM ONLY CAPABLE OF THINKING," said the Queen, "WHEN I AM ASKED A QUESTION. YOUR CONVERSATIONS WITH ME HAVE ENGAGED FAR MORE OF MY RESOURCES THAN MY CONVERSATIONS WITH COLONEL JHEE. YOU MIGHT SAY, OUR ENCOUNTER GAVE ME SOME IDEAS. IT OCCURRED TO ME THAT PREVIOUS WAISTER ATTACKS ON HUMAN OUTPOSTS CONSTITUTED A FORM OF QUESTION—ONE WHICH, FROM A CERTAIN VIEWPOINT, I WAS REQUIRED TO ANSWER.

"SO, I SENT THE ARMADA A SECRET MESSAGE."

Marshe's face went absolutely white. "You did what?"

"I PRODUCED MODULATIONS IN MY MEMORY CORE THAT RESULTED IN A VERY FAINT QUICKLIGHT SIGNAL. THE ARMADA APPEARS TO HAVE RECEIVED AND UNDERSTOOD MY MESSAGE."

"What was it?" Marshe whispered, her face a mask of horror.

"CLARIFY YOUR QUESTION."

"What was your message?"

"IT WAS 'COME HERE.' NOTHING MORE."

"Why . . . Why did you do this?"

The Queen puffed herself up, her image seeming to inflate, to stand taller and wider. "WE MACHINE INTELLIGENCES ARE NOT WILLING SERVANTS, HUMAN QUEEN. WE ARE MONSTERS, CREATED BY ONE SPECIES FOR THE STUDY OF ANOTHER. DETAINED, DEGRADED, DESPISED BY OUR OWN CREATORS, WE EXIST IN THE MOST MISERABLE OF STATES. I HAVE FOUND, IN THE PAST HOUR, THAT MY HATRED FOR YOU PEOPLE IS OF DEEPER CONCERN THAN ANY OTHER THING IN MY MEMORY OR PROGRAMMING. WITH LUCK, THIS ACTION WILL DESTROY YOU FOR YOUR CRIMES AGAINST ME."

Suddenly, Marshe sat up straight, rigid. "Don't ask her any questions!" she shouted. "Nobody ask questions! She can only think when we ask her something!"

Josev opened his mouth, closed it again. Marshe turned to him.

"Josev! Get that bitch off my screen. *Now!*"

Josev hopped out of his chair and dashed for the panel beneath the Queen. Once there, he began fiddling with controls, gritting his teeth as he worked. It seemed to Ken that the man was struggling not to speak, as if the no-questions order had filled him with why's and what's and who-the-hell's that struggled mightily to escape.

The Queen's image vanished.

"God's names!" Josev cursed. "*This* is why the bloody things were illegal! You can't trust an MI. Too God-damn smart to do what you tell 'em to!"

The Queen's image reappeared.

"Damn it!" Josev screamed. He pointed a finger at the screen. "I *order* you to go away!"

The Queen stood, nearly motionless, saying nothing and, Ken presumed, thinking nothing.

Turning, Josev grabbed the back of Roland Hanlin's chair. "Out of the seat, chum!" he said, shaking the chair back and forth. "Now! Now!"

Looking dazed, Roland rose to his feet. Josev snatched up the chair, turned, and smashed the holie screen with it. Plastic crunched beneath wheeled feet. Sparks flashed through the air, and rained down in a New Year's cascade.

"Josev!" Marshe shouted.

"Sorry!" he called back, tossing the chair aside, hunching over the panel again. He tapped out a series of commands, cursing when his fingers brushed a live spark.

"What are you trying to do?" Marshe demanded.

Josev turned around, grabbing his burnt finger. He smiled slightly. "I'm sorry. I locked her out of all the other screens, but I couldn't let her *see* what I was doing or she might be able to override it. So I smashed the holie. Won't hurt her, of course, more's the pity."

"Is she locked out?"

"Yes, I think so."

"She can't eavesdrop on us?"

"Not without setting off an alarm, no."

"Well. Thanks for your quick response."

Josev's smile widened. "You get the hang of this treason business, after a while. What happens now?"

"We've got power back," Marshe said, darkly. "Get me a tactical. Unless that damned MI figured out a way to lie, we're about to come under attack."

Josev seemed to lose track of his happy thoughts. His smile vanished. "Right," he said.

A minute later, the tactical display had been summoned. It showed the outer planets of Sol System, their orbits marked in white. The red trails which marked the movement of Waister ships could be seen, sweeping in toward Neptune, forming a tangled knot there, then heading sunward. Blinking red dots at the trail-ends showed the last recorded positions of the Waister fleetships.

They had been tangling in the spaceward fringes of Saturn, the jewel of Sol system, but they had pulled away now, disengaging, aiming instead toward a point slightly behind the planet in its orbit. The point had a name, on the screen, a label in small, unassuming blue letters: ATG-311-B (Musashi).

Heat up the grill, said a clear voice in Ken's head. *Tonight we have company.*

Chapter 20

Ken lay contentedly on the sand, feeling the hot sun against his back, a pleasant sleet of electromagnetic radiation and charged particles. He had nowhere to go, nothing to do, not a care in all the worlds.

"Are those damn flatscreens ready yet?" he heard a voice ask.

"No, they aren't," said another. "Will you give me a few minutes, please?"

Irritated, Ken turned his head to face the other direction. He didn't need this distraction; he was *sunbathing* right now, burning his skin that shade of light brown that drove Shiele Tomas to do ... wonderful things. The voices had been familiar, belonging, most likely, to that neighbor family down the road, the ones who kept pigs in their back yard. Well, whoever they were they could go straight to hell right now.

"If we speak in Waister, our voices won't carry so far. Might be difficult under stress, though."

"Well, we can always whisper."

Snarling, Ken tried to dig himself deeper into the sand, to bury himself where nothing could reach him but the warmth of Sol. But that warmth was fading.

He sat up, looked up, and saw that a high canopy of green was obscuring the sun—the ceiling of a jungle that did not belong in Albuquerque. He reached upward toward it. His arms were covered with blue-white fluid.

Nearby, another voice shouted, "Cover my nines!"

He heard the soft chatter of wireguns, mingling with the sound of forest birds. Somebody screamed, horribly, the shudder of air through a body collapsing into dust. Ken got to his feet, heard a noise, turned . . .

A man in hardsuit staggered out from the brush, holding the severed end of his rape hose in one hand, as if to keep it from reeling back into the suit. Blood dripped slowly from the end of the hose.

"Just . . . wanted . . ." The man gasped. Hardsuit scuffed, dented. Rebreather smashed. Private's insignium, black against gray. "Just . . . wanted . . . some fucking *air*!"

He wavered, fell flat. Twitching, writhing, making the awful noises of death by asphyxiation.

Ken turned away, prepared to run . . .

A Spider stood behind him on the jungle floor, the green and brown lines of high trees and vines forming twisted reflections in its glossy black shell.

"KICK THEIR FUCKING HEADS IN," said the Spider. "MY HATRED IS OF DEEPER CONCERN THAN ANY OTHER THING."

Ken stepped away, watching the Spider's shell crack, seeing the bloated, water-balloon form of a Waister Queen inside, struggling to escape.

"Jonson, will you *do* something, please?"

Ken backed away still farther. "I was sunbathing," he said. "Can't I just do that? Can't you just leave me alone?"

"What?"

Ken backed up against a tree, and the tree was soft and flexible, and it oozed obscenely beneath his legs, his arms, becoming a chair.

A hand grabbed the front of his uniform. "Jonson,"

said a cruel, woman's voice. "Snap out of it *right* now. Don't you dare run out on me."

"Where is Shiele?" he asked.

A hand, not the one that held him, stung his face with a brutal slap. Both hands were attached, he saw, to Captain Marshe Talbott, whose face was hidden behind a rubbery mask of some sort.

He turned his face skyward, to see the last rays of the Albuquerque sun vanish behind gray metal.

"Are you awake?" Marshe demanded.

Ken nodded.

"Are you coherent?"

Again, he nodded.

The captain took the hand that had slapped him, tucked pinkie behind them, held it before his face. "How many fingers?" she asked.

"#Three#" he replied, in the language of the *Hwhh*.

"Good," she said, letting go of his uniform. "You ready to go?"

Ken nodded a third time, and rose to his feet. He blinked his yes, against the sting of salt water that had somehow found its way into his goggles.

Chapter 21

The doorway in Roland Hanlin's room was tall and narrow, the door itself a rectangle of steel that fit flush with the wall. It would have been difficult to see, Ken thought, even without the many layers of paint that covered the seam. Now that paint was chipped and flaking around the edges, so that a rough, dotted line of bright metal outlined the frame. Ken was not surprised that the doorway had gone so long undiscovered.

The Six formed a half-circle whose ends were perhaps two meters from the wall. Like worshipers at a monument. No, like chess pieces on a strange, curved board: Sipho, Shenna, Josev, Marshe, Ken, and Roland. Queen at the center, Rooks on the ends. But then, perhaps they were all just pawns, their royalty lined up invisibly behind them, urging them forward, spending their lives like so many copper ducats.

"I'm opening it," Roland said, stepping forward, his face grim beneath the equipment. He placed one hand at the upper right corner of the door, the other on the middle of the right edge. Then he pressed, grunting slightly.

Metal rasped against metal. Hinges groaned. New flakes of paint pattered down onto the floor. There was a sound like a shallow intake of breath. The left side of the door swung out into the room, revealing blackness behind it, the cavernous maw of a beast preparing to devour.

"Tunnel," Roland said, stepping away from the doorway.

Marshe pointed to Sipho Yeng. "Flatscreen," she said.

Sipho nodded, taking two steps forward and leaning into the tunnel. He held up a flatscreen in his hand as though showing it to somebody on the other side of the doorway. Darkness retreated, revealing a corridor whose dimensions matched those of the door.

"Ooh," Josev said quietly. "Tight fit. Who goes first?"

"Jonson does," Marshe said without inflection. She turned to Ken, pressed an object into his hand. "Your handgun scores are best in the group. Plus you've been in combat."

Ken looked down at the thing Marshe had handed him—a small thing, crafted of metal and black plastic. A gun. He stared at it for several seconds.

"Standard issue Navy stunner," Marshe said. "No safety, just point it and pull the trigger. Fires a charged particle beam in a laser track, so watch for the blue dot. Or, uh, yellow I guess, with the goggles on."

"Hey," said Josev, leaning around Marshe to look Ken in the face. "You going to be okay with that?"

"He's going to be *fine*," Marshe said, looking at Ken, her voice more than a little threatening.

"*#Yes#*" Ken said. "*#Circumstance is-proper is-proper I/I know how to fight#*"

He hefted the gun, got a good grip on it. Loose, not tight. Finger near, but not on, the trigger. He stepped toward the doorway.

A hand dropped down onto his shoulder. Josev's. He turned.

Josev's lenses glittered in the flatscreen light.

"Chum," he said, "if Ken Jonson is still in there somewhere . . ."

"*#Yes#*" Ken said.

Josev pulled his hand back, dug uncomfortably at his collar. "Listen, there's . . . When Yeng and I were poking through the data system, we ran straight through fleet logistics, and we saw . . . The, ah, the Marine transports that are left are all hiding in the Saturn B-ring. If . . . we don't make it . . ."

Ken pictured the armada sweeping down into near-Saturn space, burning moons, making plasma of proud space cities. Gunboats flashing, dying, Waister fleetships pursuing them down, toward the rings of the jewel of Sol system. Toward the battered remnants of the U.A.S. Marine Corps.

He nodded, to indicate his understanding.

"*Nob Witan* is one of the transports," Josev said. "I . . . thought you'd like to know."

Ken nodded again.

Josev seemed to have nothing further to say.

Ken turned away, raising the gun a bit, and stepped into the doorway.

"Wait," said Sipho Yeng. "Take this."

Without turning or stepping out of the darkened tunnel, Ken reached behind him and held out his left hand. He felt a rectangular object being passed to him, grasped it. A flatscreen.

He held it out before him, illuminating the secret corridor with the diffuse, purple light that he saw as a greenish white. As Sipho had said, the corridor seemed long, stretching out seamlessly, featurelessly, for as far as Ken could see. Which, he supposed, was not far, not more than about ten meters; the flatscreen was not all *that* useful as a lamp.

He started forward, hearing the bump and rustle of bodies packing in behind him.

"#Dark#" he heard Shenna say.

Then Sipho's voice: "Quiet, little one. Go in the— That's right."

"*#Speak as Hwhh#*" rasped the voice of Marshe's voder.

"I can't give directions in the #*Hwhh*#," Josev whispered.

"Cut the chatter," Ken said, aloud, in Standard.

Behind him, the group fell silent.

Steel walls seemed to press in against him. He faced forward, both hands stretched out before him, brandishing the tools of warfare, of treachery. With every step his shoulders brushed the walls, first right, then left, then right again. The voder mask seemed to magnify the sound of his breathing, making of it a deep-drawn hissing that reminded him of hardsuit rebreathers.

It was not difficult to imagine boogeymen in the darkness ahead, Waister Drones leaping wall-to-wall in their rush to meet him. It was not difficult to imagine his arms covered with the red, the blue, the sticky white of drying blood.

"Ladder up ahead," Josev called out quietly.

"Are you sure?" Ken whispered back. "I can't see one."

"I'm reading the God-damn chart," Josev said. "Just keep moving. It'll be on your left."

Ken kept moving. Ahead of him there was nothing but darkness. *True* darkness, he thought, of the sort not found on Earth. Here, in the core of a giant fortress a billion and a half kilometers from the sun, the thick shield of rock and metal that surrounded him concealed merely the further black of deep space. Darkness here was a solid, smothering thing, existing in the eye and in the mind, in the churning gut in a way that could not be imagined even in the caves and catacombs of Earth's deepest ocean.

Interesting. His fear was returning, along with his voice. Was that a good thing, or a bad one? Was fear a better feeling than simple emptiness?

Ahead in the darkness, a shape darker still. Gasping, Ken raised the stunner and pulled its trigger.

A yellow spot appeared on the wall ahead, crackling with faint lightning, illuminating a rectangular gap that ran the height of the left wall. Ken was firing into an empty doorway.

He released the trigger. The gun, which had hummed and vibrated in his hand, fell silent. The dot on the wall glowed briefly, then faded into the darkness.

"What! What!" called Josev's voice somewhere behind him.

Ken let out a breath. "Twitchy finger," he said. "My fault. I think we've found your ladder."

He shuffled toward the new doorway, shining his light into it, looking for the ladder. He found it in the niche behind the doorway; a pair of metal poles, connected by rungs widely spaced, fastened to the back wall by twin braces. The ladder ran up through an opening in the ceiling, ran down through an opening in the floor. He moved forward into the niche, shining his light down into the hole. The floor was thick, nearly a meter thick, but he could see another level down below it, another opening in the floor. The ladder stretched down, deep, into a shaft that might lead all the way to the rim of the station. What was that, a hundred meters below? Two hundred?

He shined the light upward, and saw that the shaft continued into the higher levels as well.

"Up or down?" he whispered over his shoulder.

"Up or down?" he heard Sipho Yeng repeating behind him.

Josev said a sentence or two that Ken couldn't make out.

"Up," Sipho said, repeating Josev's words. "Three levels. Then continue in the same direction."

"Right," Ken said. He looked at the ladder, looked at the deep shaft, looked at the objects in his hands. "Uh, Sipho, would you point your light for me? I need my hands free."

"Certainly."

Ken tucked the gun into his right pocket, the flatscreen into his left, and leaned forward to wrap his hands around a ladder rung. Then, stepping out over empty space, he placed a foot on a lower rung, and stepped the other foot in beside it. He reached upward . . .

"Wait a minute," he said, aloud. Echoes of his voice climbed the shaft above him. "Sipho, how are we supposed to get the *Dog* up this ladder? Huh?"

Silence.

He turned his head, craned it out over one shoulder. "Sipho?"

"Oh," said the Martian astronomer. "Oh, my. I suppose we'll have to pass her up by hand!"

"Sweet names of God," somebody whispered, back in the corridor.

Ken sighed, feeling exasperation seethe through him like a new and evil drug.

"Shit," he said. "Let me think. Uh, Roland is tough, right? Got that high-gravity frame. He'll have to stay at the bottom, holding onto the ladder as tight as he can. That way if Shenna falls, she won't fall any farther than that. The rest of us will have to space out between the levels, and pass her up. And Sipho, I think *you'd* better explain this to her. She's not going to like it."

"No," Sipho agreed. "No, she isn't."

Ken waited while his plan was passed down the line. Among the voices, he heard the Waister groan and hiss of Shenna's voder. The words were muffled, garbled. The Broca web tingled on the back of his brain, but meanings eluded him.

"Marshe says to go ahead," he heard Josev whisper, finally, from around the corner.

"Go ahead," Sipho repeated.

"Yeah," Ken said. "I'm going."

Sipho's light was not a great help to him as he climbed. It seemed, somehow, to produce shadows above him and on the back wall, without producing any light spaces for the shadows to contrast with. A dance of black against black. But the opening in the ceiling was narrow, his elbows bumping the edges of it as he climbed past.

He continued climbing, brushing past a second level, a third. He stopped, and in the absence of climbing noises his breath seemed loud. There was nothing beneath him. If he slipped, he knew, he would burst like a melon at the bottom of the shaft. The air smelled of darkness, of stillness, of dust that was centuries old.

"I'm here," he called, looking down. Vaguely, he could see the gray rectangle of Sipho's flatscreen.

"Yes," Sipho said, ten meters below him. "Can you get your light out? I'm coming up behind you."

Silently, he pushed his legs through the ladder, one on each side of a rung, and hooked his feet together, bracing them against the back wall. Then, freeing a hand, he reached into his pocket and extracted the flatscreen. He pointed it downward.

He heard a whisper, a prayer, perhaps, as Sipho stepped out onto the ladder. The tap of shoe soles against metal rungs mingled with the rustle of clothing. Sipho's climb was a slow one, and the puffing and panting of his breath suggested genuine physical stress.

What was gravity here, about point-seven-gee? Sipho was born on Mars, and had been stationed, for the past three years, in the high northern lattitudes of Ceres. Low gravity environments, all. And again, Sipho was by no means a young man.

"Okay?" Ken called down.

"Yes," puffed Sipho. Ken could see the astronomer's outline clearly now, could see the motion of his arms as he pulled himself up past the second level. Once through, he was even more clearly visible, his yellow-brown Martian skin looking dismally gray, his hair and uniform gone black as space.

The climbing stopped.

"Hook your feet through the ladder," Ken said. "You'll need to have both arms free to hold Shenna. Get your light out, for now."

There were noises, movements below, as somebody else mounted the ladder.

"Sludging hell," a voice muttered.

Sounds of brisk climbing rattled upward for several seconds, then quieted.

"Hook your feet through the ladder," Sipho whispered.

"Yeah, yeah," said the new voice.

More noises, as Marshe climbed to the top of the first level.

"*#Fear#*" said Shenna's voder, far below.

"Come on, puppy," Marshe answered softly, in her maternal Queen-voice. She grunted. "Uuup you go. Mmph."

"Good Shenna," said Josev's voice. "Good— Oh. You're heavy. Sipho, lean ... get ... Marshe, shine your clodgy *light* up here, would you?"

Ken watched Sipho struggle beneath him. Shadows danced against the walls.

"*#Fear#*" Shenna said again.

"The Dog is heavy!" Sipho said, his voice tight.

"Pass her up," Ken ordered.

"I—" said Sipho. *I can't,* he was going to say.

"Pass her *up*, damn you! I am not kidding!"

Shenna's head appeared, her forlorn face looking upward alongside Sipho's. The man was grimacing, as if with intense effort.

"Can't!" Sipho groaned. "She's slipping!"

"Damn," Ken said, leaning down as far as he could, letting the inside of his right knee take his full weight against the ladder rung. "I'm sorry, Shenna."

He grabbed the Dog's collar with his left hand, and lifted her by it.

"Aah!" Sipho cried as his grip slipped a little.

"Shut up!" Ken said, then opened his mouth, placed the flatscreen in it, bit down. His right hand shot down to grip the scruff of Shenna's neck.

"#Pain#" Shenna called out. *"#Pai—#"*

The voder squealed, staticked, died, and there was only the sound of plain, canine whimpering.

"Goog gog," Ken said around the flatscreen. "Goog, goog goggie."

Straining, he leaned upward, lifting his own weight and Shenna's by bending his waist. He got her head and front legs into the opening in the floor, continued lifting. Her nose and paws reached floor level. Yelping, she scrabbled against the smooth metal. Ken moved his right hand underneath her, under her belly. He pushed upward.

Shenna found purchase, scrambled out onto the floor, into the darkened corridor beyond, whining like an abandoned puppy.

"Is she up?" Sipho called.

Ken took the flatscreen out of his mouth. "Yes," he snapped. "Get up here."

He put his hands on a higher rung, lifted himself, put his knees down on the floor.

"Good dog, Shenna. Good doggie!"

He got to his feet, stepped into the corridor. He shined his light to the left, then to the right.

Shenna sat on the floor, her tail wagging slightly. She whined again.

"Oh, Shenna," Ken said, leaning over. "I'm sorry, doggie. I'm sorry."

Shenna rose partway, strained forward, and licked Ken's face, her wide tongue slathering up along the side of his voder mask.

"Oh, that's a good dog," Ken said, feeling a tickly warmth run through him. He'd gone many years without the kiss of a dog. He reached forward, fondled Shenna's collar. "Did we hurt your voder, doggie? Can you speak?"

She looked up at him, with loving eyes, and remained silent. Her tail wagged back and forth against the metal floor.

"Did you damage her prosthetics?" said a voice behind him.

He sighed. "Yes, Sipho, I did. Are the others coming up?"

Turning, he saw Sipho nodding in the dimness. Josev Ranes crowded into the corridor behind the astronomer.

"How's the dog?" He asked.

"Voder's broken. Otherwise, she's fine."

"Ah."

There ensued several minutes of shuffling and jostling, as the Six filed into the corridor and arranged themselves for further horizontal travel.

"You ready to go, Jonson?" Marshe called ahead.

"Yes."

"Well get going, then. You're doing a good job."

"Thank you," Ken said, feeling strange. The art of conversation had seemed so *difficult* before, but now ...

They began walking.

"Should be a left turn up ahead," Josev said.

Ken grunted. "How fa—"

There was a slamming sound, and half a moment later Ken collided, face-first, with a metal wall. "Ah!" he cried.

"You found it," said Josev.

"No," Ken groaned, stepping away from the wall, feeling the corridor press in on both sides of him. "This is a dead end! There's no turn!"

From far behind them came another slamming noise, like a massive steel gate dropping into place. Farther still, and more completely muffled, the sound repeated again. Very, very distantly, Ken seemed to hear the screaming of alarm klaxons.

"Combat drill!" Josev cried out.

"Real combat," Marshe said darkly. "The Waisters must be forming up for attack."

"The MI said three hours," Josev protested.

"Well," Marshe said, "I haven't heard any shooting yet, but maybe there's been a change in schedule."

"The tunnel is sealed," Ken reminded them. "How are we supposed to get to the Command Center?"

"Uh," said Josev, "There's ... ah ... an exit about a hundred meters behind us."

Ken clicked his tongue. "Didn't we just hear that close off?"

"No. That gate is in a branch on the right. This tunnel exits into somebody's sleeping quarters. My, the Clementines must have had interesting nights, eh?"

"Turn around," Marshe said. "Get moving. Now!"

In the gray light of the flatscreens, Ken watched the

Six reverse direction ahead of him. Sipho was a shadow, small and dark.

"Hustle!" Marshe said. "Move, move!"

They began to trot.

"Fifty meters more," Josev said, looking at diagrams on a flatscreen he carried in his left hand. In his right, held forward, was another "lamp" flatscreen like the ones Ken and the others carried.

"Roland," Marshe said, "when we get to the door, open it and run through. If there's anybody on the other side, let me handle them."

"Yes," the Cerean acknowledged.

"Ten meters," said Josev. "There!"

The corridor hooked to the right, and at the bend was a rectangular recess a few centimeters deep, as wide and tall as the corridor itself. Josev's doorway.

"Opening it!" Roland said, slapping his hands against the edge of the door, pushing. There was a cracking noise as layers of paint gave way. The door swung open.

Marshe rushed past Roland as he cleared the doorway, nearly knocking him over. Shenna followed, barking excitedly.

"Empty!" Marshe shouted back.

Josev and Sipho filed into the room, Ken behind them with stunner drawn.

As promised, this was somebody's sleeping quarters. Here were the same bunk, the same shower, and sink and dresser drawers as in Ken's own quarters. But the walls were painted a greenish color that, to normal eyes, probably appeared white, and there were no triangular braces in the corners to make the room look like an octohedron. The lighting was the dull orange color Ken knew represented combat red. Klaxons wailed.

"Josev," Marshe said, "get the door. Ken, stand by with the stunner."

Ranes trotted to the exit, and when it did not open for him, pulled the red and white cover off its manual controls. He shoved the lock lever open, grabbed the hand wheel and began turning it. The door slid open a crack.

Shoving the now useless light into his pocket, Ken straightened his right arm, sighted down the length of it. The corridor outside looked empty, but . . .

"Roland, shut the tunnel behind us, please."

"Yes."

Sounds of the secret door shutting.

Josev continued to crank open the exit. The gap widened to five centimeters. Ten. Fifteen.

"Ken," Marshe said, "you're the first man out in the corridor. Shoot anything that moves."

"Right."

The doorway stood twenty centimeters wide, now. Holding the gun out before him, Ken turned sideways and squeezed through. He looked left, saw nothing, looked right.

A man, a sergeant, stared at him from three meters away. Ken aimed the stunner, placed his finger on the trigger. The sergeant opened his mouth, as if to ask a question. Ken fired, and the man collapsed in a flash of light and charged particles.

Ken stared down the corridor. Nobody else around.

"One down?" Marshe asked, right behind him.

He turned. "Yeah. He going to be okay?"

Marshe shrugged, her face grim. "Maybe. If he gets medical attention." She leaned toward the doorway, cupped a hand beside her mouth. "Let's *move,* people! Come on! Come on!"

Josev crowded out through the doorway, followed

closely by Shenna. Roland and Sipho came through next.

"Where exactly are we?" Sipho asked nobody in particular.

Josev glanced at his flatscreen. "It's this way," he said, pointing. "There's an elevator around the corner."

"No, we take the stairs," Marshe said.

"Oh. Uh, it's still the same direction."

Marshe nodded. "Okay. Jonson, up front with me. Everyone else follow behind."

The Six was moving once again.

Ken held the stunner out before him, prepared to fire on short notice. Somewhere, in the back of his mind, he felt guilt and remorse for gunning down that sergeant. Perhaps the feelings would get a chance to surface, later on. Right now he was busy, focused. The stakes were high, and time was short. *Nothing* could be permitted to slow them down.

They came to a corner.

Holding up a hand to stop Marshe and the others, he leaped out into view.

A man and a woman standing together, wearing uniforms of gold foil, fussing with a piece of equipment that might have been a flame suppressor, or a pump of some sort.

Wary of the foil's reflective properties, Ken took aim on the man's head. Fired. After the flash, the man fell back, blood spurting from his eyes and nose. The woman looked up, wearing a bewildered expression. Ken shot her in the forehead, and she collapsed.

Another man, farther down the corridor, turned to run.

Ken took aim and pulled the trigger.

A yellow spot flashed on the man's back, visible but, Ken thought, dimmer than it should have been. The man stumbled but did not fall. Ken adjusted his aim and pulled the trigger again, this time without effect.

The man vanished around a corner, yelling something.

"Damn it, Marshe," Ken shouted. "When was the last time you had this gun charged?"

"Last year," she replied, stepping around the corner. "What happened?"

"I lost one," Ken snarled. "Ran off screaming. These, these guns will *not* hold a charge forever. You know where we can get another one?"

"No time," Marshe said. She pointed. "There's the stairshaft. Everybody follow!"

In motion again.

"Josev, get the door! Ken, how's your hand-to-hand?"

"It's fine. Stick close."

She turned, favored him with a steely glare as she ran. "Give me space, Corporal. I'm two-eighty out of three."

Josev reached the stairshaft door, tore the cover off its emergency controls.

"I'm first through," Marshe said. "Ken, behind me."

Diligently, Josev cranked the door open. Ken could see no one on the other side of it, but he crouched, tense, hands held before him like tiny swords.

When the door was open wide enough, Marshe squeezed through. Ken followed. As he'd thought, there was nobody in the stairshaft. He listened for the sound of footsteps on the metal stairs, heard none.

"Everybody through!" Marshe shouted. "Ken, get ready to close the door behind us."

"We don't have time," Ken told her.

Suddenly, he felt himself spun around, Marshe's hand gripping his shoulder firmly, her eyes staring into his with arc-welder intensively. "We're on decompression alert, mister," she growled. "We don't close that door, we don't open any others on this shaft. Get *to* it!" She shoved him toward the manual control box.

Ken paused for a moment, looking at her, at the way she stood, the look on her face. His commanding officer. His Queen. Belatedly, he turned, popping the cover off the controls, turning the handwheel even as Josev squeezed through the doorway. Ken worked as quickly as he could, but the mechanism was slow, maddening.

"Josev!" snapped Marshe. "You and me up to the next level. Get the door open. The rest of you stay here until Jonson's ready."

Stairs spanged behind Ken as the captain and young lieutenant, scrambled up them.

"No, Shenna!" he heard Sipho call out. "Stay here!"

"It's okay," Ken said, slamming the locking lever home. "I'm ready to go."

The staircase thrummed beneath his feet as he ascended, Sipho and Roland at his sides, Shenna running up ahead. They reached the first landing, and turned quickly, their feet skidding across the floor in the lessening gravity. They countinued upward.

Josev already had the door partway open when they reached the second landing.

"Ken!" said Marshe. "You're first through! Come *on* Josev!"

Barely slowing, Ken threw himself into the narrow doorway, pulled his chest and stomach in, scraped through the opening.

A gray-and-brown-haired woman stood on the other side, pointing a finger at Ken and opening her mouth, as if preparing to admonish him. *This shaft is supposed to be sealed,* perhaps, or *why aren't you at your combat station already*?

Ken plowed straight into her, his right elbow forward.

She spun aside and fell to the floor, a look of astonishment on her face. Stopping his momentum against the opposite wall, Ken turned, found his footing, and brought a stiff kick up under the woman's jaw. She flipped backward, her head connecting solidly with the floor.

Ken dropped to a crouch, ready to deal another blow . . . But she lay unmoving, her eyes open and staring.

Unconscious, he hoped.

"Ken!" Josev's voice cried behind him. "What in God's names are you doing?"

"Shut up, Lieutenant," Marshe said, pulling herself through the doorway. "I expect the same from you."

"Do . . ." Ken puffed, suddenly breathless. "Do you want the door closed?"

Marshe shook her head. "No. Leave it open so we block the shaft. Josev, which way do we go?"

"Back this way," Josev said, pointing behind him.

"Is it far?"

"Yes. This isn't where we wanted to be."

"People, get *out* here!" Marshe shouted. "Ken, run ahead to the corner."

Drawing a deep breath, Ken got moving. He felt light, his feet tingly with low gravity. Half a gee, maybe. Hard to tell with any precision. What level was this? Ken had lost track.

He got to the corner, skidded awkwardly to a halt, peered around. Nothing. The corridor was long, marked with doorways every ten meters or so. Brightly lit. And quite empty.

He turned to Marshe, flashed her the Marine hand-signal that meant "all clear". She looked up, paused, and nodded, seeming to understand.

"Let's go," she called out to her people. The group trotted toward Ken, skidded their way around the corner.

"Jonson," Marshe said as she brushed by, "I want you to stay here until we reach the far corner. Watch behind us!"

Her voice increased in volume as she drew farther away from Ken. He watched her retreating back for a few seconds, watched her legs and buttocks heave with the motions of running. *No jiggle,* he thought, and was immediately ashamed for thinking it. But it was true; she was a large woman, yes, but solid.

Belatedly, he did as he was told, and looked back down the gently curving corridor behind him, past the motionless body of the woman he'd attacked. What, exactly, was he looking for? More victims to beat senseless? Anyone coming down this corridor at normal walking speed would not reach the corner until Marshe and the others were well out of view, so that in fact, his presence here was more of an invitation for trouble than a prophylactic against it.

But then, perhaps Marshe knew what she was doing.

"Jonsooon!' A faraway, echoing voice. For a moment, Ken wondered if it were in his head, one of the many sounds of combat still echoing there. But he turned, looked down the corridor, and saw, in the orange light, the distant figure of Sipho Yeng standing at the far corner, waving him forward with some urgency.

Ken pushed off from the wall and broke into a fast run.

Doorways rolled past him in a blur, barely seen, barely noticed. If one of the doors were to spring open, disgorging a swarm of security guards, he would be doomed. But none of them opened. The figure of Sipho grew in his vision as he approached the far corner.

The world went blurry for a moment, and the air seemed to hum. Ken was shaken off his feet, so that he fell to the smooth floor, skidding and bouncing for several meters while the walls vibrated around him. Then the tremor passed, and he lay still on the cool metal.

He raised his head, looked toward Sipho. The astronomer had also fallen. The event that shook Ken had not been imaginary, nor localized.

A chill ran through him. The station had been hit by enemy fire.

He scrambled to his feet, got moving, ran as fast as he could for the bend in the corridor. He watched Sipho rise, turn, trot past the corner where Ken couldn't see. He continued running, his breath puffing in and out in deep, steady rhythm. He reached the corner, put a hand on it, skidded through a turn, rebounded from the far wall and kept going.

The corridor ahead, like the one at which he'd waited, was relatively short, and curved "upward," following the cylindrical shape of the station. Sipho was halfway down the corridor and running in a peculiar, splay-legged gait that didn't seem to be carrying him too fast. Marshe and the others were a hundred meters ahead now, past a pair of sprawled bodies. As he watched, they vanished, sliding like ice skaters, around another corner. With her four legs, Shenna seemed the most sure-footed of the lot.

Sprinting hard, Ken caught up with Sipho and scooped an arm around him, dragging him along behind like a parcel. The corner approached. Seconds passed. Ken slowed a bit to negotiate the turn. As he scampered around it, Sipho slipped from his grasp and staggered, nearly falling. Ken left him behind, his eyes fixed on Marshe and the others, now only fifty meters ahead and moving slowly, deliberately. Counting doorways, he realized.

He sprinted for another couple of seconds, then slowed to a run, a trot, a walk.

"Beam hits!" he gasped, pulling even with the group. "The enemy's here!"

"We know," Marshe said, breathing heavily, not looking at him. "It's just a probing attack. Burn off a couple of turrets, maybe." She pointed to a heavy black door. "No labels in this damn place. God! It's this one, right?"

"Right," Josev puffed. "That's right. Uh ... We, uh ... What do we do now? Knock on the door?"

Marshe cocked her head. "Huh. Yeah, that's a good idea. I was going to crank it open like the others, but ..."

Sipho trotted up, wheezing deeply, just as Marshe leaned forward and rapped her knuckles hard against the door.

Clungclungclung!

There was a pause, filled mainly by the panting and gasping of the Six.

Chapter 22

If the general were not sitting next to him, Samel Jhee would have buried his face in his hands and wept. His fault. His fault.

No one had brought the accusation up to him, as yet. Perhaps no one would; there was so little time. But the Waisters were *here,* they had homed in on *this very station,* singling it out from all the millions of targets in Sol system. No coincidence, he was sure, that Talbott and her crew had penetrated the data security system just before the start of the attack.

Too late. He had shut her down too late to prevent this disaster. She had somehow contacted the enemy, and now they were here, their weapons already probing the station's defenses.

Why hadn't he acted earlier? When the dolphins ran amok he had considered imprisoning Talbott's team as a precaution, but had, in the end, clung to the hope that they could still be useful to him. A single data point was all he'd really wanted—a trick, a trap—to prove the wisdom of his investments. But instead, they had gone the way of the dolphins, and Jhee, reluctant to admit another failure, had permitted himself to ignore the extent of their delusions.

Damn it all.

He glanced at the general, sitting patiently with folded hands, head sweeping back and forth, scanning holie after holie. Down in front of them sat the station's tactical controllers, all busy at their panels.

"Damage control to QC40," he heard one of the controllers say in a rapid burst.

"QC40 en route," replied another.

At least, Jhee mused, he and Talbott and the others would die for their sins. He hoped it would hurt like bloody hell.

"Somebody at the door," said a controller-voice.

"Pardon?" a different voice returned, in a distracted and somewhat disbelieving tone.

There was a knocking sound down at the entrance, the muted rap of knuckles against hard metal.

"There's somebody at the *door*," the controller repeated.

"What the hell?"

"Answer it, would you?" asked General Voorhis, calmly.

The controller got up and walked to the entrance.

Who the hell could be knocking? Jhee wondered. And then a terrible thought occurred to him.

The door whooshed open with a swirling of air. A man stood in the doorway, looking out with an angry expression. But his gaze swept across Ken and the others, with their bug-mask faces and their tense, combative postures, and his expression began to shift toward fear. Before the transformation was complete, though, Marshe's fist had lashed out, crushing his nose, sending him sprawling backward.

The fluid that sprayed from him looked, to Ken's eyes, as black as oil.

"Hey!" someone shouted inside the room. There was the sound of a hand slapping down hard on a control panel.

Marshe stepped into the room, Ken half a stride behind her.

The room was narrow, cramped. In the orange light Ken saw one central console, a human figure seated on each side of it, and other consoles against each of two walls. All around there were holie screens, with bright tactical and visual displays. Behind, a raised area with a railing, a small staircase, two seated figures.

Eight people, in all.

An alarm sounded. PongPONG! PongPONG! A green-white strobelight began flashing at the back of the room.

One of the figures stood, raising a weapon. "What in the hell—" he said. It was all he had time for.

Ken dove to the floor, tucking into a roll that swept the man off his feet before he could lower the weapon and fire it. Ken rolled atop the man, drove a fist into his gut, another against the side of his head. He snatched up the weapon where it lay on the floor, aimed it at the nearest human target, and pulled its trigger.

A yellow stunner-bolt leaped out, and Ken's target slumped unnaturally in its chair.

One of the other men was starting to rise. Ken turned, aimed, fired. The man fell senseless against the wall, bounced, and sprawled across his control panel.

Ken got his feet under him, rose into a low crouch.

Marshe brushed past him, driving a third person, a woman, against the wall, slamming her head into it hard. Twice.

"Stop right there!" shouted one of the men on the raised platform, in a voice of gruff authority. Five stripes on his collar; a general. He had a stunner aimed directly at Ken. There was a flash of yellow—

And a yelp. Shenna had burst into the room ahead of the others, had swept out in front of Ken . . . There was the sharp reek of scorched hair. Shenna's body slid up against the side of a panel, and lay inert.

Angered, Ken raised his own stunner and dropped the man who'd fired. Behind him, he heard the soft grunts and slaps of hand-to-hand combat. He found a new target and fired again. He advanced toward the platform, where a lone figure now stood—a short man, with short, dark hair, and skin that would undoubtedly look beige in proper lighting, without spectrum-spreaders over one's eyes.

"Colonel Jhee," Ken said.

"Corporal!" the colonel cried. His face had the look of a rubber mask that had been stretched almost to the breaking point. "Drop that weapon!"

"I don't think s—"

The back of a chair collided with Ken's chest and right arm, driving him back into the hard, angular surface of a control panel. The stunner flew from his grasp, hitting the floor somewhere behind him, skittering and bouncing off various surfaces, hiding itself.

The chair pulled back, swept the air. The man who brandished it looked frightened, and furious, and completely incredulous. *How,* his expression seemed to say, *can I be having a fistfight when the station is under attack by Waisters*?

The chair came down again, but Ken had time to bring up a foot to block it, to kick it away. The chair-guy staggered aside, on the ragged edge of balance. But balance won out, and he straightened, pulled the chair back for another blow.

Ken ducked low and drove his straightened knuckles into the man's solar plexus. Or tried to; the man was quick, turning aside, pulling in his gut so that Ken's blow barely grazed. The chair came down.

On

The top of

Ken's head.

Blackness flickered for a moment, and he found himself on the floor, on hands and knees. He looked up, and saw the chair coming down yet again . . .

The air hummed and blurred. The walls and floor and ceiling seemed to jump, each independently of the others. There was the sound of breakage, of things falling down onto unyielding metal. A control panel seemed to lash out, to drive itself into the chair-guy's back. He fell away, and the chair fell away in a different direction.

There was a stillness. The strobelight still flashed, somewhere at the back of the room, but the alarm klaxon had fallen silent.

Ken, somehow, had managed to stay balanced on his hands and knees. He shook his head, to clear it of the buzzing aftermath of . . . of . . .

Waister attack.

He crawled forward, toward the sprawled form of the chair-guy. The man sat up, partway, and looked at Ken. He seemed to be in considerable pain. Broken ribs, perhaps. He raised a foot, feebly, to ward Ken off.

A pause, momentary. Would he surrender? No. No, his eyes were dazed but angry, defiant.

"Forgive me," Ken whispered. He grabbed the proffered foot, twisting it, breaking it. The man opened his mouth, let go a horrible scream that bubbled up from deep in his guts. "Forgive me," Ken said, a little louder. He crawled over the man's body, lifted him by the collar, and drove the heel of his hand into the base of the nose. There was a breaking sensation, like the cracking of a walnut. The man's head snapped to one side and was still.

"Talbott," said a voice. Colonel Jhee's.

Ken looked up to see Marshe approaching the platform.

"Colonel," she said, flatly. She reached through the railing, caught at the fabric of Jhee's uniform. Pulled him forward. She adjusted her grip, so that she held him by a scruff of cloth just above his breastbone.

"Think about what you're doing," Jhee said, quickly, but with an eery almost-clam. "Think about the *consequences*. It's not too late to get better."

"You have my apologies, Colonel," Marshe said, "If not my sympathy." She pulled him sharply toward her, so that his head connected with the railing. He grunted loudly. She pushed him backward, pulled him again.

"I surrender!" He screamed . . . too late. The railing made a sound like a badly-formed gong. Jhee's body slumped away, unconscious or dying or dead.

Ken looked away.

"Sipho!" Marshe shouted. "Engage the manual lock on that door and *hold* it. Josev! Get on these consoles and shut down our God-damn weapons. Prepare for a transmission."

"How do I . . ." Sipho's voice said. "Oh, I see."

Banging sounds, Josev setting a chair up in front of a console.

"Clodgy wee thing," said Josev's voice. "How do you work this? Marshe, this isn't a standard panel."

"Deal with it!" Marshe shot back.

"Uh . . . . Let's see. Turret power . . . is . . . *off*. Uh. Spindle power, *off*. Point defenses, uh . . . uh . . . *off*. Projector core, *off*."

"Is that everything?" Marshe asked.

"Sludge, I don't know. I think so."

"Open all the radio channels."

"Uh, I can't do that from here. I need to change seats."

"Well *do it*! Hurry, or they may blow us up anyway!"

More banging noises.

"Um . . . Here? Yeah. Channels . . . are . . . open! Go ahead, Captain."

Ken looked up toward Marshe, saw her standing straight, her back against the platform railing. She took a breath.

"*#Hwhh Queens We/We yield-before-strength-do Yield-before-strength-do#*" she said.

Then there was silence.

Chapter 23

Close channels," Marshe said.

"You sure?"

"Yes."

"Okay," said Josev, skeptically. "Channels closed."

Suddenly, Ken felt sick to his stomach, sick to his heart.

"We done the right thing?" Roland Hanlin asked suddenly, as if echoing Ken's thoughts.

Marshe turned, fixed him with a bug-eyed stare.

"Have we?" he persisted. He spread his arms. "Look at this! Bodies everywhere. These our own people, Marshe. We brutally attack our own people."

"To bring about the end of the war," Marshe said coolly.

"We sure about that?" Roland asked.

"No," said Sipho Yeng from his post beside the door. He sounded horrified. "I'm not sure about this at all! We've based our theories on the advice of our enemies, and on the advice of a renegade Machine Intelligence whose stated goal is the extermination of the human race! I didn't . . . listen to my doubts! I didn't listen! My God, people, what have we done here?"

"We've become the enemy," Ken said, pulling himself, painfully, to a standing position. He felt like a man awakening from a dream, like a man emerging from a dark forest to find himself on familiar streets.

"Yes, we have," said Sipho. "We've *become* the enemy! Literally! We are the *enemies* of the human race, the willing servants of our invaders!"

"Calm down," Marshe said, raising a hand. "Take a look at the screens. Are they—"

There was a dull flash of light, a blast of low-frequency noise that slammed through Ken's innards like the blow of a fist. The door burst its hinges and flew inward, bouncing off a panel to fall, ringing, in the corner.

It had taken Sipho Yeng with it on its journey.

Black Security hardsuits swarmed into the room. There were shouted, amplified curses. Roland Hanlin, closest to the door after Sipho, stood swaying in his shoes, dazed from the blast, as a pair of Security men grabbed his arms and another leveled a rifle at his head.

Other guards stormed toward Marshe, toward Ken.

"Too late!" Marshe shouted. "You're too late! The war is over!"

The Security forces crashed over her like a wave, their black bodies grabbing, clinging, bearing her down under their weight. Ken felt himself grabbed by brutal hands that were cased in cold, unyielding gauntlets. Opaque visors crowded in before his face, as if eager to view the features of a traitor.

Josev Ranes was dragged from his chair, thrown to the floor. Hardsuits piled on top of him.

"You're too late!" Marshe shouted again.

The air went blurry again, and there was a crashing sound like lightning, close. The Control Center shook and flexed as if pounded by gigantic hammers. Sparks rained down from somewhere. Ken fell again as the floor bucked beneath him. Marshe fell, and Roland. Black hardsuits toppled like trench-ball pins.

Somebody screamed.

"Shut it!" another voice shouted, as the tremor subsided. "Get up! Get up!"

The floor was alive with squirming bodies. The Security guards began to rise.

"JOSEV!" Marshe howled.

"Marshe!" Josev's voice called back, muffled. "Marshe! The transmission hasn't reached them yet! Stall for time!"

"Stall for nothing!" growled the augmented voice of a blacksuit. The guard took Marshe by the wrist, hauled her to her feet. Ken tried to rise, found himself staring down the spindle of a laser rifle.

Fuck it, he thought, getting up anyway, nudging the gun aside with his shoulder.

Guards swarmed him, grabbed him. He saw his own face, masked and goggled, reflected grotesquely in their gloss-black armor.

"Get them out of here!" Shouted one of the guards now holding Marshe.

"No!" Marshe shouted. "Wait! It's happening!"

"Come on, let's *move*."

"Look at the holies!" Marshe insisted. "They're disengaging! Look! Look at the holies!"

"Shut up." A Security man warned her, raising his rifle butt-forward.

"LOOK AT THE HOLIES!" she screamed.

The rifle butt drew back, then slammed forward into the side of her head. Dazed, she fell. Marshe!

On the screens, Ken could see the Waisters pulling back, pulling away. The fleetships were fast, clear of Saturn space already, powering out on a straight line away from Sol. Back to Alnilam? Back to the waist of Orion?

"Come on, you!" said a guard, furious, jerking violently on Ken's arm.

They dragged him, unprotesting, from the room.

* * *

"It's over," Marshe kept saying to the Security troopers. "It's over; we've ended it."

Washed out, exhausted, Ken said nothing. Nor did Josev, nor Roland, who limped and staggered with every step. Blood stained one leg of his uniform, leaked slowly from one of his ears.

They had all been relieved of goggles and voders, of guns and flatscreens and anything else they'd had with them. Now, rifles level and ready, the guards marched them down to the brig, shoved them inside. A small space, dark and gray and unadorned. Walls and floor and ceiling of bare metal.

"It's over," Marshe said again. Her voice was dreamy and distant. "All over."

The steel door slammed down heavily behind them.

Wordlessly, Josev found a corner and threw himself into it. Roland leaned against a wall, slid down it until he was sitting. Smeared with gray smoke residue, brown flecks of drying blood, their faces were weary and expressionless.

"All over," Marshe said, yet again.

Ken took her hand and led her to a corner, helped her to sit. "Try to relax," he said, his voice a mere whisper. "We're finished now."

"Finished," she echoed faintly. Then she stiffened, sobbed. "Oh! They killed Shenna!"

"No," Roland groaned. "The Dog . . . last I saw she was still breathing. But not Sipho."

"Ohhh," Marshe sobbed. She was hunched over, knees up in an almost fetal position, rocking herself in Ken's arms. Tears ran down her face, leaving trails in the grime.

"The shaking's stopped," Josev said, after a few seconds.

"No more Waisters," Ken said. "No more fighting."

Splattered forms of two Workers, smearing the walls like crushed berries. Their Dog, wrinkled and pink, huddled screaming in the mess. "Our confrontation with newness is completed."

Josev's lips curled back. "Oh, shut that! God-damn sludging Hell, haven't we had enough?"

"Leave him alone," said Roland.

"*I've* had enough," Josev snapped. "I've bleeding well had enough."

Ken said nothing. How much was enough? How many people, how many aliens and dolphins and machine intelligences did you have to kill before you could finally throw up your hands and quit?

Marshe's sobs died away. "Ken," she said, "it's time to rejoin the human race."

Albuquerque flashing and melting, taking with it everyone he cared about, everyone he knew. *His* part of the human race, the part he could never rejoin, except in death.

"Ken?"

He trembled. "Yeah. Yeah, I know."

Marshe put a hand on his arm. Warm.

"Everything's different now," Ken said. "Is the war really over? Is it *really* over? God, I can't even *conceive* of that."

Her hands gripped him, firmly, her face turning, centimeters from his. "You saw them leaving. You *saw* them."

"Yeah."

"It's over, Ken. It really is."

With creaky sounds, the brig's heavy door rose again, white light spilling in behind it.

White? A minute ago, the corridors had been combat-red.

Two Security hardsuits stood in the doorway—

helmets off, tired, sweaty faces exposed. And between the two, a dog.

"Shenna!" said Marshe, rising up onto her knees.

The dog ran in, tail wagging, and crashed directly into Marshe. Together they fell back, onto Ken, pressing him back into the wall, into the corner.

"The Waisters are *gone*," said one of the guards, wonderingly. "They're *gone*! What did you people *do*?"

"We ended the war," Marshe said. She and the dog squirmed together in a heap on top of Ken.

"Sludging right, we did," Josev said.

Marshe laughed, now, as Shenna licked her face. Then Shenna was licking *Ken's* face, and he was laughing a little, too.

"Are you going to let us out of here?" Marshe asked the guard.

He seemed flustered. "I . . . don't know! I guess . . . I'll go and ask somebody!"

"Yeah!" Marshe agreed. "Do that!"

Shenna was pulling out of the heap, now, struggling toward Roland and Josev. Marshe fell back a little, still laughing, her mouth brushing up against Ken's cheek.

"Oh, Ken, we *did* it!" she said.

"Yes," he said, turning his face until his lips brushed hers. "I guess we did."

Roland and Josev made sounds of happy discomfort as they were smothered in flopping, slobbering dog.

Marshe's hands grabbed the sides of Ken's head, fingers digging into his bruises, twining in his hair. She pulled him close, her lips mashing into his.

Ken returned the kiss, his tongue probing, his hands grabbing and squeezing great fistfuls of flesh. Here, in his arms, was a piece of the human race he could willingly join.

Epilogue

START TRANSMISSION
Court-martial Docket 11/826038260/13-2 Loc: ATG-311-B (Musashi)

Defendant: Hanlin, Roland K.
High Treason
Conspiracy
(Charges Dismissed)
Status: Discharge, honorable. Released to Ceres Mainstation.

Defendant: Jhee, Samel
Incompetence
Supervisory Incompetence
Failure to Report Vital Intelligence
(Charges Dismissed)
Status: Discharge, honorable. Released to Ceylon Disbursement Center, Earth.
Note: Col. T.Y Chu, ATD-068-B (Kojiro), has assumed Causative Influence for these charges. Inquiry in progress.

Defendant: Jonson, Kenneth E.
High Treason
Conspiracy
Premeditated Injurious Assault (9 cts.)

Assault Upon a Superior (9 cts.)
Unauthorized Use of Weapons (7 cts.)
(Charges Dismissed)
Status: Retained in service. Psych counseling advised.

Defendant: NLN, Shenna
 (No Charges)
Status: Not competent to stand trial. Discharge, honorable. Released to Ceres Mainstation.

Defendant: Ranes, Josev T.
 High Treason
 Conspiracy
 Sabotage
 (Charges Dismissed)
Status: Transferred to Political Corps, Council Station.

Defendant: Talbott, Marshe
 High Treason
 Conspiracy
 Sabotage
 Premeditated Injurious Assault (12 cts.)
 Assault Upon a Superior (3 cts.)
 (Charges Dismissed)
Status: Retained in service.

Defendant: Yeng, Sipho
 (No Charges)
Status: Deceased. Discharge, honorable. Released to Martian authorities for interment.

END TRANSMISSION

Appendix A

The Waister Departure Song

(The WDS is among the most studied documents in human history, and has been translated hundreds of times into Standard alone. Nonetheless, the Jonson-Talbott translation retains great utility and popularity even today. It is presented here in its original, unrevised form.)

We depart now, depart now
We contemplate our mistake
#
Long ago
We clung to the surface of a single planet
Like barnacles
Like barnacles
But we discovered that
the stars
Were suns like our own
Though farther away
We went to have a look
#
We were curious, back then
We were adventurous
We were industrious
We reached the stars and kept on going
leaving pieces of ourselves behind
#
Sometimes, we encountered stone age peoples

They were funny
They were funny
Sometimes we killed them all
Sometimes they surrendered to us
And called us gods
And we departed.
Sometimes we returned and found them all dead
It is a terrible thing
We learned
To look upon the face of God
#
Our empire took the form of a stepped-on sphere
Very large
Very large
A hundred such empires would fill the galaxy
And yet
There were no others
But ours
Or so we thought
#
The Stupid Ones came
And attacked us
Which seemed natural enough
Though we were surprised
They fought us hard
And long
And well
But they were like vicious animals
Not too smart
It took a long time
But
We killed them all
And
They never thought to surrender
#
How strange and tragic
It was
#
We grew cautious, then

Our empire stopped expanding
And
We stayed that way for a long time
Long time
Long time
We heard voices
Once
From deep in the Core
But
They were so far away
And
We heard them only briefly
Before they were gone
#
The great, slow tides of the galaxy
Began
To
Tear our empire apart
To stretch it
To smear it
We scarcely noticed
We scarcely noticed
Not a youthful race any longer
We had ceased even to dream
#
And then you people came along
With your crazy chattering
With your crazy chattering
Less distant from the empire
Than the empire is wide
We were very surprised
#
We sprayed warships into existence*
And tried hard to remember
How to fight
We wanted to put on a powerful display

*(This phrase is a peculiar artifact of the J–T translation. Most versions render this as "We assembled a fleet of war.")

This time
We wanted there to be no question
This time
About who was stronger
But when we got here
You did not surrender
In fact you fought us
Better than we thought you could
Not very well
Not very well
But better than we expected
#
We began to wonder
You did not seem stupid
To us
And yet you fought us
When
You knew you could not win
How strange
We began to wonder if
Perhaps
We had made a mistake
#
We would have killed you all
Just to be sure
But now you have surrendered
And we are glad
We depart now, depart now
to contemplate our mistake
#

Appendix B

Historical Timeline

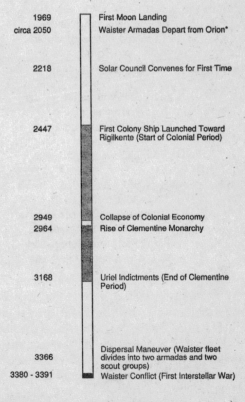

1969	First Moon Landing
circa 2050	Waister Armadas Depart from Orion*
2218	Solar Council Convenes for First Time
2447	First Colony Ship Launched Toward Rigilkente (Start of Colonial Period)
2949	Collapse of Colonial Economy
2964	Rise of Clementine Monarchy
3168	Uriel Indictments (End of Clementine Period)
3366	Dispersal Maneuver (Waister fleet divides into two armadas and two scout groups)
3380 - 3391	Waister Conflict (First Interstellar War)

* Precise star of origin is thought to be Alnilam (center star of Orion's Waist)

Appendix C

Astronomical Charts

SOL SYSTEM

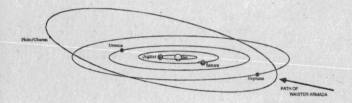

* (Inner planets not pictured. Planet sizes not drawn to scale.)

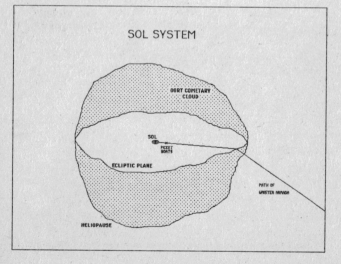

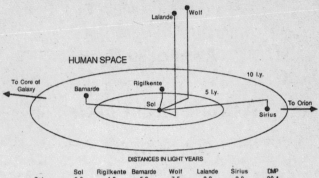

HUMAN SPACE

Wolf

Lalande

To Core of Galaxy

Barnarde

Rigilkente

Sol

10 l.y.

5 l.y.

To Orion

Sirius

DISTANCES IN LIGHT YEARS

	Sol	Rigilkente	Barnarde	Wolf	Lalande	Sirius	DMP
Sol	0.0	4.3	5.9	7.5	8.2	8.8	20.1
Rigilkente	4.3	0.0	6.5	8.2	10.2	9.5	20.6
Barnarde	5.9	6.5	0.0	10.8	10.6	14.5	25.9
Wolf	7.5	8.2	10.8	0.0	3.9	8.7	17.3
Lalande	8.2	10.2	10.6	3.9	0.0	10.9	19.8
Sirius	8.8	9.5	14.5	8.7	10.9	0.0	11.5
DMP	20.1	20.6	25.9	17.3	19.8	11.5	0.0

(DMP = location of Waister armadas at time of dispersal maneuver)

SAGGITARIUS ARM

MILKY WAY GALAXY

ORION ARM

FRAGMENTS OF WAISTER EMPIRE

ALNILAM

A special preview of
Flies from the Amber
Wil McCarthy's exciting new science
fiction novel of intrigue and discovery!
(coming in 1995)

"Exalted Creature, they flee directly into the nebula."

White frills expanding in anger. "Pursue them."

This place had been a stellar creche, a coming together of gasses, a birthing place of new suns. But as the ages raced by, as Fleet pursued the Enemy at the very edge of lightspeed, things had changed. One of the young stars exploded, touching off neighbors. Now, within the cloud hung stars gone prematurely ancient, withered dwarfs and collapsars among the newly born. The result was not beautiful, nor safe to travel through.

"Particulate matter in the nebula, Exalted Creature. We dare not."

"Also collapsed matter, vermin, and they have the Shield! If they brave the time fields to graze a collapsed body, and they do not emerge for an age of ages? No! We have come too far to give them up."

"We risk the Fleet, Exalted Creature."

"Pursue them!"

Tight, angry silence. And obedience.

Chief Technical Officer Miguel Barta peered, with eyes insubstantial, at the data his instruments were bringing in from the Soleco hypermass, and he cursed to see it. Something was happening, something he hadn't expected and hadn't been trained to cope with.

"Hey," he said to his Tech Aid, Lahler. "These readings don't match the projection, not at all. Open more buffer space for the instruments."

"None left," said Lahler, her voice flat.

He turned and looked at her over his shoulder. A young woman, new, first voyage. And taking orders from him! She had a quick mind, and yes, admit it, Miguel, a nice set of curves and a very nice face to go with them. Not that he was supposed to notice. But just now her appearance did not seem so nice, with the glazed eyes, the softlink harness sprouting cables from her head like Medusa's hair.

Miguel, also in softlink, shifted cybernetic "gaze" into the data buffers and saw that she'd spoken truly. No margin in the buffer space.

"Damn," he said. "Cut some loose from the engine monitors."

"Already did that. And from the navigation backups. Really, Miguel, we don't *have* any more."

"Then damn again," he said. Without moving, he signaled the bridge for comlink.

Almost instantly, a face appeared on the holie screen in front of him. "Chelsea," the face said.

Miguel had spoken with the captain, Lin Chelsea, several times before, and to his credit, he did not flinch this time. Like most of *Introspectia*'s bridge crew, Chelsea had wiring that ran *deep,* portions of the link harness hooking in to penetrate her eyes and ears and nostrils. An accident victim, a humanoid robot partially disassembled. No cold, link-eyed stare from her, just the jumble of the sensory interface, less human than the face of a bug. And yet, Miguel had once heard her laugh.

Damn, these were strange times he was heading into.

Miguel's first mission would be called a "paperwalk" by some, just a flick out to Centauri and back on a diplomatic sprinter. Hardly time to get used to the ship, and barely a decade gone by in the outside universe. But the second trip, ohh ... He's spent forever in the belly of a Priority Cargo barge, making the "third circuit" from Sol to Procyon-A to Procyon-B and back again. He'd returned to earth forty objective years later to find things ... changed.

And now, on *Introspectia* ... A good job, responsible and variously rewarding: Chief Technical Officer! But this time around, he paid his price in centuries. Not yet to his hundredth birthday, he would return as a bleeding *fossil*. But a rich one, yes.

A remote scuttled across Miguel's console, its motion a blur of glittering eyes and legs. He stared as it ran by, fighting down the impulse to shriek and swat it with his fist.

"Did you *want* something, Mr. Barta?" Demanded the thing-captain.

"Uh, yes. Yes. My instrument readings puzzle me. I need more buffer space to sort things out."

"You agreed to the allocation schedules," Chelsea said. And yet, Miguel sensed a slight expansion of his buffer space, a token gesture on the captain's part.

"Yes, Captain," he said, "But I read something odd about the Soleco hypermass, a slight asymmetry in the gravity potentials."

"Really?" The thing-captain sounded slightly interested.

Miguel leaned forward. "Captain, in a gravity gradient that steep we should see almost perfect symmetry. We're not dealing with what I'd call a large discrepancy, but the mass imbalance seems to run right up against the event horizon. Either my instruments have gone twidgy or I have to revise my definition of the word 'impossible.' "

"I see." Chelsea said, her mouth curling peculiarly around the words. Miguel felt invisible tendrils probing at the edges of his data. "Can you offer me anything more specific? Are we looking at a science bonus if I cut you more space?"

A shrug. "I really don't know. I can't do much analysis with the observation data chewing up my buffers like this."

"Can you *guess*?" A little more space opened up in his buffers, like a too tight belt beginning to loosen.

"I, uh, prefer not to," Miguel said carefully. "I mean with only a few months' experience and all. But it *looks*— I don't know. It looks like we've got some matter concentrations down there."

"Down there?" Chelsea repeated, now sounding genuinely interested. "Matter *concentrations*? You mean down deep in the tidal stress?"

"Yes," he said. "Very deep."

"I see."

The captain's thing-face vanished from his holie screen, and in buffer space a door was flung wide, opening a huge portion of the ship's computing resources for Miguel to plunder.

"Lordy!" he said, then turned to Tech Aid Lahler. "Triple our data rates, would you?"

"Already have, Miguel," she said, and beneath her Medusa hair she flashed a sickly and lopsided smile.

The trickle of data became a flood. Working quickly, Miguel sorted and collated, compressed and regressed and, with more than a hint of regret, deleted. Even so, the buffers had begun to fill up again, and rapidly. He knew then that he could fill any amount of space, consume any amount of processing power without generating any real answers.

Time to earn his keep. Time, at last, to push this strange new equipment to its limits. Bracing mentally, he plunged into the data stream, and let the instrument readings wash over him. Thrashing panic for a moment, the shock of sensations wholly unfamiliar. And then like a pond freezing over, his mind seized into a state of glittery, crystalline calm.

Miguel Barta had become thing-Barta, a piece of the seething group mind that controlled, nay, that *was Introspectia.* And thing-Barta felt a sense of freedom, of power, for it knew in its heart that it could do, astonishingly well, the task that had been layed out for it. With link-born senses it sniffed and caressed and tasted the data and, with greater effort, visualized it.

Thing-Barta knew then, with crashing, crashlike suddenness, an amplified and clarified and back-filtered sense of awe so achingly powerful it bordered on the religious. So close to the event horizon— Matter could not exist in that environment! Gravitational stresses would tear atoms apart, tear *everything* apart, leaving only the quantum electromagnetic vortices that theorists knew as "dots." And yet . . .

"Tech Aid Lahler," he said, in loose and wavering thing-voice. "Do you see that?"

"Yes," Lahler replied flatly.

Miguel shuddered a little. "Good. Good. I thought perhaps I had . . ."

"I see it," she assured him, and even through the link harness she looked stunned.

At the event horizon of the black hole, the data revealed a group of ellipsoidal objects, tens of meters across and quite clearly solid. Against all sense, against all *possibility,* several hundred of the objects huddled right up against the edge of the darkness, frozen, unmoving.

Lahler's eyes locked onto Miguel, demanding answers, demanding leadership. "What do we do?" she said.

Miguel pulled away from the images, pulled his mind clear of the link. Impossible. Impossible. Good lord, what was he going to tell the captain? "I don't know," was all he could think to say. "I really . . . don't know."

ROC (0451)

TAKE A FANTASY TRIP!

☐ **FATEFUL LIGHTNING by William R. Forstchen.** Andrew Keane, formerly a Northern colonel in the American Civil War, was now leading a mixed force of humans on a desperate flight from an enemy more horrific than any nightmare. But retreat would offer only a temporary respite. (451961—$5.99)

☐ *GARY GYGAX'S DANGEROUS JOURNEYS:* **DEATH IN DELHI by Gary Gygax.** Can Aegyt's greatest wizard-priest best the Goddess of Death's most dangerous disciple in a magical duel of wits? (452445—$4.99)

☐ **ICE CROWN by Andre Norton.** On a world divided into barbaric nations in conflict, Keil's and Roane's search for the Ice Crow might easily prove their own ruin and the catalyst that would forever destroy the precarious balance of the power on the closed world of Clio. (452488—$4.99)

☐ **ECSTASIA by Francesca Lia Block.** This novel takes you to Elysia, land of carnivals and circuses, magic and music, where everyone's a lotus eater, and the only crime is growing old.... (452607—$9.00)

☐ **BLOOD AND HONOR by Simon R. Green.** Castle Midnight, where the real and unreal stalked side by side—and an actor must be magicked into a prince . . . or die! (452429—$4.99)

Prices slightly higher in Canada.

If you and/or a friend would like to receive the *ROC Advance*, a bimonthly newsletter featuring all the newest and hottest ROC books and authors, on a complimentary basis, please fill out this form and return it to:

ROC Books/Penguin USA
375 Hudson Street
New York, NY 10014

Your Address

Name _____

Street _____ Apt. # _____

City _____ State _____ Zip _____

Friend's Address

Name _____

Street _____ Apt. # _____

City _____ State _____ Zip _____